Abram

Book One

The Breaking

PETER CHURNESS

Copyright © 2015 Peter Churness

All rights reserved. This book or any portion thereof may not be reproduced or used in any manner whatsoever without the express written permission of the copyright owner except for the use of brief quotations in a book review.

Cover art by Eve Ventrue (www.eve-ventrue.com).

ISBN: 1503183807
ISBN-13: 978-1503183803

FOR SANDY

Because you live in the present

CONTENTS

THE LAND BETWEEN THE RIVERS

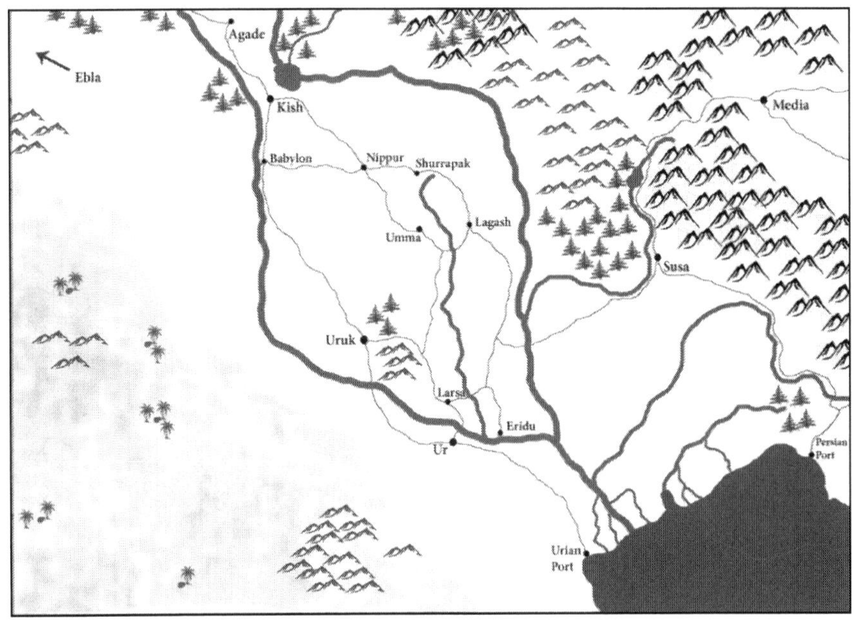

PROLOGUE

Slowly the old man edged forward. His gray beard blew gently in the breeze as he scanned the terrain below. He peered over the edge of a cliff at the valley beneath him. Lifting his gaze toward the distant horizon, he squinted his sad eyes as they stared into the sinking sun.

"Come, my son," he said softly. "Nightfall comes quickly. We will camp here for the night."

The boy he addressed was but a few years from manhood. He stood at his father's side as he gazed with him into the setting sun. Before sinking out of sight, it streaked across the sky an explosive blending of purples, reds and gold.

From the height of the mountain cleft the old man and the boy could see a vast panorama of the land below – a green, rich valley leading to a further range of mountains. This was the land of Moriah, not far from the Priest-King's city of Salem.

The old man turned to address two other companions. "One more day's journey," he said. "Tomorrow the boy and I will leave for the mountain and there we shall worship Aél. Remain here with the burro until we… return."

They set up camp and settled in for the night. Their evening meal was brief. Soon they were all lying down and fading into sleep after a hard day's journey.

The old man looked at his young sleeping son with a sad reflection in his eyes. In his gaze was a disturbed combination of hope and despair. The man lay down and closed his eyes, but this night he would not sleep. The fire slowly burned away into glowing embers as the man lay still and in thought. His mind, racing through a hundred years of life, finally fell upon a dark, brisk morning, many years before.

CHAPTER 1 – IN THE CANYONS

It was brisk, and still dark, as Enki awoke to the quiet of the early morning desert. He took a moment to savor the coolness of the cold stone beneath him. He knew the crisp, frigid air would soon give way to intense heat. Dawn began to break. He scanned his surroundings with new appreciation for the intricate maze of huge boulders and deep chasms strewn throughout the desert hills about him. After four days of venturing alone in these canyons he had acquired a new fondness for these gods-forsaken lands.

Enki was a Sumerian plainsman from the city of Ur and this was the foreign territory of the Semites – a desert people. He shouldn't be here. To disguise his identity, he had awkwardly donned the garb of a traditional Semite tribesman. He was not certain that his disguise was genuine enough to fool a true Semite of the deep desert, but thus far it hadn't mattered. He had seen no one.

Enki's anxiety and excitement was particularly heightened on this morning. It marked the fourth day he had been wandering these parts with his parchment and pens that only a person of nobility would be able to afford. If any true Semite encountered him up close, he suspected they would be able to make note of that fact.

Mapping the region had proved more difficult than he had anticipated. He had hoped to be almost all the way back to the safety of the towns surrounding his hometown of Ur by now, but his determination to complete the task for which he had come had kept him in the danger of the chasms for a precarious length of time. Surely, he was tempting the gods to his own demise this time, he thought.

He shook the negative concern out of his mind. He had almost made it. A thrill of excitement surged through him. He needed only one more day to complete his mission to map the canyons. One more day in the canyons of the barbaric Semites!

His excitement quickly collapsed into anxiety at the thought of the Semites. He reminded himself that Semite tribesmen did not typically inhabit these parts. His sources had told him they were used only as a strategic hideout in case the Sumerian armies of Uruk or Ur actually attempted a direct assault upon their scattered forces. Uruk and Ur had not been so bold, or so foolish, in quite some time and so the region was mostly uninhabited. However, because it was considered to be a secret place of refuge for the Semites, it had taken on religious meaning as well, and some would apparently make pilgrimage to the intricate tapestry of deep chasms and rocky cliffs. This is what his sources had told him and considering the price he had paid for the information – it had better be true.

Enki quietly consumed the remainder of his breakfast as the sun finally rose above the horizon. This would be a hot one. He broke camp, being careful to leave no trace of his presence. Any nearby unsuspecting Semite would certainly not be looking for evidence of a plainsman intruder. This would be unthinkable. Still it was best to be careful. Enki smiled to himself. He prided himself on doing the unthinkable. It was what gave him his edge. His father and brothers, he knew, didn't see it that way. They considered him reckless. Time would tell.

The rest of the morning was spent mapping out the remainder of the south side of the chasm he had finally stumbled upon the day before. It was exactly the type of canyon he had been looking for. He now needed to complete his task of mapping it all out by noon in order to give him enough time to evacuate the region by nightfall. He wasn't about to risk spending another night in hostile territory – disguise or no disguise. He was also starting to dream of a warm bed and a hot meal.

But while longing for the comforts of home, he had also begun to acquire a certain fondness for these *Bad Lands* as they were un-affectionately called by his fellow plainsmen of the vast land between the Rivers. There was a beauty here he had not anticipated on finding. Great boulders meshed together and piled on top of each other in an elaborate cascade of stone, sun and shadow. Small desert plants escaped the earth through tiny cracks in the hard stone, struggling for life. The musical sound of the hot desert wind blowing through the crevices of the canyons. All of it combined to give him an appreciation for why the Semites considered these lands to be a sacred place of refuge.

As noon approached, he carefully maneuvered himself between two great boulders and inched his way up to the shaded ledge above. The cold stone against his skin was a refreshing break from the relentless heat of the sun. He climbed further up the side of the cliff, and hoisted himself down into a crevice surrounded by three great boulders, but opening up downward and outward to the north giving him the last view he needed of the canyon below and the ridge on the other side. He was quite high up now and his feet dangling over the edge made him a bit uneasy. He pulled back further into the safety of his little lair.

Fear suddenly gripped him. Something was not right. The feeling and fear that he was not alone washed over him. Or perhaps he was being paranoid being nearly finished with his risky endeavor. Quietly and hastily he added the last bit of information to his parchments. He scanned the canyon below and the steep ridge on the other side one last time.

Satisfied, he carefully folded up his new precious map and stashed it away in his pack. He was now becoming anxious to leave these parts and tempt his fate no longer. The reputation of the Semites as fighters was known far and wide. That he could succeed in living four days in the canyons without stumbling upon a single wandering Semite would be quite a stroke of fortune. He dared to even hope. He considered going back down the way he came and exiting the canyon from its east entrance, but on second thought, considered climbing the rest of the way out of the canyon and traversing the south ridge to be more expedient. Also, if there was a Semite tribesman in these parts, he didn't want to find himself trapped in the canyon below with his enemy above him. He would take the high road out.

He pulled himself up out of the ledge he had been cradled in. The next set of boulders was fairly easy to traverse. With each one he found himself just a little closer to the top. Then he came to what he had thought would be the trouble spot. It was. The rock face was too steep to climb and there was a precarious drop off on either side. The only possibility was the boulder directly behind him. If he could hoist himself up on it, he might be able to make a jump to the ledge just above the rock face before him. To do so he had to backtrack down one boulder and up the other side hoping for a way up the huge stone that would serve as his launching point. The other side proved climbable. He made his way up the side of the huge rock rather easily, with only one tight spot. Four days of climbing in the desert canyons had given him a certain degree of increased dexterity and intuition. He had begun to learn that sometimes moving quicker was actually safer. He made it to the top of the boulder and then without taking time to worry about not making it to the other side, he launched himself successfully over to the ledge above the steep rock face.

He had made it! The rest of the way to the top was a

comparatively slow incline. And he had already mapped parts of the region to the south and knew he would be able to make it out of the canyons by nightfall.

He breathed a deep sigh of relief just as the attack came. The Semite wanderer had apparently been waiting for him to make the leap. It would have been a swift death had his increased adrenaline not given him a heightened awareness of his surroundings. The jagged edge of the Semite's long knife missed him by inches as Enki dodged his attacker. Although the knife missed, Enki was knocked down by the weight of his assailant. It took but a second for both to recover. Enki and his attacker now faced each other, drawing their swords.

Now that Enki actually saw a true Semite of the deep desert up close he realized how absurd his own disguise had been. His attacker wore clothes similar to his own, but he now saw the correct way he should have worn his disguise. If circumstances had been different he would have laughed aloud at his error. What he thought had been a sash was actually to be worn as the head band. And the head band that Enki wore, the desert warrior had tied about his waist. He considered how humorous he must look, but his opponent did not look amused. He saw in his eyes only a look of disgust and fierce hate. However, he also noted in his opponent what he hoped was a stance of over-confidence. Though the Semite armies were no match for the far more numerous and powerful armies of the plains peoples, the Semites regarded themselves as far superior against any plainsman in one on one combat – and for good reason.

All this he considered in the brief moment it took for

them to pull their swords and engage in battle. The sound of metal against metal echoing through the canyons was unlike any sound he had ever heard. It added to the confusion of the battle, as did the jagged terrain to which he was unaccustomed. But he held his own through the first series of attacks, parries and feints. He noted a slight sense of surprise in his attacker at the astuteness of his own defense. The look of disgust and hate was still there, but added to it was a new look of curiosity which seemed to pass over his face and then disappear with a renewed determination to end the battle quickly.

With this look, the attacker came at him, using the terrain expertly to his advantage, and striking with deadly precision. Enki broke off the attack with an astute dodge and roll into the side of the cliff. Then using his momentum against the stone to hoist his body up, he launched himself into the side of his attacker.

Enki now had the advantage, as his opponent was forced to defend his ground against the on-coming plainsman. Enki allowed himself to feel a glimmer of hope as he extended his advance, but the Semite's defense proved to be as skilled as his attack. The Semite with a swiftness and apparent recklessness that surprised Enki, thrust himself along the edge of the cliff and then down onto the ledge from which Enki had come, jumping from ledge to ledge like he was taking a stroll in the gardens of Lagash. He soon had himself back on the high ground facing Enki as the two took a moment of pause before the next engagement. He noted that some of the disgust had dissipated with what was an apparent look of respect for a worthy opponent. Enki considered this and wondered whether he would speak well of him once the Semite had killed him.

The Semite nodded in respect to Enki as he fell upon him with a new fierceness. The sound of metal rattling throughout the canyon was deafening. Back and forth they parried. It took every ounce of Enki's strength and courage to remain engaged. He found himself being driven back further and further toward the edge of the cliff. The Semite was holding nothing back now. Enki knew he could not overcome his attacker by either stealth or strength. He also knew the edge of the cliff behind him was growing closer. He decided to take a final risk. In swift succession he allowed his sword to be knocked into the air by the Semite even as he drew his own knife and lunged himself into his attacker. His sword flying into the air was just enough of a distraction to give him the needed window to thrust his knife home into the Semite's upper body. He could feel the knife go fatally deep into the desert warrior. But then as Enki fell back away from the Semite, he left himself exposed to one last desperate slash by his dying opponent. The slash ripped across Enki's abdomen. Enki and his rival fell to the ground, the Semite breathless and Enki wallowing in a pool of his own blood.

No greater pain had Enki ever known. He tried only once to raise himself up from the ground before collapsing to what he knew must be his final resting place. The contrast of the silence and stillness after the chaos and clamor of the fight was even more unsettling than the battle itself. He thought he could almost hear himself bleed.

As he lay there, a detachment came over him. He considered his situation objectively. *I am going to die. My body will never be found. No one will ever learn what happened to me.* The detached objectivity soon dissipated into personal despair. *All my training – meaningless. All my life has been for nothing. My dreams go unfulfilled. My name will disappear into oblivion. I will not be remembered. No wife. No children. The youngest son of my father, I am expendable. My brothers will carry on my father's name. I will be forgotten.*

He considered these and other thoughts as he lay there feeling the life drain from his body. The bleeding had slowed a bit, flowing freely at first due to the swiftness of his heartbeat in the midst of the battle. He had watched men bleed to death before. He knew what to expect. A faintness would soon wash over him. He would not be conscious for the final moments of his life. He considered that he had perhaps twenty minutes of consciousness left. Such an odd thought. All his life coming down to this – a handful of minutes. A wave of fear struck him. And will that be it then? Enki had never put much stock in the gods. Too remote, too distant. Why even his cities own god, the moon god Nanna, was nowhere to be seen. He imagined the moon later that evening shining down on his dead body. What god had ever saved a man from death and decay? He considered praying, but thought better of it. *I've not started yet, why should any true god be fooled into thinking I followed him now?* And yet, in this tragic moment he suddenly and passionately yearned for a god he could believe in. He considered how fragile his whole human life had been. All of it thrown away by a single slash of a sword. Why had he never considered this moment before? It was bound to come!

He could feel his heartbeat slow. He didn't have many minutes left. He began to lose some of his alertness. His vision started to cloud. In the distance, he could hear the cry of a desert hawk, but the sound was faint, though he could see the bird was closer than the sound coming from it. He closed his eyes awaiting the inevitable.

The voice that he heard at that moment was the deepest, richest, most wonderful voice he had ever heard. It was as if the sound of the words washed over him and through him like a cleansing stream. There was only a single phrase and he heard it only once.

Come away with me.

He opened his eyes with a shout. "Who's there!?"

The action of speaking, and shouting at that, brought a new wave of pain throughout his body. But the pain jarred a bit of renewed alertness back into him as well. In spite of the excruciating pain, he risked another shout, "Who's there!? Help me!"

The words echoed throughout the canyons. He didn't bother to consider that it would most certainly be another desert Semite who would hear his cry, if anyone was really out there. He settled back down fearing to even hope. No answer came. Minutes passed. Still no answer. He realized he must have imagined the voice. Other dying men had hallucinated on the battle field. He recalled one man staring at a tree and cursing his father as the life slipped away from him. He would not go that route. He resolved that he would die with as much dignity as remained to him.

"Ho there!"

The voice had come from above. Harboring fears that another hallucination was upon him, he tentatively glanced up at the cliff above him. A head was peering over the edge. The face was too ordinary to be a hallucination. Certainly not one of the gods. But not a Semite either by the look of him.

"Hold on friend! I'm coming down!" the man said in Enki's own Sumerian tongue. Then the face disappeared.

Several minutes passed and Enki was again beginning to believe he had imagined the whole thing. But then the man returned and began lowering himself down the side of the cliff. The distance to the cliffs top was perhaps only twenty feet from the ledge upon which he and his dead foe lay, and the man should have been able to lower himself slowly through the crevices in the mountains side without the use of a rope, but he opted for using a rope nonetheless. A new weariness suddenly came over Enki as he watched the man descend. He let his face rest down again in the dirt and closed his eyes. The faintness was increasing when he suddenly felt the hands of the stranger upon him. The man carefully turned him to expose the wound. A groan escaped Enki.

"I am skilled in the treating of such wounds, but yours is deep. I will do what I can," the man said.

Enki felt him tear away the clothing from around the long cut. The feeling of the desert wind against his open wound was disconcerting. The stinging kept growing stronger and stronger and then rose to an intense level as the man applied some kind of ointment to the laceration. Enki could feel a massive flow of blood rush to his head. He must have lost consciousness at that moment, for the next thing he was aware of was being buckled over in some kind of harness the man had constructed to hoist him up to the top of the cliff. Enki was fading in and out at this point. Something was wrapped tightly around his abdomen to stop the flow of blood. He noted how soaked through with blood the makeshift bandage was, but that the flow of blood seemed to have slowed. He again faded out of consciousness.

The next thing he was aware of was water dripping down his chin as the man attempted to force some down his throat. Regaining some consciousness now, Enki gratefully drank from the man's cup. He noted how terribly thirsty he was. The feel of the water as it trickled down his dry throat was wonderfully soothing.

"That's enough for now," the man said. He lowered Enki's head back down to the ground. "Try to sleep if you can."

It was not a hard command to obey. Enki was almost immediately unconscious again as the man spoke the words.

When Enki finally awoke, it was evening. He could see the moon shining down on him. He noted gratefully that it was shining down on a warm body and not a cold one. He hoisted himself up slightly on one elbow and took in his surroundings – his curiosity greater than the pain he knew it would cause him. He was under a lone tree in a field some distance from where he had been pulled out of the canyon. A fire was burning and he could smell the wonderful fragrance of roasted meat. The man sat opposite the fire watching over their dinner.

He now got a clearer picture of his rescuer. He was a tall, sturdy looking man with shoulder length black hair and piercing blue eyes. Though he looked to be perhaps twenty years older than Enki, there was something in his countenance that gave him an ageless quality. He looked both young and old at the same time. Enki had never seen anyone like him. His facial features were different than any of the kingdoms or peoples of which he knew and yet he could almost catch a glimpse of each of them in this mysterious traveler.

The man seemed to be fixated on their supper. He was carefully applying various herbs and spices to the meat roasting over the fire. He appeared to be so distracted by this activity as to take no notice of Enki's consciousness. But as Enki lay back down, the man spoke.

"There really is nothing quite like the meat of the desert hares. It's certainly not what you'd expect to find in these parts. I look forward to catching some every time I pass through this region – the meat so tender and sweet. I've learned over the years just the right combination of spices to perfectly draw out the meats full flavor. You're a fortunate man to be alive, if for no other reason than to taste my cooking."

Enki raised himself back up and then leaned himself up against the tree. The pain of his wound was not as intense as he expected it to be. Enki allowed his body a few minutes to adjust to the change of position before speaking.

"I feel it's futile to express the level of gratitude I feel toward you. I had certainly resigned myself to death." Enki's words felt strange and awkward as he finally spoke after so long a silence. The man simply smiled in response as he continued his work.

Finally the man said, "No need to direct your gratitude toward me. It's a sign of Aél's favor upon you that I was in these parts to hear your cry."

Another awkward silence settled upon them for a few more minutes. Then finally when Enki's curiosity could stand it no longer he broke through the quiet.

"If you don't mind my asking, what were you doing in these parts? You are clearly not one of any of the Semite tribes I know of, and to my knowledge, no one but the desert peoples dare to venture in these lands."

The man responded with a smile. "No one but a Semite tribesman like yourself, you mean?" he said.

Enki recalled his absurd attempt at trying to pass for one of the desert peoples. He also smiled, but before he could respond, the man continued.

"I am called Sadiq by some. And it is true that no one passes through these parts, at least not without the desert peoples' consent. Let me just say that it is a consent that I pay for dearly. But it's made me quite successful as a tradesman to pass through these lands rather than through the normal trade routes to the north. My travel time is often cut in half by passing through the Semite's territories. However, as you can perhaps imagine, I lose half my merchandise each time through as tribute to these peoples. But it has been well worth it each time and they have come to trust that my allegiance is to no people but to the profit I gain and the joy of traveling the forbidden lands. They've also come to learn that the profit they can gain for themselves each time I pass through is far greater over time than if they were to execute their normal tradition of claiming ownership of anything and anyone they come across on their lands."

Enki didn't even try to hide his skepticism. "The barbarous desert peoples actually allow you to pass through their lands?" he asked. "You mean to say you always come through with something to trade?"

Sadiq broke away momentarily from his preparation of their meal and paused thoughtfully. When he finally spoke, Enki saw a look of tenderness in his eyes.

"Most people do not understand the Semites. You would do well to learn that they are actually an honorable people. They may not have a written code of laws as you do, but they have a code nonetheless. Once you understand their ways, and can show them that you respect their ways, you will find no greater ally."

Their conversation again dropped into silence. He could hear the distant sound of a desert owl against the backdrop of a gentle breeze through the tree above him. The stars were growing brighter as the night sky grew darker. Sadiq continued his cooking without another word for several minutes. When Enki again could stand the silence no longer, he raised the question that was most eating away at him.

"You are a mystery to me, Sadiq. You travel the lands of the desert peoples, yet you are not a Semite. You ally yourself with them by paying them tribute, and yet you rescue the slayer of one of their own. Have you no fear of losing their protection and friendship? And you've yet to even inquire as to who I am or what I was doing in these lands. You say your allegiance is to profit and to the joy of traveling these lands. Have you not risked both by saving me?"

Sadiq again smiled. Without looking up from their supper he responded, "You are from Ur of the royal house of Eber. You are most likely a son of Terah himself, high king and ensi of Ur. You're too young to be Haran, his eldest, and Nahor is known to be a practical man whose passion is my own trade. I can think of no practical reason why Nahor would venture into these parts, though I've already noted I believe you could do well by the desert peoples if you gained their respect and honor. Coincidentally, had any of their kindred witnessed you slay one of their own, you would have achieved great honor and respect in their eyes. It's a shame that your fallen foe was a lone wanderer. Then again, you'd most definitely be dead if there had been more. But you'd have been respected in death for what it's worth."

Sadiq paused before continuing. "My guess is that you are Enkidu, youngest son of Terah, prince of Ur. If not a son of Terah, it's possible you are from Kosh's line and a nephew to Terah, but I deem that unlikely for I believe that you are either too young or too old, and anyway your skill as a swordsman and cartographer reveals training in Ur's royal court."

Enki was silent with amazement at Sadiq's deductions.

Sadiq then concluded. "Plus, there's a note in your pack addressed to *Enki*."

Enki allowed himself to laugh, though in doing so a wave of pain rippled through his body. Enki's laughter soon faded away to embarrassment as he considered the foolish mistakes of his endeavor. Mistaking how the desert warrior garb was to be worn was perhaps a forgivable mistake, but forgetting to carefully search his things and remove any sign that would link himself back to Ur in the event of his death or capture was simply reckless. He cringed at the thought of what his father would say, let alone Haran, his eldest brother.

Sadiq, as if reading his thoughts, said, "Don't be too hard on yourself. It's doubtful that the Semite you killed would have been able to read the note. He would most probably have concluded that you were a criminal from one of the plains cities and were fleeing for your life."

Enki accepted this. Then Enki said, "And what do *you* think I was doing in these parts?"

Sadiq smirked, then said, "Getting yourself killed and doing a fine job of it. Now stop asking so many questions and try some of this roasted hare."

Enki ate obediently. The taste even surpassed the rich fragrance that had been filling the air and Enki gratefully stated this. The meat was both tender and sweet. As he ate, he felt a warmth flood through him as his body absorbed the much needed nutrients of the meal. Enki leaned back against the tree as he ate. The stinging pain of his wound had subsided to a gentle throb. He allowed himself to relax. Curiosity about Sadiq was still prevalent, but he had saved his life and so felt safe in his presence. But he still needed to find out more about this mysterious traveler.

He again broke the silence. "I've never seen you in the courts of Ur before or anywhere else for that matter. How is it that you have come to have such a great knowledge of my people?"

Sadiq was now cleaning up after supper, washing the various pots and utensils he had used for the small feast. He continued this work while he spoke. "When you travel as a lone tradesman like me, it serves you well to have an extensive knowledge of the politics and customs of the lands through which you travel. Remaining independent of any trade federation, kingdom or city has had its obvious monetary benefits, but it has also required that I keep a low profile when traveling through the various lands where I do my trading. It's best that Uruk not know of my profit in Kish, for example, and vice a versa. I know the source of your curious questions about me. You fear that others will now find out about your exploits which will ruin your plans. You need not fear that I might speak of our encounter. We both now possess information about the other that we'd rather not have made public knowledge. Enki, you have your map, and though I don't know the full extent of your plans, I have my guesses. I advise you to consider well what I have said about the desert peoples. Bias between the plains folk and the desert lands is strong and blinding to both sides. The advantage to you if you were to gain them as an ally, rather than as a defeated or half-defeated foe, is great. Consider well my counsel."

After a few more moments of silence, Enki responded, "Sadiq, you of course can be assured that I will make no mention of you in the courts of Ur or anywhere else publicly, if that is your wish. And as you've discerned, this is to my advantage as well for I would have a difficult time explaining what I was doing during the time in which you rescued me. But you saved my life. You saved the life of a prince of Ur. I hope that all my questions have not hidden the fact that I am grateful beyond all words for what you've done. Come with me to Ur, at least in secret, and I will make it worth your while. Let me at least try to offer you some reward for your service to me."

Sadiq considered this, then said, "Enki, I thank you for your offer and I do hope and expect that our paths will cross again someday, but I'm bound with my cargo for Kish. You can travel with me as far as the western villages of your own land, but I think it's best for both of us if we part at that point. Now, the first day of traveling with your wound is going to be a painful one. I advise you to get as much rest as you can tonight."

And with that their conversation ended for the evening. Enki lay back down as Sadiq finished cleaning up and prepared his own place of sleep for the night. Laying there near the warmth of the hot coals, full from a good meal and grateful for his good fortune, Enki allowed hope and ambition to once again flood back into him. Thoughts of his precious map passed through his mind and the plans that it would now support. A wave of excitement rushed through him. He was still alive! He would still have time to marry, to build a name for himself, to fight other battles. He indulged himself in one of his many fantasies – this one of himself as a great general leading an army in fierce battle. The fantasy faded into a dream as sleep finally took him.

CHAPTER 2 – UR

When Enki awoke, it was before dawn. Sadiq was already up and preparing them a quick meal. Enki felt much rested from the night's sleep, but he soon discovered how weak his body was when he tried to stand up and nearly collapsed into the fire. Sadiq explained that his feebleness was a combination of the wound and the ointments he had applied to it and that he should feel most of his strength return by tomorrow when they would reach the western villages of the Urian realm. At that point they would be forced to part company. But for today Enki could ride one of Sadiq's mules.

After breakfast, they packed up and headed down a short way southeast to a small hidden canyon where Sadiq had his trade caravan stationed the day before. Enki could see now that Sadiq was indeed making a good profit on his risky ventures through the desert lands. Having come out the other side now on his way to Kish, he still had nine camels and six mules weighed down with merchandise sure to bring a healthy profit in the land of Uruk's chief rival to the north.

Traveling in his caravan were also two young men. Both were Egyptians. Sadiq explained that they were orphaned brothers whom he had acquired on one of his various transactions. Curiously Sadiq seemed to treat them more like sons than slaves. Indeed, they appeared even genuinely glad to see that Sadiq had returned safely to them after having been gone for an unexpected day and a night.

After introducing Enki to his two slaves, they hoisted him up onto one of the mules and headed off north. About mid-day the desert terrain began to give way to vegetation. The sight of green things after so much rock and dirt brought a new wave of gratefulness to Enki.

As they traveled, Sadiq was in a talkative mood and told them of many stories and adventures he had been a part of during the years of his travels. Assuming the stories were true, Enki concluded that Sadiq had traveled farther and knew more about the various peoples than any other single person he knew, even more than good old Shulpae in Uruk.

For his part, Enki told Sadiq bits and pieces about his family. Enki was the youngest of the three sons of Terah, king and ensi of Ur, which Sadiq had already deduced. Enki considered his father Terah to be a wise city ruler, but a bit old-fashioned, lacking in far-reaching vision and with very little ambition. He seemed to be content to rule his lone city and the small villages surrounding it. Ur was no small town,

Sadiq pointed out, and so his assessment of his father as lacking ambition and vision was perhaps a bit unfair. Ur was the greatest city of the southern part of the united realm of New Sumer. The city of Uruk in the northern part of New Sumer was the preeminent city in the realm, but Ur in the south was a close second. Terah as king of Ur was the closest ally and most trusted advisor of High King Lugulbanda of Uruk. Ur had one of the greatest libraries of any of the known lands surrounding her and its temple was one of the great architectural breakthroughs of its time. Terah commanded great respect not only in Ur but also in the other cities and surrounding villages that identified themselves as part of New Sumer. However, Enki considered him overcautious, slow to speak his mind and slow to act.

But Haran was worse, Enki continued. Haran, Enki's oldest brother and Terah's heir, was even more set in what he perceived to be the *old ways* than his father, if that were possible. Haran was a stern faced man, quite a bit older than Enki and already with a family of his own. Haran's personality and ruling style could be summoned up in one word – honor. Enki thought Haran was obsessed with this invisible thing called honor. It never allowed him to enjoy himself and it rarely allowed him to laugh. It robbed him of all vision and ingenuity. Haran looked like a king, but Enki perceived that he would never be a great ruler. He lacked the needed political savvy and intuition needed in these more complex times.

Now Nahor, Enki's other brother, had political savvy. Unfortunately, he used it only to further his own financial holdings and those of House Eber. These of course were not bad things, but they often blind-sided him, keeping him from seeing the bigger picture. He had a strong wit, an easy laugh and a terribly irritating suction noise that he made when he ate.

Sadiq listened to Enki with great interest, making his own comments here and there, and asking questions occasionally. He thought the bit about the suction noise was information he would rather have gone without, but as to the rest, he noted that Enki was a perceptive man for his age, and that in years to come, that intuition would serve him well. However, he cautioned him against himself being blind-sided by placing changeable people in unchangeable molds.

The days travel took them from the edge of the desert into the irrigated fields of the plains peoples. That night they set up camp just half a days walk from Ur on the outskirts of one of the western villages. Enki's mule ride compounded with the soreness of his wounds resulted in one seriously exhausted Sumerian. Enki ate gratefully as usual but then was fast asleep as soon as he hit his sleeping mat.

He slept soundly and it did him good, for he awoke feeling almost his normal self, greatly refreshed, and eager to forget his near death experience and to take on new challenges. He fingered his precious map excitedly as Sadiq's servants broke camp. Having finished breakfast and with Sadiq's caravan ready to head north toward Kish, the time of their parting had come.

"You are truly gifted and blessed, Enkidu of Ur," Sadiq said as they prepared to say goodbye. "But beware of using your ambitions unwisely. I have seen many promising young men meet with grave misfortune because they placed too much confidence in themselves. Confidence and ambition are good things, if one doesn't forget one's own mortality. You are flesh and blood and you can be killed. I trust you won't soon forget your Semite friend's single slash of the sword. To help you remember, I had the foresight to collect your fallen foes sword when I rescued you. It is a fine piece of metal – Amorite in its make if I'm not mistaken. Take it now as a reminder."

Enki winced at the memory of his last encounter with the sword. As he took hold of it a brief sting of pain washed across his wound. "Thank you, Sadiq. I won't soon forget the sharpness of this blade or its signature across my flesh."

"Remember also what I've said about the desert tribes. They may not have a written code of laws as you do, nor great cities and armies, but if you can earn their trust and respect, you would find for yourself no greater ally."

"I will consider your words, Sadiq, and also all the counsel you have given me."

Enki then reached for Sadiq's arm clasping him firmly above the elbow in the traditional Urian way.

"Thank you, Sadiq, for everything," he said. "You've given me more than good counsel. You've given me my life and I am forever indebted to you. The gods be praised that there exists in this world such men as you. The city gates of Ur are always open to you and I hope to someday repay the debt of my life I owe you."

"Oh, I think that we shall indeed meet again," Sadiq said

with a twinkle in his eye. "Enkidu son of Terah, I am your servant. Be blessed and receive the favor of Aél."

Sadiq's caravan headed on up north as Enki began to make his way on foot back to Ur. His body still felt stiff and sore from the wound, but he was eager now to reach home as soon as possible and decided to bypass the western villages. He actually gained strength as he walked. It was a beautiful day. The sun was warm and the sky was a deep, bright blue as it rose above the forests to the north. He walked through vast grasslands interspersed with small wooded areas. At one point he had to head a little south out of his way to bypass a huge herd of wild gazelle feasting in the plains. He soon met up with the Orin canal, one of the many waterways built to carry the life giving water of the mighty Euphrates to the fields and farmlands of the western villages. Now, he was on very familiar territory and began to run across various farms of which he knew some of the inhabitants. But he bypassed all these, making straight for Ur.

He began to think through what story he would give his father and brothers for his long absence. His usual story was that he was out for an extended hunting trip. He supposed the story would work again, though he wished he could be a bit more creative.

Ur was in sight now, still perhaps an hour away but gaining in size with every step. Its mighty temple rising above its great walls was now visible through the trees at times. He was in a thoroughly good mood. Not being dead was only part of it. The feeling that nothing could stop him flooded over him. He had killed a desert Semite, and an Amorite at that, if Sadiq judged correctly! He had survived four days in the forbidden canyons. Unthinkable! But he had done it. And he had his map. He reached for the map and ran across the note that he had failed to purge from his pack before his adventure had begun. He decided to read it again to add to his pleasant mood.

My Dearest Enki,

I am submerged once again into the course of my studies, but as at all times, my thoughts are only of you. Your last letter and the beautiful carving you made for me have both found a permanent place in my parlor, where I can view them at all times and think of thee. I just reread your last letter to me for the fourth, maybe fifth time, and it was as if I were hearing you speak those words to me afresh, for the very first. So long I have loved you, as you know, even when you and Gil would torment me with your pranks – alas, my love for you only grew stronger. To know that this love is now returned in fullest measure has given me a heart that is ready to burst with joy and tears ready to spring forth in sweet relief.

Our time together upon your last visit to Uruk is time that I cling to now in my continual remembrance of it. I hear other maidens speak of you longingly. They admire your strength. They know your courage and talents would win them a high place in our kingdom, be it in the court of Uruk or Ur, they care not. But I am drawn to your tenderness, to the real Enki that they know not, but that I have always seen since I was but a little girl admiring my older brothers devoted friend and fellow adventurer. Yes, I too am drawn to your courage and strength, but it is your tender heart that moves me. Gentle and strong is my Enki. He will be great not because of his skill with the sword or his valor in battle, but because of the greatness of his heart.

Know then the depth of my love for you sweet Enki. I am for you. I am your servant. I am your devoted friend. And if one day you should take me for your lover, I will be then in the flesh what I have always been in my heart – a maiden in love.

Aya

And with that last line read, Enki stumbled over a log and into the muddied trail. Cleaning himself up only slightly, he continued on his way, his pace quickened, but his heart light. Thoughts of Aya flowed over him as he walked. She was truly beautiful. He thought of her gentle, love-filled brown eyes that melted his heart every time she looked at him. He longed to once again hold her in his arms, to run his fingers through her hair and to feel the closeness of her body next to his.

Then he laughed as he thought of how he and Gil used to treat her, the little sister who had always tried to tag along on their adventures. She was but a girl then, and he had not foreseen the woman that was emerging. During the last few years, Enki's family had made few trips to Uruk, and when they had, Aya had always been away in Lagash receiving her education. And so, a year ago, when the two royal families reinitiated close ties with one another in Uruk, Aya had taken him completely by surprise. It was as if he had never known her before. She was beautiful and bright, gracious and kind. She had an easy laugh, which Enki loved, and an inner strength and confidence that shown in her eyes. And she was, of course, now a woman. They spent many days together during those two weeks. Gil felt a little jealous at first that he was spending more time with Aya than with him, but it soon both delighted and amused him, and he reveled in poking fun at him and Aya. Since then, he had had many extended hunting trips to the north, which invariably led him to visit Uruk.

But now he was heading home to Ur. The city was now in full sight, unobscured by the woods out of which he had just emerged. Segments of the working populace milled about the outskirts of the city walls. Small flocks of sheep and goats were grazing on a nearby hillside. He was coming into the city from the south and knowing that word would reach the court of his return, he decided to modify his story from hunting in the northeast, his usual story, to fishing in the marshes of the southwest. He didn't know if he was ever believed, but he cared not all the same. He was becoming his own man and his father and brothers knew that, to the obvious dismay of Haran and probably of his father as well. Nahor always seemed a bit more understanding for some reason.

He was recognized by certain city dwellers and was given a full salute by the guards at Ur's south gate as he passed into the city. The city streets were fairly crowded. It was approaching the noonday hour and Ur's citizens were partaking of their various errands that would end their mornings work before the noonday meal. He passed through the temple complex on his way to the palace noticing the obvious looks of disapproval from the various priests on duty. He had, of course, removed his desert disguise the day before and wore his normal traveling clothes, but his hair was disheveled, and dried mud from his recent fall still crusted his tunic. He looked down quickly to make sure no blood from his still healing wound had made its way through that mornings bandaging by Sadiq.

Thoughts of Sadiq crossed his mind and he wondered again about this mysterious tradesman coming out of the desert at just the right time. He also considered how surprisingly quick his wound was healing. He had never really believed in the gods, but decided that if they were concerned with the dealings of men, that he must have had their favor during these last few days. And so in an act that was really an act of sincerity, Enki ascended the platform of one of the statues to Ur's moon goddess Nanna and placed his lips to her feet in thanksgiving. The priests merely smirked reading the act as an attempt to appease the priesthood, but Enki didn't care. He didn't really need the priesthood, if he could gain the favor of the people, the palace and at least a few of the noble houses. And even if he did end up needing the priesthood to further his ambitious plans, he knew which priests could be bought.

Enki continued on his way through the temple complex. The temple compound consisted of a vast courtyard filled with various buildings for administrative purposes, homes for the priests and their families, storehouses for food and clothing in times of famine or flood, and of course many shrines to various gods and goddesses strung throughout the grounds. In the very center of the complex was arguably the greatest ziggurat ever constructed. It was magnificent. The temple had been begun by his great-grandfather, Serug, but was completed by his grandfather Nahor, whom the people called and history would remember as Ur-Nammu. Now his grandfather was a true king, very much unlike his father who he considered to be simply acting as custodian of his ancestors' ambitions. His grandfather, Ur-Nammu, had completed the temple, improved and expanded the system of canals, and had even rebuilt the Urian port. And he had built a fleet of ships for trade with the mysterious kingdoms in the east as well as with Egypt. He did not remember much of his grandfather, only faint images and feelings. His grandfather had died passing the throne on to his father, Terah, when he was still learning to speak. He regretted never having the opportunity to really know the great Ur-Nammu.

His thoughts now turned to his father Terah. Aside from all his criticism of his father's rule, he really did love and respect the old man for other qualities. His father had a wisdom and a kindness, perhaps not befitting a king, but certainly sufficient for being a good father. He recalled the times that Terah had taken to spend only with him after his mother had died. He remembered now very little of his mother, since she died when he was only four. His father did not leave his upbringing solely to the nurses and tutors as many of the noble classes tended to do. He had spent time with him, had taught him to fight and had shared with him his love for history and for the sciences. Indeed, his father probably would have been content if he had been born to be but a tutor in some royal house. Instead, he was perhaps the second most powerful man in the realm, at least in title. But, in Enki's mind, he was king of a city and land he had no real ambition to rule. Nonetheless, he did rule to the best of his ability and gave his whole self to what he thought to be the good of the kingdom. But Enki could see that his heart was often elsewhere. There was a sadness in his father that he never shared – like he'd been robbed of something dear to him but could not speak of it.

Just as Enki was thinking these thoughts, an out-of-breath page ran up to him from his right. It was his personal servant Malki, a lad a few years his younger, a gift to him from his father on his twentieth birthday. That had been a year ago now, and since then he and Malki had developed an unusually strong relationship for a master and his slave. Malki had been competent in all he had called upon him to do, and Enki was beginning to place more and more trust in him. Malki was proving to be an able and devoted servant, loyal in every way, but also shrewd and intelligent, in his own way.

"Master! …I've been searching... all over the city... for you," Malki said. He gasped the words out between breaths. "Are you just now… returning? Your note said you'd be back two days ago. You haven't been fighting again in the Umma games have you?"

"Malki, my friend, you worry too much," Enki said. "No trips to Umma this time – just fishing in the south for a few days." Enki didn't like lying to his slave who had been so loyal and he decided he would fill Malki in on the truth later.

"What terrible tragedy in the kingdom has sent you running all over the city looking for me this time?"

"Master, the council! You promised that this time you wouldn't forget. And this time with the trip to Lagash coming up by weeks end. Your father and brothers sent me early this morning to fetch you."

"Ahhg! The council is today! I'm a day behind myself. I was thinking it was tomorrow! I'm sorry, Malki, I did promise I'd make it to the next dull council. And it's actually essential that I make it to this one. Let's get to the palace – the east gate – fewer observers. Help me get cleaned up."

Enki and Malki hurried now through the streets toward the palace. Underneath great arches and past impressive three storied structures they ran, dodging caravans, slipping through the crowded marketplace, and diving into less traveled alleyways wherever possible. It was only a few minutes before the palace loomed into sight. Though not as inspiring as the temple, it was nonetheless a thing of beauty. It was a many-storied structure with numerous wings enclosing a vast inner courtyard. Enki and Malki slipped in through the east entrance, not without some notice of course, but certainly not as much as if they had come in from the west or south.

"Ah, master Enki. So good of you to pay us a visit," a voice suddenly said. It was Larzo, captain of the palace guard, who had playfully spouted out the sarcastic greeting.

"Not now Larzo. You can berate me later."

They continued on without stopping.

They sped in through the atrium and up the wide spiral

staircase to the second floor. Then down a narrow hall which led to the servant's quarters. They headed up the servant's staircase the rest of the way and then crossed over on the fourth floor over to the south wing where Enki's rooms were. There he washed up, asking Malki to clean his equipment in the next room so as not to reveal to him his wound. He didn't want to have to take the time to explain it.

Enki dressed himself in his dark green trousers with a gold and brown embroidered tunic covering a white blouse. He thought dressing like he was actually royalty might soften the blow to his father and brothers when he made his belated entrance.

Malki returned having cleaned the main essentials of his equipment and handed Enki his sword and dagger.

"Your sword and dagger appear to have been used, master," Malki said perceptively. "Were you battling the fish of the marshes?"

"Malki, I promise I'll fill you in later on my recent adventures. I should know better than to think I can fool you with my stories."

"Well, you're not fooling anyone else either, master. Please let me help you next time to come up with something better."

"Agreed. Now wash the rest of the clothes in my pack while I'm in council and don't let anyone see the blood."

"Master?"

"I'll explain later," Enki said and then he was out the door on his way toward the administrative wing.

Enki made his way through majestic halls richly decorated

with large beautifully weaved tapestries covering walls of deep dark wood constructed from imported timber from the vast forestlands of the northwest. Fine pottery, sculptures and carvings of various styles and ages strewn the halls and reflected brilliantly in the carefully positioned lighting.

Enki ignored all of this as he hastily made his way through the palace. He cared not about most of what would go on at the council that day, but there was one issue he needed settled. And so he sped on, walking briskly through the less populated regions of the palace until he came to the administrative wing where the number of servants and officials milling about increased substantially. Now he slowed to an easy pace to hide any sign of urgency and he composed himself with the carefree confidence for which he had become known. As he casually strolled down the last hallways on his way to the council chamber, he occasionally stopped to chat with a lower official, always aware that others would notice this and conclude he was unaffected by any pressure from his father and brothers. They would conclude that Enkidu was his own man, dependent upon no one. Enki allowed his own self-perception to be built up by these thoughts as he finally made his way to the council chambers two huge doors. He gave one final yawn before he opened the door and slipped in.

The chamber inside was not a huge room, but sufficient for a table large enough to seat twelve to fifteen comfortably. The central table itself was an elegant thing, richly carved from the lighter colored wood of the forests around Susa. It had engraved on its surface great battle scenes from Urian history and legend, with a flat surface around the border to facilitate writing. There were two large windows on either side of the room, letting in sunlight. His grandfather had designed the chamber concluding that "...decisions about war would be made in this room and so should have no look of gloom affecting our decisions." Terah had quoted this to him the first time he'd been allowed into the chamber.

As Enki slipped into the room, his brother Nahor was speaking. Scrolls and parchments were strewn across the table. Most sitting around the table were peering into a particular parchment as Nahor spoke. He was speaking of the trade talks in Lagash that would begin by weeks' end. Nahor, along with the economic advisors, had drafted his proposal and position for the talks and the meeting this morning had been for the purpose of hammering out the details for the upcoming trade gathering. Enki breathed a sigh of relief as he realized he had missed the driest part of the meeting.

He looked around the table and noted those present. His father Terah was at one end of the table with his brothers Haran and Nahor on either side of him. Next to Haran sat Krishnu, Regional Commander of the military responsible for Ur's local defense. Krishnu was a stout man of medium height with an impressive look of importance about him that covered up his general incompetence as a military leader. Enki wondered about the absence from the gathering of Calderach, the High Commander of the military. He allowed himself to hope that Calderach was where he thought he was. He would find out shortly.

Next to Krishnu, and sitting on the other side of the table opposite Haran, was Graco, priest, scribe and Chief Administrator of the realm. Graco always attended these advisory councils on behalf of the High Priest Ultaro, who regarded such an advisory role as beneath his grand position as head of Ur's religion. It was also generally known that Ultaro despised Terah and his ruling house. But the reality was that Ultaro hated anything and anyone that threatened his power base. And it didn't help that Terah's grandfather had brutally purged the priesthood of corruption and had limited their power, taking for himself the title of ensi away from the priesthood.

Ultaro used Graco as his eyes and ears in the council, but the reality, unbeknownst to him and Ur's best kept secret, was that Graco had secretly allied himself to Terah and the royal family. Graco had his own personal hatred for his superior Ultaro, but Graco lacked the power base to challenge his position.

Next to Graco sat Lord Micah, Terah's political advisor and chief of domestic affairs. Micah was also Terah's source of information and advice concerning the maintenance of his own power base over the other noble houses of the realm. Micah's own house had aligned itself to House Eber during the days of Serug, Enki's great-grandfather. He exercised considerable influence within the kingdom and was a powerful and able ally to his father.

Finally, sitting in between Lord Micah and his brother Nahor was Lord Salzarto, Foreign Minister of Ur and head of another noble house aligned to his father. As Terah's chief foreign advisor, he brought a wealth of knowledge concerning the customs, religions and ambitions of the rival kingdoms to the north and east. He was also an able economist and was Nahor's chief aid in drafting the proposals and positions for the upcoming trade negotiations.

It was to these documents prepared by Nahor, Lord Salzarto and their advisory team, that Nahor was currently referring to as he apparently wrapped up their discussions concerning the talks.

"...so in the interim, assuming Kish's recent alliance does not interfere, we'll continue with the agreed upon transfer of barely for wheat to Shurrupak, but I must return to and finish out these discussions with my initial point concerning last year's Umma treaty, that we must not allow Kish's political dealings to interfere with our economic advancement, even if Kish is to profit from those advancements. Our economic lead is sufficient to guarantee our near security, and our advancement will give us greater stability into the future, so long as economic trust is not broken with the northern cities, especially with those that have now politically aligned themselves with Kish..."

Halfway through Nahor's final statements, the participants began noticing Enki's entrance into the chamber, and Nahor broke off from his train of thought to acknowledge him.

"...well, my dear brother! How honored we are at your presence. How blessed that you would grace us so. So was it women or game that has kept you occupied these last few days?"

Enki said, "Brother, I receive your gracious welcome, and I'm sorry if your own impotence keeps you envying my own virility. Unfortunately, it was only fish in the south marshes that I caught this time."

Nahor gave out a hearty laugh, but Haran's scowl gave way to speech. "How dare you insult this council and the honor of your father the king with such irresponsible and irreverent speech," he said. Haran would have continued had Nahor not cut him short, still laughing.

"Let him be, Haran, he speaks the truth. I do envy his sway over the maidens of our realm."

That broke the tension and the other members of the council relaxed their embarrassed looks. Terah, having masterfully kept himself from laughing out along with Nahor, finally said, "Enkidu, my son, I'm glad you are here, even if you have once again masterfully avoided the financial reports. Nahor, do you have anything further to add? If not, I'm pleased with our positions, while acknowledging Krishnu's objections. Commander, you may convey to the military assurance that I will conduct all dealings at Lagash with our strategic defense in mind, of course. However, unless further information becomes available in Lagash, I am in agreement with Nahor and Lord Salzarto and we shall proceed according to their direction."

Nahor said, "No father, I have nothing to add and am grateful for your approval."

Terah said, "Then let us move on to the other matters at hand. As you know, raids upon the western towns have increased, and we now have it confirmed that a number of the desert tribes have united under a leader whom we believe is behind these raids. Commander Krishnu has Calderach's report. Commander?"

"Thank you, My Lord," Krishnu said. "Our sources confirm the reports of the last few weeks that a desert warrior by the name of Zoreth, a name by now recognized by all of us, has united several neighboring tribes with his own, and is the chief instigator of the recent raids upon Ele, Yurat and now upon Roeth. Indeed, the devastation upon Roeth was particularly severe. Our western town's people are terrified. Our forces in the west are very limited at this time, being stretched thin over the entire western region. At the king's command, High Commander Calderach has the bulk of our army in the south guarding the port from any surprise raid which would damage our position at the trade talks. Our position in the south is now secure, but the west is vulnerable. We don't know when or where Zoreth will strike next. There has been no logical pattern to his raids. He attacks a town and then disappears into the desert before we are able to gather our western armies to confront him. We currently have units near each of the western border towns, but this has spread us thin. The canals are also vulnerable. We've been forced to choose between security in the west and security in the south as noted earlier by his majesty, and I would add that Ur's own defense could be jeopardized if we extend ourselves to the fullest in defense of each and every town and canal. We're dealing with limited resources in the face of an unexpectedly unified force out of the desert. Ultimately, the threat is not significant of course, but the trade talks demand concern in the short term. It would seem that we've been forced to sacrifice local security in order to secure potential stability in our positions at the talks."

"You disapprove then of the decision to give the port the priority," Terah said. He said this more as a statement than as a question.

"My Lord, you know my position," Krishnu said. "Zoreth needs not just a victory, but a high profile victory. I agree, attacking the port successfully would fulfill this for him, but just as beneficial to his position would be a successful destruction of one of the canals or some other destructive measure that would communicate our inability to insure the barely crop in the quantities that you're relying upon for the talks. I can't insure even a relative security in the western reaches without forfeiting the security of Ur itself. And if I were Zoreth, I would consider pushing my way to within even an arrow's shot from Ur's city walls to be a prize beyond any of his other possible targets, even an outright conquest of the port city. You must decide between security of the western towns and canals and the security of Ur itself. I simply cannot defend it all!"

"Then don't defend. Attack!" It was Enki who interjected this.

After a moment's pause, Nahor broke in. He said, "Don't be foolish, Enki, this isn't the Umma games we're discussing."

Haran just looked at him with added disgust.

"Master Enkidu," Krishnu said. "There is no army to attack." Krishnu was speaking more patiently but somewhat patronizingly as well. "If it were simply a matter of engaging in a conventional campaign, we would not be having this discussion."

"I'm not suggesting you actually launch an assault upon an invisible force in the desert," Enki said. "But at least look like you're prepared to attack. Give the enemy the impression that you're thinking offensively and not defensively. In doing so we can put the enemy on the defensive or drive him to attack us where we want him to. Commander, that's a line right out of one of your lectures at the academy. As it is now, we're playing right into Zoreth's hands. If we give Zoreth the look of an army stretched to its limits, we're just inviting further raids."

"What are you suggesting, Enki?" the king asked.

Enki paused in feigned thought before he continued. "Commander Krishnu, you said it yourself, that if Zoreth had the chance to fight his way to within even an arrows shot of the walls of Ur, he'd have made his point, advanced his position among his tribal peoples, and weakened ours at the talks. If that is what you suspect, then release no more forces to the west. Stay in Ur, awaiting his attack."

Enki then turned to Terah and said, "Father, give me charge of the forces currently stationed in the west. No more. I'll give Zoreth a show of force throughout the region. I'll look like an army ready and willing to attack. He won't call our bluff. He'll assume that the presence of the mighty King Terah's youngest and most inexperienced son amidst the armies defending the western towns must mean that his military position is more than secure. I'll station myself in

Roeth. We'll pull the central division of the rege out of Yuret and lead Zoreth to believe they're with me along with other forces pulled away from Ur to secure my position. But, we'll actually send them to Ur to add further strength to Krishnu. Zoreth, knowing Calderach is in the south at the port will be forced into choosing Ur as his target, should he choose to attack anything at all. If he does, Krishnu will sweep out of the city and deal a decisive blow to this desert upstart."

There was several moments pause as the others considered Enki's words. Terah was the first to speak. "Enki, my son, I confess your plan may have merit, but do you truly feel ready for such a command?"

"You would have to put on quite a show, Enki," Lord Micah said.

Haran then broke in. "Are we really even want to consider this? The boy can't even fulfill a commitment to council, and when he does, he fills this sacred chamber with irreverence for family and crown."

Nahor said, "Enki, no one questions your valor or skill in battle. You proved both at the Akkadian campaigns last spring, and I'll finally admit, despite my disgust with your insistence on sneaking off to the Umma games, I've profited from your victories every time. But you're talking about command of an entire rege. Did you even command anything larger than an erst against the Akkadians?"

Enki said, "Brother, the whole point of this plan is intimidation. I won't be commanding anyone into battle. I'll be prancing around from town to town like an over-confident Kishite."

"I must admit, the plan has merit," Krishnu said. "It would give us the advantage of knowing with relative certainty the locale of the raids. I also do not question Enkidu's courage and strength in battle, but would it have to be Master Enkidu?"

Terah said, "Lord Salzarto? The desert peoples are not your expertise, but you probably have a greater grasp on their mindset than the rest of us. What are your thoughts?"

Salzarto said, "In order for the bluff to work on someone like Zoreth, it would have to be one of your own family commanding the western rege. I think you know the answer to your question before I give it. Nahor is the author of our trade positions and is indispensable at the talks. You, My Lord, must be there to lend absolute credibility to our agreements, and Haran as heir must be there to provide assurance of the talks vitality into the future. Enkidu is the only one not absolutely needed at the talks, though I would dearly love to see him gain the kind of experience he could gain at the Lagash summit."

There followed silence then as Terah considered the matter. When he did speak he spoke with finality. "I'll endorse the plan if Lord Micah agrees to accompany Enki as chief council."

Enki almost spoke out in objection, but then thought better of it, deciding to be content with the decision and concluding he could deal with the Lord Micah problem later.

Micah said, "I of course am ready to serve the crown in whatever capacity the king think best."

Poor disappointed Micah's going to miss another chance

to prance about the Great Library in Lagash, Enki thought to himself.

"Then it's decided," Terah said. "Graco, have the plans distributed to the usual quarters and blessed by the priests. Also, let's make our departure a high profile event. What are the high priests views on the talks? How much is it going to cost us to acquire his personal blessing and presence at the sendoff?"

Graco said, "More than what you'd be willing to pay, as usual, My Lord, but if you accept his price, I'll see to it that only a reasonable percentage actually makes it into his treasury. Ultaro's almost as ancient now as he's pretended to be for decades. He hasn't been able to read one of my reports for years."

"It's hard for me to imagine what kingship would be like if I had to deal with that rascal Ultaro myself," Terah said. "Praise the gods for you Graco."

As the meeting broke up, Enki endured the expected rounds of sarcastic praise to his new title of rege commander. Nahor kidded him the most, but Enki knew he was generally on his side when it came to most matters. Humor was just his way. Haran, in true form, gave him a formal blessing and issued a word of forgiveness for all past grievances if he would only now embrace with nobility this new role of service to the kingdom thrust upon him. How big of him, Enki sarcastically mused. As each began to leave, Terah asked for Enki to remain a moment.

When they were alone, Terah said, "Enki, I hope you

understand why I've ordered Lord Micah to assist you. It's more to lend credibility to your mission with the council than a need of my own to see you supported. You should know, Enki, that I regard your military prowess highly. You should also know that Calderach has given you secret praise in my presence. He has high hopes for you, as do I."

Enki considered this. Then he said, "Thank you, father. And I do understand why you think Lord Micah should accompany me. I consent to his being my counsel, but will it truly be that? Will it be counsel and not control?"

"I've made you rege commander, Enki. What general does not take on such responsibility without wise counsel? Lord Micah is there for that purpose. Do you question my motives?"

"Of course not, father, but Lord Micah has known me since I was a boy. He even acted as guardian those two years after mother died. Don't misunderstand me, I feel a certain fondness for the old man, but he I'm sure still looks upon me as a boy. His interaction with me will affect my ability to command the rege. My ability to maintain the highest level of command might be affected."

"Enki, you said it yourself, you're not going to be leading the men into battle. I hardly think that your stature will be diminished beyond the level needed to carry out the plan."

"But, father, surely you see that it is completely essential to the bluff that our forces maintain the highest level of readiness and morale. They must truly be ready to attack. Otherwise Zoreth may call our bluff."

Terah said, "Lord Micah's presence will only strengthen

the bluff. Zoreth will be more likely to consider that we're thinking offensively if wise and experienced counsel is with you."

"Agreed," Enki said, "But the question of who's commanding who will still remain, regardless of what title you've given me."

"What more can I give you?"

"The signet ring. Let all know that I have your full authority in the west. And make this known to Lord Micah personally that he is under my command."

Terah paused for a moment. Then he said, "Very well, Enki. If you feel such a need I will give it to you. But I think you may be over-reacting to Lord Micah's presence. However, I suppose I should be grateful that you are thinking so thoroughly about your command. I will do as you've requested."

Enki left the chamber with a sigh of relief. The last remaining barrier to his plan had been lifted.

CHAPTER 3 – VICTORY IN THE DESERT

The ceremony of blessing and sendoff for those heading off for the trade talks lasted nearly three hours. Ultaro the high priest was in lavish form and reveled in the attention. Once completed, Enki stole away to his upper chambers. From his window high above the city, he watched the extravagant company being paraded out of Ur. Huge jubilant crowds followed them hoping their mission to Lagash would bring even greater financial gain to their already swelling prosperity. It was indeed a time of unprecedented abundance in the Urian realm. Not since the days of Ur-Nammu himself had the kingdom seen such rapid growth. But there were danger signs as well. Some of the people grew soft, and a wealthy realm was sure to draw the attention of ambitious peoples awaiting a moment of governmental weakness. Would his father have the strength to lead the kingdom should times of war come? Enki knew he sometimes underestimated his father – Sadiq had been right on that point. But his doubts persisted all the same.

Perhaps, it didn't matter with Lugulbanda on the throne in Uruk. Enki had to admit his admiration of His Lordship, High King of the united realms. He had always been impressed by his best friend's wise and cunning father. Of course, he was also afraid of him like everyone else in the realm. Lugulbanda was not known for mercy. He was a hard, but strong ruler. Enki, intrigued by the high king, would often ask Gil or Aya about their father. So often they gave very little information because they had so little to give. The king of Uruk spent all his time governing, growing and expanding his realm. Aya hardly considered him her father, so little time had he ever spent with her. There was always a formality between them, she had said, that though not uncommon in the realm, was nonetheless painful to bear. Gil as his heir had spent more time with the stern ruler, but such time usually involved various exercises in the art of diplomacy or trade or some other such nonsense that little interested his underachieving friend.

Just then a final trumpet blew and the noise from the distant crowds now at the edge of the city rose to a momentary roar. Enki could see distant banners and bright colorful streamers being waved in excited anticipation of a successful mission. Enki wished them well, but was glad to be staying back with a mission of his own. His heart was already starting to beat fast as he thought about his risky venture. Just then, Malki entered.

"Malki! What is our situation?" Enki asked.

"Everything ... prepared as you directed, Master."

"And the couriers?"

"Sent off day before yesterday..." Malki said hesitantly.

"But...?"

"But, are you sure you won't reconsider going through with this?"

"Malki, my worrisome friend! This is going to be my finest hour. Did you brief Lord Micah on our plans?"

"Brief him?! If you mean, did I lie to his face, then, yes, I've done as you instructed."

"Do you think he suspects the truth?"

"I don't think so, but I'm not a good liar."

"Nonsense. You're a wonderful liar. Now, fetch me the clothes we came by yesterday."

"Master, are you certain you won't let me wash them first?"

"Malki, I can't just look like a peasant. I've got to smell like one too. You didn't try to mend anything did you?"

"It was tempting, but no."

Malki returned in a moment with a set of dirty, moth eaten rags once worn by a now very well dressed pig herder from Ele. Enki tried not to cringe as he converted himself into a commoner. He was determined to enjoy this.

"Who did you send off to find the central command?"

"Regino."

"Perfect. He'll raise just the right kind of suspicions. And you delivered the package to Captain Larzo along with the orders?"

"As you instructed. He left for Tor day before yesterday.

Are you sure Krishnu won't get suspicious?"

"It's worth the risk. Larzo's the only one I trust to find Yani. Besides, when he finds out what's going to happen, he'd never forgive me if he ended up stuck at Ur wasting away guarding an impenetrable palace."

"And what of Yani, assuming Larzo finds him. Are you sure you can trust him?"

"Of course not. But I trust his greed. He'll do it."

Enki the peasant quietly slipped out of the palace just before the noon hour when the city streets would be most crowded. He decided to test out his new identity by venturing into the main marketplace. At first he felt naked, as though every man, woman and child in the crowd knew exactly who he was. At any moment he expected someone to expose him. But his paranoia soon faded as he attempted to do the same into the crowd.

He passed through the city streets, trying to mimic the walk and demeanor of the peasants around him. Feeling momentarily the weight of his own plans he almost wished he truly could be but a simple farmer concerned with nothing but the price of barley and the impact of the flood season upon his crop. But Enki shrugged off the feeling. He had a great destiny to fulfill, greater than any these simple folk could fathom. And yet it would be these around him who would one day praise him, not for being prince, which they did already, but as something much greater. He saw it in his dreams at times. "Enkidu, great father of deliverance!" they would cry. And not in Ur only. Together with the help of

Gil and the current prestige of Gil's royal blood, he would recapture the greatness of Old Sumer, surpassing even Ur-Nammu in grandeur. Even Sargon's name would one day seem small and forgotten next to his, cursed be the tyrant's name forever!

The sun was at its peak as he left the cities confines and slipped under the cover of the royal forest through which the western road made its course. He traveled quickly, knowing that Lord Micah would be departing well before nightfall, scheduled to arrive in Roeth by next mid-day. Enki had till dawn to meet up with him.

The road to Yurat was quiet for the most part. He ran into the occasional cart laden with vegetables which grew best in the western reaches. Most had finished the journey into Ur by mid-day, so contact with late travelers was at a minimum. He had also left prior to most of the farmers who would be returning that day back to the western towns. Had speed not been required, he would have taken greater care with his role and taken with him an empty cart, or one laden with city goods for the smaller villages to which he was headed. Some travelers no doubt wondered at his business, but there was nothing terribly unusual about a lone traveler un-laden with goods. No doubt, each came up with their own scenario for his errand, and did not bother with questions. Privacy was respected among the western peoples. A man's own business was his own.

The sun was already setting by the time Enki reached Yurat. Yurat was one of the greater towns in the west and chief of the central region. It had a great marketplace and even its own temple. There were no town walls, but sentries were posted at every route into the village. These ignored him as he passed into the town.

The streets were crowded with activity as merchants and tradesmen peddled their goods to farmers and artisans whose own daily activity allowed them only this time before dusk to mingle with the populace and make purchases while the evening meal was being prepared. The noise and bustle of the town, though similar to a scene in Ur, was also different in some respects. It seemed more chaotic, but also more lively, more ... happy. Occasionally, two parties haggling over a price for some good would rise above the others, pass into violent threats, and then end in happy agreement. So went the bartering of the border towns, similar to that in Ur, but more extreme in every way.

It had been some time since Enki had been in Yurat. It took him some time to re-familiarize himself with the place and get his bearings. Once he did though, he began to thoroughly enjoy his secret mission and his new identity. He even tried his hand at bartering with the commoners, trying to surpass the locals in their own extremism. He was certain that he failed to do so, but considered that he passed the test of peasantry.

It was now nearing the time he was to meet up with Yani. He cringed to think what his father would think if he knew the relationship he had with the desert scoundrel and he hoped that for Larzo's sake his father would never find out. It had been Captain Larzo who had accidentally introduced them one day years before. Larzo had been at that time regent of the northern region and Yani was one of his chief informants concerning news from amidst the desert peoples. One day Enki had been tagging along with Larzo on one of his excursions into the western reaches when Yani came to report to him. Larzo, being fond of the lad Enki, and having an instinct regarding Enki's potential and future, had cautiously encouraged the relationship to develop. Now Enki would find out if that relationship would pay off.

Enki slipped into the crowded pub which was to be their meeting place. The main room was crowded with tired farmers and merchants huddled around variously strewn tables. Tired though the working populace was, it didn't hinder their speech. The noise level of conversation and laughter was near deafening, which was why Enki had picked the place. What was spoken between Enki and Yani must not be overheard.

Enki found Yani sitting alone at a small table near the fire pit in the center of the chamber. He was sipping what looked to be his third beer. His beard was gray and his wrinkled face reveled one who had born the desert sun for many years. Yani looked up and a critical grin cracked through his hard demeanor as Enki sat down.

"The court of Ur can't afford any better wardrobe for their young prince than these rags of yours?" spouted the desert scoundrel.

"Why Yani, this is the latest fashion at court. Soon all the princes of the realm will be dressed in such fine garb."

"Be careful of such statements," Yani laughed. "Such is

the daily prayers of my people for yours."

"Speaking of such fine clothing, you could have given me some clues as to how to wear those desert rags you supplied me with last month! I met one of your people while dressed as one of you. Your kinsmen I think rather despised me when he saw me wearing the head gear about my waist. I shan't tell you how I was wearing the waist band."

"Ha!" spouted Yani as half swallowed beer flew from his mouth amidst his laughter. "That's a sight I would have paid good money to have seen."

"Yeah, well for the price I gave you for those few pieces of rags you would have had plenty of good money to pay with."

"Hey, you get what you pay for. That wasn't some half-desert tribesmen's garb like my own I gave you. That was authentic costume from among the tribes of the deep desert. I didn't charge you enough!"

"Well, Yani, if you were displeased with your payment, I have a job for you now, and if all goes well, you'll be able to retire in style with what I'm going to offer you."

"Oh? It would take quite a bit to compel me to retire."

"Do you still have enough credibility with Zoreth's captains for them to believe inside information brought by you?"

"Most of them still trust me. I know which ones to avoid."

"What is their current intelligence? My father has leaked certain information that he has hoped will be believed. Do you know what that information is?"

"How badly do you want to know?"

"Never mind that right now, Yani! You'll receive whatever payment you require. The situation is at a critical hour and I'll be willing to pay you whatever you ask."

Several moments passed as Yani considered this. Then he said, "Very well. They know that you, Enki, are coming with full counsel to take control of the western forces. And they know that the central command will be pulling back to lend you strength in your southwestern region."

"And do you know their plans?" Enki asked. "Are they preparing to attempt an assault upon Ur?"

Yani's initial look of surprise faded into a sly grin. "What are you up to, you clever young prince? Yes, I'm fairly certain they will attempt some kind of assault upon Ur, though of course they are well aware they would not be able to take the city, as you also must know."

"What if I told you, that the central command wasn't actually being sent to Roeth to join my southwestern forces?"

A moment's pause gave way to a grinning Yani. Yani asked, "You're pulling them back to Ur?"

"Yes," Enki said.

"And you want Zoreth to know the central command is pulling back to Ur. Why?"

"That's not your concern. It's better if you not know. Will Zoreth's command believe the news?"

"You want him to attack you! You want him to attack you in the west and not at Ur."

Enki said nothing.

"If this is a trap, and if you're successful, it will become known that I had part in betraying my people."

"Which is why I am offering you 30,000 pieces of silver and a permanent place on the palace payroll. I'm offering you retirement in style in Ur."

Yani's mouth nearly dropped and there was several minutes pause as Yani considered what was being presented to him.

"And what if this plan of yours, whatever it is, fails?" Yani asked.

"Life is risk, my ancient friend," Enki said. "There's a chance that I may be killed and unable to meet my commitment to you. But if my plan succeeds, you'll never need to lift a finger for the rest of your days. But it has to be now. You have to leave this very minute. Zoreth must know tonight."

Another surprised grin broke across Yani's face. He said, "That's the rub, isn't it? This is your plan, not the kings! Terah doesn't know anything about what you're up to, does he?"

"Yani, believe me when I tell you, that I will not fail. I will succeed. And you will live the rest of your days like a king."

After several more moment's pause Yani cursed himself. Then he said, "Larzo always did see something in you, told me once he did. If you can beat Zoreth at his own devious games... Oh, I'm a fool! I'll do it, fool that I am. I'll do it."

***

It was nearing midnight as Enki approached the rendezvous point. He had at first had difficulty making his way through the thick of the forest as he searched for the interior path. Once he had found it though, his progress was swift and silent as he made his way to the old stone hearth – ruins from a forgotten age. The captain of the central command was standing there, ready and alert, but clearly impatient and annoyed at this summons. He was a tall beardless man, too neatly dressed for a true captain of the frontier, Enki thought.

When he saw Enki approach, he appeared ready to unleash the flow of words he'd been rehearsing.

"My prince, this had better be important!" he whispered harshly. "How can I be expected to secretly withdraw the central army to Ur, if I have to this very same night prance around the Old Forest to appease your majesty's fancy!?"

"Settle down, Eldoreth. Your orders have changed."

Eldoreth asked, "What are you talking about?"

Enki said, "Here, take this." Enki handed him a folded parchment which Captain Eldoreth promptly opened and read with obvious displeasure.

"Larzo?!" Eldoreth said. "Who issued this command? I only see your mark. What of the king's?"

"I have the king's authority," Enki said. "You are under my command. When you arrive with the central army you will transfer your command to Larzo and follow his directions. He will explain things further."

"I can't believe that this has the sanction of the king. Where's Lord Micah?"

"He also is under my command and his orders and wishes are not your concern. You will follow the orders as I've given you and you will do so this very moment."

Eldoreth became flush with anger. He said, "Calderach would never approve of this."

Enki said, "Calderach is not in command of the western rege. I am, and I have the full authority of the king."

Enki then revealed to the incredulous captain the signet ring of King Terah of Ur.

Eldoreth gasped.

He said, "May the gods help us!"

***

The camp began to awaken as sunrise approached. Already the eastern horizon was ablaze. The morning dew had soaked through the tents strewn throughout the compound. Sentries of the morning's final watch were sipping hot tea and trying to keep warm. The horses began to stir and snort in dread of the next leg of the journey to Roeth. Malki was bringing a pail of hot water to Lord Micah's tent when he was hit in the head by a small stone. Turning angrily he saw Enki peaking from behind a tent.

"Ashima protect us!" Malki said. "Why could I not have been left a slave in Damascus?"

"Settle down, Malki," whispered Enki. "Everything is going perfectly. You're going to live through this."

"Yes, I'm sure I will. I'll be personally preparing Zoreth's bath no doubt. That is, if Lord Micah doesn't sell me off to

Kish like he's been threatening. You know he blames me for your feigned excursions."

"But he's not suspicious of anything else?" Enki asked.

"Oh, he's suspicious of everything else," Malki said. "And I'm running out of creativity in trying to cover for you. Nabu only gives so much craftiness to each one of us. I believe I'm beginning to try his patience."

"Nabu could learn from you, Malki. You are one of the gods in disguise. Now which one is my tent?"

"The farthest away from Lord Micah's of course. The one to the right of the stables. There's hot water and the most obnoxious looking robes I could find laid out for you. I'm not sure which you'll look more ridiculous in. The pig herders' clothes you have on now, or the opulent garb I found in the palaces east wing."

"Perfect. I can't wait to try it on. You know I can't even smell myself anymore I've grown so accustomed to these peasants' clothes."

"Consider yourself fortunate." And with that, Malki continued on to Lord Micah's tent.

Enki slipped into his own tent and out of his peasants' rags, grateful for the piping hot water with which to disinfect himself. The clothes Malki had brought along for him truly were opulent and would definitely make an impression upon the people of Roeth – and more importantly upon Zoreth's spy's in the crowds. He had a great performance to enact today. He had to show himself to be the pompous fool and coward that he hoped Zoreth already suspected him to be – him being the youngest son of royalty living his days in a soft palace with no real command experience. He hoped he could pull it off without further raising the suspicions of Lord Micah.

The hot water over his face reinvigorated him and Enki soon felt refreshed and ready to continue his adventure. He had managed a few hours' sleep in the forest before making himself known to Malki and he hoped it would be enough for the day.

When he made his appearance, most of the tents had already been collapsed and the horses were being made ready for the day's journey. Lord Micah was finishing breakfast when he approached. He nearly choked on his food at first sight of the prince.

"I'm too old for this!" Micah said. "When did you get here? And who are you supposed to be? The son of Sargon?"

"Hey, the success of our mission depends upon our making an impression upon the populace," Enki said. "And yes, I agree, you are too old for this."

"Enki, this isn't some game. This isn't Eridu or one of the other towns of the interior. Anything can happen out here. This is serious business. I can't have you running about the western reaches without attendants. Not under the present circumstances!"

Enki sat down and began eating off Lord Micah's plate.

"Enki, what have you been up to? You're up to something, I know it. Malki is a good liar, but he's not that good."

"Oh, please don't tell Malki that. I've been trying to build up his confidence."

"Oh, be serious for a moment, Enki!"

"Listen, old man. You've nothing to worry about. I'll behave myself once we've reached Roeth. These are good eggs!"

Micah eventually gave up, as Enki predicted. He was indeed getting too old for this. The camp finally broke as the sun rose fully above the horizon. Lord Micah and Enki rode side by side with Enki trying to nurture his dwindling patience. Malki rode behind them trying not to be noticed by the old duke. The contingent was not large, no more than a hundred men, but they were heavily armed and well equipped with the usual fanfare of royalty. It was well after the noon hour when they finally approached the outskirts of Roeth.

With banners unfurled and trumpets ablaze, the populace of Roeth, came out to greet them. With them was the southern army's commander with one of his units leading the way to welcome their arrival. Roeth had been the most recent casualty of Zoreth's raids and had endured heavy losses to infrastructure and to the lives of those farmers brave enough to put up a resistance. By the time the southern command arrived, Zoreth had already disappeared into the desert. Several units remained in the town to help rebuild what had been destroyed and to lend comfort to a terrified populace. Enkidu was glad his arrival would further strengthen the morale of the town, but his choice of Roeth was more strategic than compassionate. It was unlikely Roeth would be a target for another raid any time soon. A coward of a prince would therefore pick such a city as his base. At least that's what Enki hoped Zoreth would think. Also the strength of the southern army stationed in and around the town would lend to his feigned image of an inexperienced and naive prince leaning on a strong show of arms to bolster his confidence.

The southern army's commander, Captain Tereth, was a good man, brave yet sensible, and most importantly, loyal to Larzo. Enki hoped that Larzo had been able to connect with him the day before when he would have passed near the city and to fill him in on the plan. Larzo at one time had told him that he was a man who could be trusted. Enki remembering those words had taken a risk and instructed in his orders to Larzo for him to gain Tereth's help if possible. The captain was now the first to reach Enkidu and as he did so, he respectfully dismounted and knelt before Enki and Lord Micah.

"Greetings My Lords, and especially to you, oh prince," Tereth said. "I bequeath my command into your royal hands."

Enki said, "Riseth, oh faithful Tereth, loyal captain of the southern lands, given to my fathers from the gods in long ages past. Rise and receive my favor." It was the most pompous voice Enki could come up with and he thought it came off rather well. Lord Micah simply rolled his eyes and looked away. From behind, Enki heard a nervous cough, presumably Malki's.

By Captain Tereth's own performance it appeared that Larzo had indeed filled him in on things. Enki was grateful to have an ally.

Tereth said, "The southern army has secured the entire perimeter of Roeth. Our forces here in the south are strong enough to repel any assault from the desert." Tereth gave his update loud enough for any in the gathering crowds to hear.

Enki said, "Excellent!" Enki tried to match Tereth's volume and direction of voice as he spoke. "Then we shall feast tonight and celebrate the gods' goodness to Roeth in blessing this land with my presence. Where is the steward of this fair town?"

Tereth said, "Regent Kiath is awaiting your arrival within Roeth. He has himself been directly overseeing the preparations for a great feast in your honor."

Enki said, "Then let us not keep him waiting. Lord Micah, fall in line with Tereth's troops in the rear. Captain Tereth, you will ride at my side."

Lord Micah's blank stare gave way to lethargic obedience as he turned his horse and made his way for the rear. Malki thought he heard him mumble under his breath something about the Great Library in Lagash. Tereth's men also fell in line behind the troops already traveling with Enki making his numbers now 800 strong as they made their way toward the city gates. Enki lowered his voice as they rode and tried to glean from Captain Tereth a survey of their situation.

Enki said, "Thank you Captain for your performance. Larzo told me you were a man who could be trusted, but he didn't tell me what a good actor you were."

Tereth said, "Thank you, My Lord. Larzo and I go way back. We were at the academy together. I could tell you stories of his own acting sometime if we have opportunity."

Enki said, "I hope that we shall. In the meantime, what can you tell me of Roeth's regent? I've never met him."

Tereth said, "Kiath? He shouldn't give you any trouble. Sure, he's corrupt along with all the rest of the city councilors of the region – you have to be to survive in power out here. But every town's chancellor's dream is to find an administrative post in Ur as you probably already know. He'll be bending over backwards to please you."

Enki and the captain rode on, Enki filling Tereth in on additional aspects of the plan he felt safe to disclose, and Tereth filling Enki in on Larzo's *acting opportunities* at the academy. Enki hoped he and Larzo lived through the next twenty-four hours so that he'd have opportunity to harass him about the stories Tereth told him.

They entered the city within a half hour. The populace of the town had gathered into the main square where the town regent awaited Enki's arrival. Enki was struck by the devastation he saw to property and lives as they entered through the city gates. The fields outside the town perimeter were completely burned up. Many town buildings within the walls were destroyed. Roeth's walls were not much of a deterrent to attack, more of a boundary marker than anything, and were now in complete shambles. Tereth's men had been in the region for a week assisting the rebuilding of the devastated areas and Enki could only imagine how much worse things must have been immediately following the raid.

Enki dismounted with the help of Malki as they

approached the central part of the main square where the regent Kiath awaited them. A temporary platform had been erected to raise the central figures above the crowd. As Enki pompously ascended the dais, Kiath bowed in humble, though certainly feigned submission and respect. Enki gratefully played along.

Enki said, "Rise faithful Kiath, steward of my father's people and lands. Rise and be recognized for your trust."

Kiath said, "Not I, sire, but you, we acknowledge as our sovereign lord. Hail to you who the gods crown our prince."

And so they continued to speak, each delivering speeches aimed at the populous, though Enki's true audience was Zoreth's spies in the crowd. All and all, Enki thought it went well. Lord Micah no doubt was now thoroughly confused by his performance. Enki was certain he was successfully coming across as a pompous fool of a prince and a coward hiding behind a powerful military. After the festivities and the long banquet that followed, Enki tried to explain to the old man that he was simply trying to exude a sense of confidence as planned. Micah clearly didn't buy it, but what could he do or say? Poor fool. He was trapped between the king's orders and the signet ring now in Enki's possession. He had had to play along and Enki knew it and so he had not been too concerned with placating the old duke. But now was the time approaching for Micah to be pushed over the edge. He knew there was only one thing that would do it and cause Micah to play his wildcard.

Enki lay down that evening hoping to at least get a few

hours' sleep. He considered how remarkably smooth all had gone. This would all be over by the end of the next day – assuming all his sources and spies were correct. He considered then how complex and confused war and diplomacy had become and wondered if Ur-Nammu had to be so devious in his own exploits. Enki was certain he had been, despite what the histories said.

It was Lord Micah who woke the prince close to midnight. Captain Tereth was with him as well as Malki.

"My prince, there is troubling news from the north," Lord Micah said. "Our scouts report that Zoreth has a strong force heading for Ele."

Enki asked, "How strong?"

"Two, maybe three divisions," Micah said.

Captain Tereth then stepped forward. He said, "If our scouts are correct, they should arrive at Ele within a few hours. Our northern forces are too spread out guarding the canals to be an effective defense. We must move the bulk of the southern command at once to engage the enemy. Zoreth's force is substantial."

Enki jumped to his feet in feigned excitement and eagerness. He said, "Excellent! Malki, prepare my battle guard! Captain Tereth, will you ride at my side?"

Expectedly, Lord Micah broke in. He said, "Master Enkidu, signet ring or no signet ring, I will not allow you to ride to battle against that desert rogue! I've been complacent long enough, but now the situation is critical. You are not ready for this challenge. Captain Tereth and I will lead the southern army to face Zoreth. You will stay here in Roeth."

Enki said, "Listen old man, I didn't ride all the way out here to the edge of oblivion to shoot desert hares! I will lead the army!"

Micah said, "You'll do no such thing. If you were to get killed, not only would I never be able to forgive myself but it would provide Zoreth with the greatest of all possible victories he could achieve. Now is not your time." Micah then softened his voice a bit. He said, "But your time will come soon enough, young master. But not now. And not without your father's consent."

Enki said, "But I have my father's consent. The western rege has been entrusted to me and me alone!"

Micah said, "Your father entrusted you with a mission to be a decoy. That mission is no longer valid. Zoreth has called our bluff. Stand down Enki, lest I claim *urgarith soonti*!"

Enki said, "You wouldn't dare!"

Micah said, "Don't underestimate my power, Enki, or my willingness to use it. Avoid the embarrassment and stand down."

Enki forced himself to redden with feigned fury. His sullen look was masterly performed, Tereth would later tell him. After several moments of further silence posited for dramatic effect, Enki relented speaking slowly and with clenched fists.

Enki said, "Very well old fool, but I shall never forget this and the day will come when you will regret your action here today. Take the rege and be gone!"

And with that Enki stormed out of the room, with no real

place to go, but feeling elated that he had made it through the exchange without giving himself away. And to think Micah had actually used the word *decoy*, he thought to himself. If he only knew!

Lord Micah was heading north with the troops within the hour. Enki went back to bed. He figured he had another good three or four hours. He slipped quickly into a troubled sleep.

***

When Malki woke him, it was near dawn.

Malki said, "They're coming. Just like you said they would."

Malki's voice was calm with only a hint of anxiety. No doubt he had resolved himself to the tide that had been unleashed and could not now be stopped. Now they had to see this thing through to the end and their very lives swayed in the balance.

Enki continued to lie in silence and in the dark. It felt suddenly to Enki that time was standing still. Gone for a moment was his confidence. He suddenly felt a wave of fear sweep over him. What if he were wrong? But he shook the thought away. He had a destiny to fulfill. He started to rise, but he stopped himself. Was he ready for this? Too late to back down now he knew. He continued to lie in darkness and silence. Malki did not speak but waited on Enki. Finally, an unusually reflective Enki broke the quiet. Still with his eyes closed he spoke slowly and softly.

He said haltingly, "I heard a voice when I was last in the desert."

Enki paused for several seconds before continuing.

"It was after I had killed the Semite. I felt sure I was dying – perhaps I was. I've been assuming the voice was a hallucination due to the loss of blood ... but now I'm not so sure."

Malki said nothing. Outside the feint caw of a crow was heard breaking the silence of the pre-dawn hours. A ray of light invaded through the window, but then was dimmed by distant clouds.

"*Come away with me*, I heard the voice say."

There was silence again as another minute passed. The distant sound of a multitude of horses could now be heard ever so faintly in the background.

Finally Enki spoke again. He said, "The voice was ... wonderful."

Enki let the description roll off his tongue reverently as he savored the memory.

"Master, they're coming," Malki said again at last, quietly but firmly.

Enki said, "I know."

More silence.

"Do you think I can pull this off?" Enki asked at last. It was the first time he'd allowed himself to express doubt to another.

Malki replied with surprising forcefulness. He said, "Master Enkidu, you are the most foolhardy, careless soul

I've ever known – it was the gods curse upon me that I became your slave. But know this – I would go to the ends of the earth with you, not because you are my master, but because I believe in you. For all my worry, there is in me a relentless foreboding that you have a destiny to fulfill. Whether you get yourself killed before you're able to fulfill it is another matter, but if anyone could pull off this ridiculous scheme of yours, then yes, I believe it would be Prince Enkidu of Ur."

Enki had opened his eyes by now and was staring at Malki incredulously. Something passed between them there in that brief instant as both shared a look of mutual admiration and affection for the other. It was a moment of which they never spoke of again until years later in what would seem another lifetime.

Enkidu then rose slowly from his bed, leaned back like a catapult being prepared to fire and gave out a great yell that woke half the city. A surge of excitement exploded through his being as all his suppressed stress found sudden release. Then he kissed Malki on the cheek and ran out the door.

"I wonder how cruel a death Zoreth will give me," Malki then said to no one in particular. "At least I can be sure he won't kiss me." And then he sped off to catch up with Enki.

Enki gathered the small garrison that remained. Forty or so soldiers on horseback were ready for flight with their prince. Enki climbed atop the watchtower. Zoreth's forces were a cloud of dust in the fast shrinking distance. A faint rumble was growing steadily into a terrifying roar. They were coming in from the east and north, cutting them off from flight to anywhere but the desert. The sun was now making its ascent across the eastern horizon. Some of Zoreth's forces formed an eerie silhouette against the bright morning sky.

Enki mounted his horse, now dressed in full battle garb. Malki was at his side as he led his small cavalry unit out of the city limits in swift flight. Zoreth's forces, closer with each passing minute, changed their course upon seeing the garrison depart. Zoreth's full force was heading toward the fleeing prince and his small contingent. A few units then appeared to break away from Zoreth's army and head once again toward the town, no doubt to verify that the prince had not remained behind in hiding.

Enki could feel his heart pounding within him as he knew his life now hung in the balance. There were so many things that could yet go wrong. He tried not to think of such things, but to enjoy the chase. The desert air was already warm against his face as he sped on at a frantic pace. He knew that he had to stay well ahead of Zoreth's forces for the next few hours. Fortunately, Enki's men's horses were well rested and Zoreth's had already been traveling for some time by the time the chase began.

Enki led his men southeast for about half an hour, then made a sudden turn south. Zoreth would no doubt think he intended to fly toward the Urian port far to the southwest. Calderach would be there with the bulk of the southern army, but it was a full day's journey away still. Enki knew he would never make it, cutting through the hot desert wilderland as they were. This was Zoreth's country. Zoreth's men would make their way swiftly through the region while Enki and his men struggled for their bearings.

A segment of Enki's pursuers now broke away making a sharper southwest trek. Their intentions were to cut off Enki's escape route to the port and Enki knew they would succeed. Now there truly was no turning back. Embracing his fate, Enki sped on with a war cry which frightened Malki, but stirred his men on to greater fervor. His men knew their odds of escape were now negligent. They embraced their fate as well, hoping that their flight and final valiant fight would earn them a song.

Another frantic hour passed. Zoreth's forces showed no signs of slowing and had even gained on them. Zoreth's contingent to the northeast had gained such ground by now as to force Enki to veer slightly eastward again toward the desert. Another hour passed and Enki was beginning to worry they had veered too far eastward when he finally saw off in the distance what he'd been straining to see through most of their flight. The faint outline of the desert canyons could now be clearly seen through what must have been a sandstorm breaking up. The storm was steadily dissolving with each passing minute as the canyons likewise emerged.

Enki allowed himself a quick glance at the copy of his precious map to verify his bearings. He adjusted their course slightly and sped on with all haste. The canyons were not as close as he had at first thought and it was an additional hour before they had reached the outskirts. The ground had now become rockier and their horses stumbled from time to time. The more difficult terrain forced them to slow their pace, which allowed Zoreth's army to make quick gains on them.

Still Enki allowed himself to hope. If he could just make it to the canyon he'd discovered the previous week. He passed by several entrances to similar canyons, each time wondering if he'd been mistaken in the distance to his intended target. Passing each such entrance by, his mind would be routinely tortured as he allowed himself to second guess himself until the entrance of the next.

Finally, he made out the two lone trees he'd isolated those weeks before as his landmark. The hills to their right as they continued on south had risen in both height and steepness. The jagged cliffs took on a menacing look as he sped along the outskirts, eager for the break in the mountains wall.

Enki almost missed the entrance as his eyes were focused somewhat beyond the actual point of entry. He signaled quickly to his wearied men. Enki led them in a sharp turn to the right and then into the canyon's shadows. At first the way was narrow, but it soon widened, allowing more light and revealing the interior valley. All around them steep cliffs rose to the skies. The main floor of the valley was mostly flat, but was interspersed with various mounds and hills along with pockets of dry shrubs.

Zoreth was now close enough for him to hear the battle cries of his men. Already the closest of Zoreth's forces had entered the canyon. Their voices echoed throughout the canyon interior.

Enki continued to lead his men deeper in. They were

now at the widest point of the valley. From this point on, the cliffs on either side would grow closer and closer until they merged into a veritable dead end.

More of Zoreth's men had now emerged into the canyon and Enki in looking back could for the first time make out the faces of his pursuers. These were stern faced men, hardened by the elements and by a strict, regimented life in the desert wastes. They were dressed similarly to the Semite he had killed in the very ledges now above him the previous week. Recalling the battle skill of that one unfortunate warrior, he cringed at the thought of being trapped by a whole host of such men.

He was now nearing the eastern end of the valley which ended in an enclave of rock and stone. The cliffs towered all about them from every direction except from that of his pursuers. Enki waved his men come to a halt, but it was a needless command as there was nowhere left to go, but turn and fight. But Enki on this option held his men at bay. He gave the command to withhold attack, and he made the command clear enough for his attackers to see their intentions.

Zoreth's men had now begun to circle around the trapped men. They withheld attack as Enki had anticipated. With Enki and his men momentarily withholding hostility, Zoreth's men would wait for Zoreth himself to arrive. Enki and his men were on slightly higher ground and so could see over the heads of the Semites enough to observe a final segment of Zoreth's army enter the valley with what Enki assumed to be Zoreth himself. Soon a whole host of Semite warriors were gathered around in a vast semi-circle, each crying intonations in their own tongue. Enkidu guessed that their total numbers were three to four hundred. These finally parted at one point to allow a central figure and several of his aides to make their way through the mass of horses, swords and shields.

Zoreth was a huge man. His bulk was mostly muscle, though it was clear he had enjoyed a fine meal from time to time. He was taller than most Semites and his horse was a massive creature clad in armor. His thick black beard hid most of his face, but his eyes shown through with a penetrating stare. His age was difficult to discern, but there was a certain maturity about him. He carried himself with great confidence and tenacity as he strode toward the mound upon which Enki and his men awaited their fate.

"Prince Enkidu!" Zoreth said. He spoke spitefully in rough Akkadian, the common speech of the land. "Terach's boy! So are you really the fool I've heard reports of, or is there indeed any manhood in you?"

Enki's men began to grab for their swords until Enki quieted them in Old Sumerian.

Enki then, "So you're the great Zoreth who's been striking terror in my people."

"I accept your praise, but it will not save you." Zoreth's speech was again in the common tongue, but it was clearly not his first language and he spoke with a strange accent. The deep desert peoples had their own speech, which Enki now heard from time to time coming from Zoreth's troops all about him. Zoreth spoke in such a tongue now back in reply to some captain near him . Then he turned back to Enki and spoke again in Akkadian. He said, "I've not yet decided how I'll kill you. You would I assume bring a great profit were I to hold you ransom. Perhaps you'd like to begin the bidding yourself?"

Enki's men were now extremely restless, eager for a final fight, but no doubt anxious in their knowledge that it would be their last. Enki again steadied them with a wave of his hand. Then in a firm, confident voice he spoke. "Zoreth," he said, "I see that you are a great leader. I've decided that after I have killed you, I will spare your men in your honor. Let us avoid a bloody war here and settle this ourselves. I will fight you, the winner to determine the fate of the other's men."

The proposal stirred angry laughter amidst Zoreth's troops. Enki sounded confident, but his mere forty men against several hundred desert tribesmen did not lend much weight to his offer.

Zoreth scoffed then. He said, "You and what army is going to force our hand this day, as if we were your pitiful plains peasants who grovel at Ur's gates?"

Zoreth was indignant in his tone and brought the tension of the moment to a breaking point. The critical moment had arrived.

Enki waved his hand at the canyon cliffs above him. "This one!" he said with a shout.

And in response to his signal the central army hiding in the cliffs all about them rose and peered over the cliff. With a deafening roar they shouted and brandished their swords and spears and their archers all about aimed with deadly precision upon the now unfortunate desert army poised below. Enki could make out Captain Larzo in a crevice near at hand. He was no doubt clearly enjoying this bit of action after such a long imprisonment as captain of the palace guard. Enki's forty men about him were no doubt thoroughly confused as they had not been let in on the full plan. Enki would make it up to them later. Malki simply let out a sigh of relief.

As for Zoreth's army, angry and incensed cries rose from the trapped desert warriors all about. Every warrior let out his angry protests except for one who gave out a hearty laugh. It was Zoreth laughing with great abandon as his sharp mind quickly came to terms with the intricate trap that Enki had carefully laid out for him.

"I am the fool this day!" Zoreth said. He heartily voiced this as the roar about him quieted to hear the coming exchange. Enki allowed himself to relax his own nervous stance as he permitted himself to hope that this plan of his could yet be pulled off without bloodshed. Zoreth continued with an address to his men. He said, "My desert brothers, we were wrong about this Prince of Ur. No coward or fool have we here but one of our own kind. If death be our fortune this day, we fall to a worthy foe."

Enki then picked up on this overture of Zoreth's toward avoiding conflict, grateful that Zoreth's mind was indeed as sharp and as astute as he'd heard it was. Here was a master of men's emotions. Sadiq was indeed right in his assessment of these desert peoples and Enki now sought to implement his advise. If he could gain Zoreth as an ally...

To the surprise of all of his captains and most of his men, Enki addressed Zoreth now as his equal. He said, "Master Zoreth, we can end this conflict this day in one of three ways. Fight we can, and as you now know, we will win the day, but certainly not after a great loss to our own lives as I concede to you your superior skill in this your land. For indeed, in the week before this one, I nearly lost my life in a noble battle with one of your own in these very canyons. It is his sword that I now hold in my hands."

Murmurs of disbelief rose from Zoreth's forces who were unwilling to believe that a desert Semite had fallen to a plainsman in single-handed combat in the Semite's own land. Enki knew he would need to move on quickly to his next point lest his boast be called further into question.

Enki continued his speech. He said, "Or you can still accept my initial offer. I will fight you Zoreth, and should I kill you, I for my part will allow your men safe passage homeward. I expect that as a man of honor you would do the same for my men should I fall and you be victorious."

There followed a mixed response from both armies and each protested with steadily growing murmurs. Neither army would trust the other to carry out such an arrangement, Enki knew, and certainly upon the death of one in such combat, battle would almost certainly ensue. Zoreth no doubt knew this as well, as did his captains. Enki raised his voice above the growing disquiet and presented his third option.

Enki continued, "Or! Or we can end this standoff now and embrace each other, if not as friends, then as respected allies!"

That brought a stunned silence for a moment, giving Enki the momentum to continue with his plea. Enki said, "I did not lead you into the desert to destroy you, though I am prepared to call upon my army to do so!"

Enki paused for a few seconds to allow this fact to sink in. Then he continued. He said, "We each have something to offer the other in exchange for peace. We of Ur desire safety and security for our western borders, free from the worry of raids. Our real rival is to the north and east, not from you our neighbors." Still silence. He'd not yet lost his audience. He continued on confidently hoping his men would not protest this next statement.

"You would desire, I believe, and we would welcome, you as a recognized people and a partner in trade. There is greater prosperity that could be won from one another as friends, than as foes."

At this a quiet murmur did arise from portions of his own army all about, but this was quickly quieted by Larzo and the other captains. There was silence again as Enki dismounted, lay down his sword and held out his hand to Zoreth. Enki addressed Zoreth. He said, "Master Zoreth, would you embrace us as an ally this day? I offer you this sword as a token of my good will."

A nervous, tension-filled moment grew to further intensity as Zoreth himself dismounted and walked over to Enki's dropped sword, picked it up and then approached Enki. Something passed between the two as each seemed to read the other's mind. Each was playing upon the emotions of his troops. Each was now trying to avoid a devastating battle without losing face. Enki's forces would indeed win such a conflict, but it was likely that both Enki and Zoreth would die in such a battle. Enki and Zoreth both knew this, which seemed to unite them in a common goal.

Zoreth examined Enki's sword. Then he shouted to his men. Zoreth said, "It is indeed one of our own! The prince has spoken the truth. He has defeated one of our brothers in combat. A worthy ally he would be!"

Zoreth then drew closer to Enki and raised the sword. Several archers far above readied themselves to save their prince, but Larzo quietly restrained them, correctly interpreting the situation. Then to the horror of Enki's troops, Zoreth swung with all his might missing Enki's head by a hair. Enki remained frozen, unmoved. Somehow he maintained his confident stance. Still his hand was outstretched. Zoreth said, "And truly, a man of courage you are, Prince Enkidu! Worthy of our friendship!"

And with that Zoreth threw down the sword and clasped Enki's hand.

***

The rest of the day was spent by Enki and Zoreth convincing their respective captains that their move had been a wise and honorable one. Enki's men soon relented, but it would be his father and brothers who would need the convincing. Zoreth had a harder time with his men until Enki pointed to the portion of the canyon where he'd slain his foe the previous week. There they found the decomposing corpse and the evidence of the battle Enki had testified to. Most were then apparently satisfied and even allowed Enki to take part in the funeral rites as they buried their fallen brother.

Later that night in a tent in the middle of their camp, Zoreth and Enki and their captains hammered out an initial agreement whereby Zoreth and his forces would cease all raids upon the western towns and would act instead as a buffer to hostile tribes of the deeper desert. In exchange, Enki, using the full authority his father had given him, officially extended recognition to Zoreth's people as a legitimate power, and relinquished all claims to the silver mines of Zoreth's realm. In addition they signed an agreement of free trade between the towns of Ur and Zoreth's own tribal clan. Afterward they exited the tent and announced the agreements to both armies, now each much more agreeable after a hearty meal supplied by Enki's army and strong drink supplied by Zoreth's.

It was indeed an agreeable picture and Enki and Zoreth noted it well. There were now campfires and tents strewn throughout the valley. Around each fire were groups of Semites of the desert and Sumerians of the plains of Ur enjoying song and drink together. What had nearly been a bloodbath had turned into a night of levity. Enki and Zoreth sat around a fire as well. With them were Malki, Larzo, and a close captain of Zoreth's named Hamud. They drank in silence admiring the stars above, drained from the excessive stress of the day's happenings, and still letting the strange turn of the day's events to sink in. Zoreth finally broke the silence.

"Prince Enkidu, tell me truthfully," he said. "Will our decisions this day truly survive your return back to Ur and the critique of your father?"

Enki, awoken from deep thought quickly responded. Enki said, "I spoke the truth in our conference this afternoon. My people will welcome peace. They grow soft and desire to conquer economically, not through bloodshed. My father and brothers will have to concede this, though they may not initially agree with the terms. They will accept it."

"And are you to tell me that you too desire to go this *road of peace* that your people desire? Are you also grown *soft*?"

Enki was silent as he considered how to answer the desert Chieftain. Enki decided to throw it back to Zoreth. Enki asked, "And what do you think?"

Zoreth seemed to look deeply into Enki's eyes just then. "I think," Zoreth said slowly, "that you are not *soft*."

A few seconds of silence passed before Zoreth continued. Then, staring again into the fire he continued. "I think you are an ambitious young prince and that you will not for long settle to be leading regiments to clean out the swamps of your south. I also think that no one will be fooled again, as we were, into believing you to be a nave. I fear your days may be numbered."

Zoreth looked up again at Enki and met his gaze for several seconds. Zoreth's words were not spoken in spite, but they made Enki uncomfortable nonetheless. He decided to change the topic.

Enki asked, "Tell me, Master Zoreth, how is it that this day indeed ended as it did? There was a time not long ago that I would never have welcomed such an alliance as we are now forming. But somehow, deep within me, I am compelled to ... to trust you – you, who I was intending to lead to the slaughter."

Zoreth turned back to the fire and smiled. Zoreth said, "It is a question I have also been asking. I am a judge of men. Such a day as we have had reveals much. I am able to discern a man's nature. I quickly knew what kind of a man you are. I am only a little surprised that we have embraced one another so swiftly. More surprised am I that our men have done so. It is true that less separates us than one might think. In generations past, our peoples were completely separate. In these days of change, our peoples begin to mingle. There is desert blood in many of your men, and some of ours come from the land of the River. Many of my people no longer even maintain their own tongue. Akkadian is spoken even in parts of the deep desert."

"It is the same for my people," Enki said in mournful agreement. "There have been many a priest who have tried to revive Old Sumer, and to discourage the common tongue that has invaded our land as well. It always fails. Like holding back the tide at the gulf, all resistance to this tide is doomed to fail."

Zoreth asked, "And would you too like to see Old Sumer rise again?"

Enki said, "Sumer yes. Old Sumer no. Sumer is greater

than the classic tongue of my ancestors. The priests are content to try to revive the past. I desire to surpass it."

Zoreth said, "Ha! You *are* an ambitious young prince." Zoreth laughed and then turned to Larzo as the next target of his speech. He said, "Tell me Captain Larzo. What will you tell your king when he asks you what kind of a man his fool of a son has made an alliance with?"

Larzo was taken only slightly off his guard. He recovered quickly. Larzo answered, "I will tell him that he has got himself a sly old fox of a man and a scoundrel at that for a new friend!"

Fortunately Zoreth laughed at Larzo's bold remark with understood appreciation for the brash Captain. Larzo continued, "But I will also tell him that he has an ally who is a true leader of his people, and a keeper of his word. I too am a judge of men."

Zoreth gazed keenly into Larzo's eyes nodding his head and then responded thoughtfully.

Zoreth said, "Many a surprise have we had today, not the least of which is that there still exist men of the *Old Ways* even in our own corrupt times. Glad am I that I had no need to kill you, but such a fight I would have cherished."

"Aye," Larzo agreed.

"And what about you, curious slave?" Zoreth asked as he turned his attention suddenly to Malki.

Malki straightened up abruptly after having been bent straight over and gazing intently into the fire lost in thought. Zoreth continued, "How is it that you, a slave of the prince, share his fire like one of his captains?"

Malki turned helplessly to Enki but received no rescue. Enki was curious about his answer.

Malki finally found his voice and was once again his obstinate self. He said, "Of the peculiarities of my prince I have no answer. But as for me, I was a man before a slave and when I am dead, a man I will once again be."

Zoreth then spoke to Enki. He said, "Perhaps you *are* soft to let such disrespect go unchecked."

Malki bowed his head at this, but Enki gave him a reassuring glance before Zoreth continued.

Zoreth said, "Enkidu of Ur you are a curious mix of a man. I concede to you that you have beaten me. Our agreement is not one I would have sought, but I will indeed carry it out, and believe it yet will benefit my people at least as much as it does yours. Nevertheless, you have forced my hand, something no one has ever done before. Many of my own people have tried and failed. They are all dead."

As Enki considered this, Zoreth continued. He said, "And yet there is something quite ... unfinished about you. Your youth betrays you. I don't know what you will one day be, or if indeed you will survive, for I foresee turbulent years ahead for you. But this I will say. If indeed survive you do, then the gods beware of what havoc you will wreck upon their world."

***

As the evening progressed their conversation grew lighter. Soon they were telling of past adventures, highly embellished but entertaining. Even Malki joined in the amusement, once it was clear Zoreth had accepted the role Enki had allowed for him.

The next day, they broke camp late and after a hasty breakfast, prepared to depart. The previous evening's revelry amongst the two armies did more than the signed agreement to mold the resultant alliance. There were many a Sumerian and Semite who parted friends that day and many more with a fond respect for their would-be opponents. Enki rode at the head of his troops and waved his battlements in hearty salute to the desert Chieftain as Zoreth and his men headed south and west into lands unknown to the plains people of Ur.

Enki and his men traveled all day and it was near sunset when he and his troops finally reached Roeth. Word had preceded them. The whole city of Roeth, along with many from other towns as well, gathered to welcome them. As they entered the town they were soon surrounded by a whole host of grateful devotees. Soon their cheers blended into a steady chant.

They shouted, "Enkidu, Enkidu, abram teshua! Abram teshua! Abram teshua!"

Enki leaned over to Larzo in bewilderment. Enki asked, "What are the people shouting?"

Larzo, too, was awe struck.

"It is an ancient title," Larzo said. He spoke haltingly as if recalling something. "They are calling you, *abram teshua.* It means *great father of deliverance.*"

CHAPTER 4 – A HERO'S WELCOME

The whole east sector of Ur was near vacant as King Terah and his entourage made their passage through the east gate and into the city proper. It was near mid-day and yet the city streets were empty. Terah looked at his son Haran, who in turn looked at his brother Nahor, who in turn looked at Lord Salzarto, each with questioning eyes. They had approached the city expecting huge jubilant crowds, but instead were greeted by song birds and the sound of the wind. But the city populace was clearly somewhere! From time to time they would hear the distant rumble of a pleased crowd rising in ecstatic celebration before declining again to a low steady roar.

Terah was the first to verbalize their confusion. He said, "Surely word would have preceded us concerning our successful mission!"

"So one would have thought," Nahor said in perplexed

agreement.

"The sound of our people appears to be coming from the west sector," said Haran. "Perhaps, they await our entry there."

"If so, then I would wonder at their jubilant cries in our absence," retorted a cynical Nahor.

"Perhaps, the desert chieftain Zoreth did indeed attack Ur in our absence and the people celebrate Krishna's victory," Lord Salzarto said.

Terah finally tired of bewilderment and asked someone. He spotted a store keeper locking up his shop and shouted to him across the way. He said, "Here old man! How came the streets to be so vacant at this most busy of hours? Where are the people assembled and to what end?"

The storekeeper looked up at first in annoyance and then in fearful shock as he recognized who was addressing him. He responded nervously, "My Lord! You've returned! Forgive us, your people, for not being ready to receive you. The people are assembled at the west gate to receive and celebrate the prince's victory! I was just heading there now."

Haran then stepped forward and said, "But the prince is here at the king's side. If the people wish to celebrate Prince Nahor's diplomatic victory at the Lagash summit, then why are they not awaiting him and us here at the east gate?"

The storekeeper was now even more nervous and responded with hesitant fear. He said, "My Lords, the people celebrate Prince Enkidu's victory in the desert. Surely, My Lords have heard the news?"

"What ... news?" King Terah asked slowly.

"Why Prince Enkidu planned and led Zoreth and his army into ambush. In so doing he won Zoreth's tribe over to our side and has secured our western frontier. Surely his plan had the sanction of your majesty? The people celebrate the prince's victory in the name of the king."

A moment's dead silence was ended by Nahor as he broke into hearty laughter. Haran was visibly enraged. Terah also appeared angry, but there was a touch of pride in his eyes as well and his demeanor continued to soften as he spoke. He said, "Go on good citizen. Enjoy the festivities as we rejoice today in many good tidings. I bid you only speak not of our return. We wish to surprise the prince and celebrate his victory in like fashion."

"As you wish, My Lord," he said. And with that the storekeeper scurried off quickly wishing to avoid any further inquiry.

Nahor's laughter was beginning to subside when Haran heatedly spoke. He said, "Father, you mean for us to slip into the city like outcasts while this son of yours receives the praise that is our due!?"

Terah was staring off in the direction of the celebration as another wave of noise from the distant crowd erupted. Still gazing, he spoke. "We shall receive our praise in due time, my son. Let Enki have his day. Come! Let us steal away quickly before we are further noticed. We will await Enki in his quarters."

Nahor was still chuckling as he wrapped his arm about Haran. He said, "Come, my brother. We have been outwitted. Let us accept our brother's good fortune. If anyone has been wronged it is I, and I release our brother in the hopes that he will have a grand tale to tell us while we feast tonight on song and drink."

It was nearing sundown when Enki finally arrived at the palace having thoroughly enjoyed the throngs of Urians celebrating his victory. The receptions that he'd received, first in the western towns and now here in Ur itself, far surpassed his highest expectations. Lord Micah had been just as bewildered by the strong show of support for Enki and had been forced to withdraw his harsh critique of the prince for his wild scheme. Malki, at first in a daze at the huge lively crowds, soon joined them in hearty celebration of their prince. Captain Larzo had perhaps celebrated the most and was now thoroughly drunk and no doubt lost in some dark quarter of the city.

Enkidu was nearly drunk himself as he stumbled into the palace. He somehow made his way up both flights of steps to his quarters and was about to throw himself with complete abandon upon his couch when he noticed it already occupied by his father. The fright nearly sobered him as he leaped aside and into his wardrobe forcing it down upon him. The sound of the crash was followed by Nahor's easy laughter and Haran's predictable sigh of disgust.

"Brother, if only your throngs of admirers could see you now," laughed Nahor.

A bewildered and fallen Enki shook the pile of clothes off him and rolled to his feet.

Enki said, "Father! When did you arrive?"

"We just did," Terah said. "And none too soon. Had we delayed any longer we might have found ourselves allied with Kish as well." Terah spoke with feigned anger but a glimmer of pride shown through his eyes.

With more realism, Haran continued his thought. He said, "How dare you make alliance with an enemy of the state without any consultation with our lord or the high council!"

Enkidu tried to compose himself and regain his edge. He stood up and straightened his clothes and walked across the room flinging himself confidently down upon the only unoccupied couch. With hands behind head and feet kicked up in abandoned leisure, he spoke with biting sarcasm. "Come, my brothers," he said. "Do not be jealous of your kid brother. I only did what any other humble prince of the realm would do – seeking to serve our people and bring prestige to our father's name."

Terah said, "The only thing you'll have brought your father is an early death."

"Alright, Enki," Nahor said. "Let's have it. And embellish no detail. We'll be getting Lord Micah's side of the story later."

Enki then launched eagerly into the account of his tale. Often leaping from his couch and prancing about the room in extravagant dramatics, he stretched what could have been a short tale into a several act drama. Nahor later conceded privately to Lord Salzarto that Enki was magnificent in his performance. He was particularly brilliant in presenting his encounter with Zoreth. Had Enki not been born a prince, he would have made a fine bard.

As Enki finished, Nahor broke out in riotous applause while Terah tried to look unimpressed. Finally, Haran spoke, unable to hold back his predictable verdict. He said, "A fine adventure Enki, but did you ever consider the consequences of failure? What if you'd been captured or killed before reaching this canyon you speak of? How careless could you be!? I concede to you, your actions reveal a certain level of courage that I had not given you credit for, but this only highlights the crime against our father's good name that such courage inborn to all of House Eber should be put to such foolish means! And to let this Amorite chieftain live – do you have any honor whatsoever?"

"Oh, let him be," Nahor said with a lighthearted chuckle. "It's our fault for not letting him go with us to the trade talks. In response to our slight, Enki held some trade talks of his own. The irony alone was worth the risk."

Enki, having ignored, as usual, Haran's critique, bowed low now in response to Nahor. He said, "Thank you dear brother."

"My pleasure, oh great Guardian and Savior of the West," said Nahor with more than a touch of sarcasm.

"Actually, they are calling him *abram teshua*," a voice said. It was Lord Micah who just walked into the room. "It means *great father of deliverance* and it makes me sick every time I hear it."

Nahor once again broke into laughter.

Lord Micah extended warm greetings to King Terah and his sons and then broke into grave apology for allowing himself to be so carelessly manipulated. But the kind, old man could not be convincingly vicious toward Enki and his own pride in the prince's deed shown through.

Terah shone with pride as well as he arose and walked over to Enki. Then, his expression became more serious. He said, "In all seriousness Enki, I agree with Haran, you should not have let the Semite lord live. But what's done is done, and we will honor the agreement. It will be welcome news if such an agreement holds for even a year, giving us at least a modest break from concern about the western reaches such that we can focus on more pressing matters."

Enki said, "Father, the agreement will hold, and longer than a year. I vouch for the desert chieftain."

Terah said, "We shall see. In the meantime, we must prepare for the High King's coming next week. I do not believe he will care for your embracing of this desert tribe any more than I, but it will seem a minor matter – there are indeed more pressing matters that beg our attention."

Lord Micah perked up at this with sudden interest. "What pressing matters, My Lord?" he asked.

"We heard some troubling rumors from the north when we were in Lagash," said Terah. "We await confirmation, but it appears that the Ebla Coalition is collapsing."

Lord Micah gasped and then sat down. Then, after a few moments silence he spoke. He said, "By the gods, I knew this would happen. But I did not think I would live to see it. This is indeed troubling news, and especially now with Etana on the throne in Kish." As he spoke, Lord Micah sounded old and tired. Enki noted that he had never seen the old duke so gravely concerned.

Enki's father's response was equally disconcerting. He said, "Indeed. Nor did I think I would live to see it either. It may be that our days of peace will soon be over. I had hoped to go to the grave in the peace and security won for us by Ur-Nammu. But now it looks as though my final years will be as troubling as his."

"Father, we will meet whatever the challenges be together," said Haran. He spoke with confidence and sincerity.

Terah looked about at his sons and then clasped Haran on the shoulder. He said, "Indeed we will. And this troubles me as well. It is a more uncertain world that I will leave to you my sons. I wish it could be otherwise. But there is yet cause for hope. Come, let us prepare for Lugulbanda's coming." Then smiling and turning to Enki, he said, "That is if the great *abram teshua* will still take orders from an old man."

"For now, father. For now." Enki was smiling in jest as he said this, but his father and brothers would secretly wonder all the same.

The following week was something of a letdown for Enki after the high drama and exciting events of the week before. He spent it mostly with Malki going over revisions of the desert treaty which he would soon formalize and present before the high council. The news from the north was sure to guarantee easy passage of the pact. Ur needed peace on its western frontier more than ever. But still he struggled through its wording. He wanted to do an adept job with the proposal and so show his father and brothers that he was competent with the pen as well as with the sword.

Adding to the difficulty of his present task was the distracting news he'd heard of Aya coming to Ur with her father. He'd been expecting Gil and old Shulpae to be along, but had thought Aya would still be with her tutors in Lagash. She hadn't mentioned coming in any of her letters and had probably wanted her coming to be a surprise. He was both excited and anxious at the news. He desperately wanted to see her, but this would be her first trip to Ur since their romance had begun. He didn't even know if his father and brothers knew of their relationship. He quickly repented of that thought – of course they must know. But it would still be somewhat awkward all the same. He hoped Nahor would behave himself and not embarrass him.

When the time of their arrival finally came, Enki was in the southern part of the city. The first trumpets sounded forth from one of the high watchtowers, but soon the whole city resounded in jubilant acclaim of the High King of Uruk's arrival. No doubt they were still a good half hour from the city when the first watchtower spotted them and sounded forth the announcement. Enki tried to restrain himself from rushing excitedly to the northern gate. He would have time to arrive ahead of them and there was no need to reveal his anxiousness to the commoners. The people must know that even the High King held no sway over him.

And so it was that Enki was one of the last of Ur's elite to arrive at the northern gate. Nahor noticed him first. "See, father. I told you not to worry. Here's the Great One now."

A relieved Terah then made his desperate plea. "Please, Enki, behave yourself," he said.

Enki said, "How could I possibly do otherwise?"

Terah simply sighed in defeat and turned to await Lugulbanda's arrival.

Great crowds had assembled to welcome the most powerful man in all of New Sumer. Banners were unfurled and trumpets continued to sound forth in happy acclaim. The contingent from Uruk looked to include a good fifty or so, mostly on horseback, with a few carriages as well. King Lugulbanda and his son rode at the front of the entourage and soon broke into a gallop to arrive ahead of the rest. King Terah of Ur then rode out with his sons to greet them.

Enki remembered now why he was intimidated by the great king. Lugulbanda was a big man, tall and strong, and though probably about his father's age, he looked as though he would live forever. His majestic garb was not needed. He would have looked majestic without them. And his eyes blazed with a fierce intensity. Here was a great king of the old kind. He belonged to the ages.

"Hail your majesty! My friend and my king!" Terah said. Terah's greeting was strong and confident.

"And hail to you, lord of the southern lands," Lugulbanda said. "We of the north embrace you our brothers!"

Enki knew Lugulbanda spoke for the sake of the crowds assembled, as did Terah, but he could not help but be caught up in the majesty and history of the moment. Here was solid evidence of the existence of New Sumer, the united kingdom centering around the cities of Uruk and Ur.

The alliance between the southern and northern cities had begun during the days of Rue. During those years, following the collapse of Kish's Empire, King Rue of Ur and King Anu of Uruk had redeemed the ancient custom of assembling the kings of Old Sumer at the priest city Nippur. Fearing that Kish's power in the north might be regained or that the growing restlessness of the eastern peoples of Susa might threaten their independence, Anu and Rue had led their peoples and the peoples of several other cities into a union of necessity. With Uruk as the closest of the great cities to their more prominent enemy Kish in the north, King Rue of Ur gave his support to the supremacy of Uruk's royal line as overlord of the new coalition. Thus began the great union between House Anu of Uruk and House Eber of Ur. Down through successive generations the union had remained intact and House Eber had maintained its loyalty to Uruk even though Ur could boast that it was Uruk's equal in culture, power and population. Ur-Nammu had come closest to straining this relationship as he led Ur into an unprecedented renaissance of expanding power and culture that made some in Uruk nervous. Yet all knew that civil war would mean national suicide. Kish in the north, Susa in the east and Amorites and other desert tribes from the west would quickly swallow up Sumer should she lose her unity.

But not all the cities of Old Sumer had joined Uruk and Ur in the union they now referred to ambitiously as New Sumer. Lagash had opted for independence and had grown to be a great economic center, in spite of the troubling years of war with Umma. Umma had also remained an independent city-state along with Shurrapak, the ancient city of the legendary Utnapishtim. And Nippur as the ancient priest-city had also remained allied with no one. But joining Ur and Uruk were Eridu and Larsa and together with their surrounding villages they maintained the most powerful and prosperous coalition ever produced through peaceful means. Ur-Nammu had considered tipping the balance of power in Ur's direction during the final years of his reign, but was prevented from doing so by declining health. Terah's one independent move away from his father had been to re-strengthen ties to Uruk and House Anu upon Ur-Nammu's death.

This strengthening was now evidenced by the warm greeting and embrace of the two great kings. Lugulbanda and Terah both descended from their horses and firmly clasped hand to forearm in symbolic display of the kingdoms unity. The crowds round about cheered, knowing the prosperity a stronger alliance would continue to produce. Enki, Nahor and Haran also dismounted and stood by their father's side. Next to Lugulbanda stood Prince Gilgamesh. Enki and Gil waited patiently for their fathers to finish with the formalities before they would be free to embrace one another.

Terah then continued the exchange. He said, "And we embrace you, our brothers of the North. I am gladdened and strengthened by the continued favor bestowed upon Uruk, the Great City of the gods. Your increase is our reward."

Lugulbanda said, "Which we return back to you, in gratefulness for your own strength and power which you lend to our united peoples." Lugulbanda's reply was quick and gracious. Then he continued, addressing the crowds now gathered with a loud booming voice. He said, "And to you, oh people of Ur, great city of the southern reaches, favored ones of the great goddess Nanna, whose beauty, serenity and eternal light is reflected in this, your great city, and in you her people, we of Uruk, declare our allegiance to you!"

Loud cries of approval rose and then fell as Lugulbanda continued.

"We are for you, O people of Ur!" Lugulbanda said. "We are indeed your brothers, not in speech alone, but in deed and action, united forever! And to your great king, to Lord Terah be ascribed great praise from our people, and to the princes and lords of this land!"

Terah then concluded the refrain. He said, "And we join with you by praising Uruk, our protector and deliverer, our strong right hand! And we unite in proclaiming the great eternal destiny of New Sumer to be forever unleashed upon the earth! We unite in praising our king! Hail! Hail! Hail! Hail, to His Highness, the exalted King Lugulbanda forever!!"

And with that the crowd erupted into jubilant cheers and joyful noise which continued as the two kings turned to continue their trek into the city.

"Well, thank the gods that's over with," said Lugulbanda speaking freely now that the crowds were no longer within ear shot.

"Oh, it's not quite over with yet," Terah said. "At the palace gate we've yet to receive the queen. Without a queen of our own, Ninsun has developed quite a cult following in our land." Terah spoke with amusement.

"So I've heard," Lugulbanda said. "Well, she's going to hate whatever it is you have planned."

"I've no doubt she will," Terah said. "But it's not my plan. It's our high priest Ultaro's way of taking part in the festivities without actually affirming my reign in any really constructive way. You've no idea how much I had to pay for his support when we left for Lagash."

"Oh, please let's not talk about the priesthood," the High King said. "I've enough troubles of my own back in Uruk. But speaking of Lagash, congratulations and honor to you, oh prince, on your performance at the trade negotiations." Lugulbanda now addressed Nahor who bowed low in grateful acceptance of the High King's praise.

Enki, who by now was walking alongside Gil but still waiting for a chance to speak freely with his old friend, was suddenly caught off guard by Lugulbanda as he turned to address him.

Lugulbanda said, "And to you young prince – *abram teshua* they are calling you. Tell me, what great deliverer ever let his enemy live to strike again?"

Enki blushed at the sudden attack, but before anger had a chance to replace embarrassment Lugulbanda continued. He said, "Peace, Enki. It was a masterful bit of soldiering, well redemptive of any potentially harmful political consequences. And who knows, your bold move may yet yield a good return. We shall see. That aside, I've no doubt your brief campaign will be the talk of the academies from Ur to Nippur for some time to come. With more years bringing you greater wisdom, you will no doubt become a powerful weapon in fulfilling our destiny as a united people."

Gil was beaming at his father's approval of his best friend. But Enki had no chance to respond before Lugulbanda moved further ahead with Terah and Nahor, turning to speak to Haran now, the man who would one day rule Ur in his father's place. Enki and Gil did not keep up their pace and so fell behind gaining opportunity at last to speak freely.

"You've no idea the excitement you've stirred up in Uruk!" Gil said, with an excitement of his own. "I still can't believe you did what you did."

Enki said, "Gil, I still can't totally believe it myself. It's as if the gods themselves were guiding my way. Everything fell into place far greater than I had hoped for or even planned."

Gil said, "Tell me, what kind of a man is this Zoreth?"

Enki said, "Remarkable. I'd never met anyone like him. You know, in spite of what your father says, or even mine for that matter, I really believe he's a man of his word."

Gil said, "Enki! A desert barbarian? You trust him?"

Enki said, "Oh, I didn't say I'd trust him. But, I believe in this case he'll do what he has said. They appear to have some kind of code of honor, these desert peoples, though certainly not as advanced as ours, it's noble in some savage way, nonetheless."

"The gods help us, you're sounding like your brother Haran!"

"I did just use the word *honor* in a complete sentence,

didn't I? Please don't tell Nahor, he'll badger me about it for weeks."

Gil said, "Your secret is safe with me."

"Speaking of secrets," Enki said. "Is Aya really with you?"

"Oh dear, how did you find out? You will pretend to be surprised, won't you?" Gil asked.

Enki said, "Gil, I fooled Lord Micah, my father, my brothers, the regent of Roeth, and even the Amorite Zoreth, but I'm not so foolish to think that I can act well enough to fool a woman, especially your sister!"

Gil said, "Enki, you're a wise man."

The crowds continued to grow as they made their way toward the city of Ur and in through the north gate. Great throngs of Urians lined the streets and hung out of the windows in buildings above, crying out in praise of King Lugulbanda and his people. But if half the city had come out to escort the king of Uruk, the other half had assembled at the palace awaiting the arrival of the queen. These were bolstered further by the presence of the priesthood. A temporary dais had been raised to elevate the extravagantly garbed high priest Ultaro. Graco sat helplessly at his side and rose together with him and the rest of the priests as Lugulbanda's entourage arrived. Terah and Lugulbanda, together with their sons, ascended the platform and received the proscribed blessings from Ultaro and the other priests of the sacred council. Lugulbanda in return, paid tribute to Ultaro and especially to Nanna, the moon goddess of Ur.

The pleased crowds exulted in Lugulbanda honoring their deity, but their cheers rose to even greater levels as the last carriages finally arrived bearing Queen Ninsun, wife of Lugulbanda and mother to both Gil and Aya. As she descended the carriage, great banners bearing the symbol of the moon goddess were raised and waved in her honor, hailing her as the unwitting incarnation of the deity. She quickly realized what was happening and reluctantly played along, giving a fine little speech of her own – Lugulbanda was not the only eloquent one of House Anu. The crowds would have gone on in celebration for much longer had not Ultaro, tiring of the attention being given to someone other than himself, wrapped up the ceremonies.

As the crowds began to disperse, the two royal families made their way through the palace gates and into the inner courtyard. It was there at last that they were free from the crowds demand for formality and could address one another with greater liberty. Lugulbanda, Terah and their sons dismounted and awaited the queen's carriage. The carriage arrived and Ninsun gracefully descended. She too seemed to have an ageless quality about her, similar to her husbands, but quite different at the same time. Here was grace and beauty and honor all wrapped up into one solitary figure. Enki allowed himself a glance away from her and caught the admiring gaze of his two brothers. Indeed, they each one still mourned the absence of a mother and queen of their own, theirs having died giving birth to Enki. But it was his father Terah's look of pained sorrow as he gazed upon Queen Ninsun that shook Enki the most. The sad look of pain and loss flooded over Terah's features for only a moment before it was gone and covered over once more by the feigned look of a composed king of a great city admiring and welcoming a neighboring ally.

Terah said, "Greetings and warm welcome to you great Queen of the North. Your unsurpassed beauty as always has been eagerly anticipated in our land." Terah spoke with both formality and warmth, but there was also still that touch of pain and loss that did not escape careful observance.

Ninsun seemed aware of the pain and responded in like manner. She said, "And to you My Lord, I am always gladdened by your presence and have longed to see you again. It has been too long."

"Indeed it has," Terah said.

They were still gazing at one another as Lugulbanda approached the queen's side, having been distracted by the formality of reviewing the palace guard in these first moments after their arrival.

Terah and Ninsun both seemed to awaken as if from a slumber as the High King placed his arm about the queen and spoke. He said, "Terah, you keep the finest guards anywhere, as always. That Captain Larzo of yours is worth fifty men. Why is it you have him locked away in your palace?"

Terah then, back to his normal self said, "Larzo's a great warrior. But warriors need a war. I'd rather not have a war right now, so I find it best to lock old Larzo away lest he find one."

Larzo said, "I heard that remark, your majesty." Larzo yelled from across the courtyard as he was dispatching his men. "I'm a delicate rose, great king. Don't let My Lord deceive you."

"Perhaps," Lugulbanda said laughing. "But the rose I'll deem has thorns. Come, let's invite Larzo to join us tonight as we dine. I'd like to hear his account of the mighty *abram's* victory in the desert."

"It shall be so," Terah said lightheartedly. "But first, let us retire to court. We've a few minor items of business I'd like us to attend to in preparation for tomorrow's High Council. We can complete these before we recline for our evening feast."

"Excellent," Lugulbanda said approvingly. "You recall my obsession with disposing of the mundane before all else."

Terah said, "It's a good obsession. And it will give us freedom tonight to enjoy one another's company without the dread of unpleasant dullness early on the morrow."

Ninsun then spoke as they all turned to follow Terah inside. She said, "Gil, would you and Enki watch out for Aya's carriage. She should be arriving anytime now. You wouldn't mind would you, Enki?"

Enki said, "It would be my sacrificial duty, my lady."

"I'm sure," she said.

"I hate it that your mother is so aware of my feelings for your sister," Enki said once the others were inside. "Have I been that obvious?"

"It's a woman's gift. My father doesn't have a clue. He thinks all your visits to Uruk this last year has really been to see me."

"Why is Aya's carriage so far behind, anyway?" Enki asked.

Gil said, "Oh, you know Shulpae – he's making her stop at various points along the way and giving her a history lesson here and a botany lesson there. It was all I could do to convince him I had to ride ahead at my father's side."

Just then, the sound of Aya's carriage was heard coming through the tunnel which led into the palace inner courtyard. Trumpets then sounded forth announcing the arrival of the princess and her elderly tutor. Enki's heart began to beat faster. He was suddenly struck by how anxious he felt. What was this power that women held over men, he wondered. He then realized he had greater confidence as he faced Zoreth, the barbaric desert chieftain, than he did now facing a ninety pound girl.

The carriage came to a halt there in front of Gil and Enki. A page traveling alongside the carriage quickly jumped down from his horse and opened the carriage doors. Shulpae was the first to exit the vehicle. He was a kindly looking old man with bushy eyebrows and a thick gray beard. He was short and stout and slightly hunched over, but a loveable figure nonetheless. And he was indeed a walking history and science text. Shulpae was always a welcome sight, at least for Enki, since he wasn't his tutor, and so need fear no lesson other than a drawn out tale of the old days. Gil and Aya however had a slightly different perspective.

Shulpae said, "Master Enki! Fancy meeting you here. I suppose it is your city, but I thought you'd be out enjoying the praises of your adoring people. Can I still call you Enki, or should I now address you as *Abram*?"

Enki said, "Not you too, old man? I'm wondering now if all the abuse I've taken from you and my family has been worth this rise to fame."

"Ah my boy, best enjoy it while it lasts," Shulpae said. "The memory of the masses will fade at the first crisis and you'll go back to being a normal prince again."

Just then, Aya's lovely head popped out of the carriage. She said, "I'll take a normal prince over an *abram teshua* any day."

"Aya!" Enki said.

"Oh please, Enki," Aya said. "Don't try to act surprised."

Enki said, "Not surprise, my lady. Delight."

Gil groaned in disgust. He said, "I'm leaving."

"No… Aya's leaving," Shulpae said. "You know your father's rules on completing assignments prior to festivities. If you want to spend some time with your adoring little friend here, then we best be off to your quarters to complete your lessons. Why it was that your father allowed you to go on this little trip, right before examinations, is beyond me."

Aya said, "Oh please, Shulpae, we just arrived. Just a short stroll around the grounds here?"

Shulpae said, "Batting those pretty brown eyes of yours might work with the young prince here, but I'm far past the age of being swayed by the dangerous weapons of woman."

Aya said, "Really Shulpae! You're no fun." She spoke with disappointed compliance.

"I'm not hired by your father to be fun, my lady," Shulpae said. "Come now, Enki. Where in the palace have you placed us?"

Enki, who had already resigned himself to the fact that they would not be able to be together until after the banquet, had already motioned to a page to deliver their baggage to the guest wing.

Enki said, "Aya my love, we best comply with the tiresome old fool lest he get excited and die on us."

Shulpae said, "Die on you!? Why I could still take you out in a fight!"

"It is true, my darling," Aya said joining in the attack. "We best humor the gentle Shulpae while he still has breath. It won't be long 'ere he moves on to the land of shadows."

"Humor me?" Shulpae said. "Why I'll out live the three of you!"

Gil could not be left out. He said, "Enki, perhaps you should beckon another page to come and carry the fragile creature to his room along with the rest of the baggage."

"Alright, that's enough!" Shulpae said.

And with that Shulpae took Aya by the arm and began guiding her in the direction of the page carrying their baggage. He continued ranting on about something but it was lost amidst a chorus of laughter.

CHAPTER 5 – A WALK IN THE GARDEN

The Great Banquet Hall had been built by Enki's great-grandfather Serug II. Great columns lined the interior of the vast chamber. Expansive tapestries hung from every wall. The floor of polished marble reflected the ornate ceiling high above. Magnificently carved statuettes, fashioned from onyx and fine granite, portrayed the great heroes of the Eber royal line, as well as other figures from antiquity. Indeed, in this chamber, there were statues of each of the kings of old, dating all the way back to Eber himself. These now lifeless kings looked on with stern faces as if in judgment upon the dealings of the day. Lightening the mood of the hall was the presence of desert flowers in exquisite vases. Adorned on every table, these added life and vitality to an otherwise austere chamber. Musicians who were gathered in one corner of the hall provided an atmosphere both festive and majestic. Old anthems and songs of war and remembrance rang out throughout the chamber. But these did not drown out the lively conversation which rose from every table as if in a chorus of their own.

At the far end of the chamber there arose a gold crested dais upon which rested a great table of stone. This was the table of honor reserved for the royal families and their guests. Enki was already seated here with his father and brothers and various members of the ruling classes. Together they awaited the official entrance of House Anu. This came with two great trumpet blasts and the steward giving them their unneeded introduction.

"All rise for the High King! Hail Lugulbanda the Great!"

Great cheers arose as the king and his family entered the chamber. Various members of the nobility seated at nearby tables reached out their hands in hopes the king would recognize them and thus grant them prestige amidst their fellow countrymen. At the kings side was Queen Ninsun, followed by Prince Gilgamesh and Princess Aya. The Queen was dressed in a long flowing gown of velvet and lace dyed purple to mark her stature. Gil wore baggy breeches like himself, with a shirt of white lace and a burgundy cape. But Enki saw only Aya. She was beautiful. Her elegant gown flowed down her slim figure in a cascade of color. Her bare arms and shoulders added the golden brown of her soft skin to the deep black of her hair and the bright blue of her gown. She walked like a gentle breeze and bore on her breast a necklace of pearls from the sea. She gave Enki a warm smile that completely undid him. He managed an awkward smile back. Nahor nearly lost it at the amusing sight of the obvious demise of his would-be warrior little brother. No one else seemed to notice the awkward exchange except for Ninsun who looked away to keep from laughing.

Once introductions had been made and Lugulbanda had been seated, the rest did likewise. A seat next to Enki had been reserved for Gil. On the other side of Enki sat Larzo, looking rather out of place amidst such personages of nobility and finery. He didn't seem to mind though. Just like Larzo to not care how he was perceived, Enki thought. Enki tried not to look directly across the table to where Aya sat. Aya for her part was already lost in conversation with Lady Toeri, wife of Lord Micah, and Lady Zerea, wife of Lord Salzarto.

Enki noted that Graco the priest had been seated next to Shulpae. A long friendship those two had enjoyed over the years. Next to Shulpae sat Lord Micah and Lord Salzarto. They were already lost in talk of politics and distant wars. Next to them and taking part in the speculative diplomacy was Ur's High Commander himself, Calderach, back from defending the port in the south. Calderach was indeed an imposing figure. His hard, worn face looked as if it had born the brunt of a hot desert wind over long decades. It had.

On the other side of Enki and Gil sat Enki's brothers and father conversing with Lugulbanda and his accompanying aids. Soon their conversation dominated the table as other voices began to die down to listen in and take part in the fellowship of Sumer's inner circle.

"Nahor, you keep telling us to not give credence to Kish's control of the River, but how can you be so certain that our economic positions will not be threatened once the floods come?" Speaking was one of Uruk's high noblemen, Lord Kalat, who had accompanied House Anu on this visit to Ur. He was perhaps the greatest landowner between Ur and Uruk and so had gained a strong hearing in the presence of the king and his advisors.

Nahor took a full bite of roasted gazelle before speaking. He said, "Lord Kalat, you need not fear the floods this year. Kish will not have the economic leverage to affect the southern flow of the River in any detrimental way to our trade. The trade guilds of Kish and Agade would never allow Etana to disrupt their profit. Now I'm not saying we should discount the threat indefinitely, but Etana's power is not yet absolute. He still needs the support of his nobles."

"And what makes you certain his political control has not yet surpassed the economic force of the guilds?" Kalat asked.

"Ah, that's where Lagash comes in," Nahor said. "They are always the wild card. The beauty of the whole summit was that with all attention centered upon our dealings with Lagash and the eastern cities, no one noticed our pact with Kish's wheat and barley guilds! It's probably just starting to hit them now, in fact. Etana must be furious."

Lugulbanda then joined in the conversation. He said, "A grand bit of economic diplomacy my good prince, as I noted to you earlier. But tell me, Nahor, what do you make of these strange new observers from the east? They say they're from Susa, but their accent is strange."

Nahor said, "Your highness, if you're implying a takeover of Susa by the eastern peoples beyond the mountains, I deem you are correct. But I think it matters little. Surely they observed our united front politically, and no doubt saw the economic advantage of greater contact with their new neighbors. What think you, Sal?

Lord Salzarto was ready with reply. He said, "I think that Susa is nothing to be concerned about. Not yet at any rate. They're the new player. Now it's true the surprised lion is most apt to attack, but it is they who have sought us out, not we them. I think that after their change of government that they will need time for consolidation. We need not fear our eastern neighbors. There is rather the great potential for profit, if we are able to secure their markets. Lagash is no doubt a step ahead of us, but we need not overtake the League. Indeed, we need their strength as a buffer to guard our flank from Kish. We've enough of a distraction with the desert tribes. We don't need Kish, or Susa for that matter should I be incorrect in my assessment, swooping down on us uninvited and unimpeded from the northeast."

Nahor said, "Ah, but the desert problem has been eliminated by the mighty *abram* here!" Nahor's sarcastic jab resulted in a ripple of laughter throughout the room. Enki politely laughed with him, but was inwardly angered by their underestimation of his exploit.

Lord Kalat then made it worse. He said, "Ah yes indeed, the *abram teshua.* Our generals would indeed like to have a word with the mighty prince who doth leave his enemy not only to live, but also to reign as an equal, free to strike another day."

Enki, strongly tempted to lash back in self-defense, deprecated to a chorus of supporters on his behalf rising from various corners about the room. Larzo became their spokesman. He said, "Be careful to not pre-judge the young master, Lord Kalat. Many a campaign have I seen in my day, and many a young warrior have I observed, some fierce but naive, others shrewd but cowards. In Enkidu son of Terah you have a warrior prince both brave and shrewd. His mind and heart have secured us peace, albeit by means I would not have sought myself."

"Well said," Haran said. Enki was surprised, but grateful, at the sudden support of his elder brother. "The young prince, my brother, is of the great house Eber of Ur. His blood and our honor will be offended should you, Lord Kalat, question so freely an Eberew of the highest order."

Lord Kalat then, wise enough to play the game, relented. He said, "I am dethroned, My Lords, and I withdraw my critique then. But rest assured that a question of the prince's courage was left out of the critique from the start. It was a masterly bit of soldiering, all are agreed."

Terah then joined the chorus in support of his son, unable to join the fray till now. He said, "My son, though young, has acted where we all have been content to talk. Perhaps we all have rested secure for too long and have been too reluctant to engage our challenging times. And now it appears that the time of security and peace is quickly passing away." Terah paused tiredly as the rooms other conversations quickly sank to an even quieter hush as all knew where the head table's conversation was now going. Terah, turning to Calderach, motioned to the silent but stern general. He said, "Well, Commander, I suppose this is as good a time as any to discuss the fall of Ebla and what this may mean for us."

The High Commander Calderach was a man who spoke few words, but when he did, all listened. He was indeed a warrior of the old stock. He was a soldier zealously committed to the Sumer of Old, but needing to command forces in defense of the Sumer of the day. Though he was High Commander of the armies of Ur under King Terah, he also commanded great influence throughout the cities of New Sumer and was the ranking member of Sumer's joint military council. Even Lugulbanda seemed to perk up attentively to hear the old general's words.

"Long have we expected this hour would come," Calderach said. He spoke slowly and deliberately. "We are not surprised, but grieved that it should come in our day. It will indeed mean an end to the relative peace that we have enjoyed these past generations. With gratefulness we have enjoyed the passivity of Sargon's descendants – cursed be his name forever – these past years. But it is true. And all our sources have confirmed it without question. The power of Ebla appears to be crumbling. And the coalition will surely fall with them. It's very possible that the stage is being set for a great civil war in the far north. These wars will not affect us directly, but it does indeed mean that Ebla's hold upon Kish will finally come to an end, perhaps forever.

"Now Kish will never be strong enough, I believe, to actually regain its past glory. But I believe that Etana thinks it can, the poor fool. And his generals I know for a fact are simply feeding him the thought of eventual attack. He will not wait long, though we may yet have a few years. He must at least know that he is not yet ready. We shall see." Calderach then turned to Lugulbanda. He said, "Your majesty, I deem you must have further news to give us. Let us have it all, lest we lull ourselves into false confidence as our unfortunate ancestors did in the days of the evil one."

The High King rose from his seat, for now all was indeed silent and no longer was this a discussion for the head table, but all the ruling classes were now attentive to the conversation at hand. Indeed, Enki perceived that the whole occasion had been staged for this very purpose – to convince the nobility of Sumer of the criticalness of the northern threat and to rally support among the landowners. Lugulbanda, whose greatest strength perhaps lay in his kingly manner and force of person, used these now to his full advantage.

Lugulbanda said, "The general speaks the truth, and now you all know it." As he spoke he was now addressing all assembled in the chamber. "But what Calderach has spoken of as possibilities, we can now confirm as fact. Our sources tell us that not only has the coalition fallen, but the city of Ebla has been completely destroyed."

Gasps of shock could be heard throughout the room. Not many had actually ever been to the great northern city, but those who had had spread word of its great wealth and power. To hear now of its complete demise was indeed a shock to all. Even Calderach was slightly taken aback.

Lugulbanda continued after a brief pause to allow the shock of the news to sink in. He said, "And it is not truly civil war that has brought Ebla to an end, though some disunity may be cause for blame. We don't know much about Ebla's conquerors except that they come from beyond the mountains of the far northwest. But it also appears that this new power, though fierce, is not so advanced as to extend any level of consistent rule much beyond Ebla's borders. We are, of course, looking into such possibilities, but the word we have as of yet received, indicates that we need not fear directly this new barbaric power.

"But Ebla has become their prey, and the danger to us is clear as Calderach has noted. Kish is now free to once again seek to rebuild the empire it once lost. This we must not allow! We will do all in our means to disable the threat without war, but I deem that war may indeed be coming. However, I agree with the General that the threat of Kish may yet be years away…"

Just then a fragile looking Lord Micah arose, interrupting the High King's next thought. He began haltingly. He said, "Your majesty, if I may?"

Lugulbanda sitting down motioned Lord Micah to take the floor.

Micah said, "Your Highness, I fear I must add to the adverse news of the day." He paused as he stepped over to the great map hanging near Lugulbanda's end of the table. Pointing to a position on the northern edge of the map he continued. He said, "Just this morning we received further troubling news. It appears that the Old Forest… has been retaken by Kish."

Lord Kalat said, "The gods help us! The Cedar Forest? Are you certain?" Kalat voiced his shock and concern on behalf of all the rest assembled. The Old Forest and the centrality of the Great Cedar as a cult rallying point for the great oppressive empire of Sargon of Kish in a past century was so etched into the minds of society through song and tale, that the news, though less significant than that of Ebla's fall, created an even greater emotional stir. Enki noted Lugulbanda's lack of surprise. This was evidently not news to him.

Lord Micah first looking at Terah for direction and receiving some signal continued. Micah said, "I'm not at liberty to divulge my sources, but I can confirm that the report is indeed true. And the act is having its desired effect. Large masses of Kish's populace assembled last week in the name of Shamash to reinitiate the Sargonist Rite."

Terah then stood up and joined Micah at his side. Micah, responding to Terah's nod, took his seat as the host king continued. Terah said, "They've been moving quickly to secure the Forest. Apparently, there was little resistance, which as far as I'm concerned is the most troubling aspect of this news. The Old Forest's strategic value of course is its lumber. That the northern tribes should allow it to be so easily retaken is indeed a sign of their increasing weakness. We suspect that Ebla's conquerors may be posing a threat to the northern tribal alliance as well, forcing them to pull out of the plains completely."

There were several minutes of silence as all allowed the rapid succession of news to sink in. Finally, Lugulbanda spoke. He said, "It was important that we gather you together here to hear of these new threats as one united body.

We are one people. This Union formed by our great ancestors will hold secure and we will overcome all threats, be it Kish or even this new force further north. This is no time for fear. But we must also not be lulled into an over confidence. That is why I am reconvening the Great Convention."

Nods of approval could be seen throughout the room as Lugulbanda paused and then continued.

Lugulbanda said, "Tomorrow we shall reinitiate the ancient code, and plot our course to greater security and strength in the face of our newly empowered neighbors to the north."

Then, Lugulbanda, always the master of men, softened his features and in an instant transformed himself from stern king to kindly father. Enki observed his performance with awe as he continued with a comforting, almost homely voice. He said, "But let there be no more talk of war or threats this night. Tomorrow will be a day of wise council and swift decisions. Let this night be a time to strengthen the heart. Let us remember our forefathers. Let us remember the price they paid for our security. Let us celebrate the gods who have given us the victory in the past over our foes and who will grant us victory again." Turning then to Terah he said, "Terah, have you a bard gifted to lead us into such sanctuary of song as we toast the divines?"

Terah motioning to a ready respondent in the back replied quickly. Terah said, "Indeed I have. I present the great Tolethanki, one of our very own and one of the very best of New Sumer. Come, friend Tol, sing for us one of the songs of old."

Enki, knowing well enough all the players involved this evening, was aware of the performance of Lugulbanda, his father and the rest, and not easily moved thereby. However, the dinner hall was filled with entranced lords and ladies eagerly embracing the patriotic call. They beamed as the nearly legendary Tolethanki, a native Urian who took the music halls of Lagash by storm in recent years, took to the center platform and who with his lyre began to weave a spell upon all his hearers. The other musicians joined him with their stringed instruments, but only enough to accent his skilled and melodious sonnet. Underneath it all was a barely audible drum beat, steady like the heartbeat of the Union itself. The song he played and sang now was not one of his own, but was an ancient melody transmitting the favorite patriotic account of New Sumer. He sang of the great uniting of Old Sumer in the days of the decay of Sargon's legacy. He sang of the overthrow of Kish's hated grip and of the uniting of house Anu and house Eber, of Uruk and Ur into a union of strength and power that would grant Sumer security to the very day.

The clouds were dark, the skies were gray
As dim fog rolled that dreadful day
The smoke arose to greet the gods
And tell of Sargons fall

Freedom to the southern lands,
As strength and power rise
Forever we will sound the cry
Forever we will reign

Praise be to An, and to his son
Enlil, we lift his name
Tis justice that the evil fall
Forevermore disdained

The statue of the cursed one
Has crumbled into dust
The Hurrians have led the way
And Kish has had its day

Sumer arise and greet the sun
Let Nanna rest her weary head
And to Dilmun may she retreat
Until our need again be great

Sumer arise and greet the moon
As Nanna turns to take her seat
Upon the plains her glory shines
And Ur and Uruk rest tonight

Lord Uruk-Anu and Rue of Ur
The Great Ones gather to Nippur
As kings of old assembled there
And Sumer rises once again

The Uruk-Kai and Uruk-Kin
Have gathered there as well
To bless the union of the gods
A people now reborn

O Desert lands and Mountains fair
O Sea and Sky and Rain
Confess thy place be underneath
The glory of the plain

Enki had slipped out as planned sometime around stanza thirty-eight – he had no intention of sitting through the other 462 verses, especially with the knowledge that the last hundred or so would be in Old Sumerian. He made his way to the palace garden, their rendezvous point. Aya was not able to escape till around stanza eighty-seven, but he soon heard her gentle footsteps nearing the garden's entrance where he stood. As she rounded the corner he jumped out from behind a bush pulling her quickly and playfully into his arms.

She feigned surprise and said, "Oh, My Lord! I beg you to release me this once!"

Enki said, "I'll release thee for a kiss my lady. A simple return of affection is all I ask of thee."

Aya said, "Good Lord, my father the king I deem would not approve such free affection. His daughter is not a temple servant of Nanna."

Enki said, "Concern for thy father, my good lady, has never stopped thee before."

And with that Aya playfully slapped Enki across the chest pulling away briefly. But then, reversing her façade, she now allowed herself to be drawn intimately into his arms. Enki could feel his legs start to give as his body took in the full impact of her womanly embrace. She then raised herself up through his arms till on tip toes she placed on Enki's cheek a gentle kiss.

Looking deeply and lovingly into his eyes as she returned to her feet, she spoke in her usual playful way. She said, "There My Lord, you have your kiss. But I withdraw my demand for release."

Together they strolled through the garden grounds arm in arm as Enki recounted for her his adventures of recent weeks. He only embellished a few things. She asked him questions along the way and was able to draw out some further details that Enki had withheld from his father and brothers in his earlier account.

Aya, though clearly proud of her warrior lover, could not help but scold his carelessness. With greater seriousness than before she implored him and said, "Enki, what if you'd been killed and I lost you forever?" She placed her head upon his chest and continued her entreat. "I would not be able to bare such news. I would be forced to join you in the land of shadows if such ever happened."

Enki, ignoring the tenderness of her entreat, brushed it aside brashly. He said, "Nonsense, Aya. You would have a thousand princes seeking your hand the moment I was gone. But you need not fear such a dilemma. It will never come.

I'm a god, Aya. I can't be killed."

Aya said, "Enki, you mustn't speak so! Nanna is overhead even now. She will challenge your brashness."

"Aya, Nanna is my equal," Enki said easily. "She's received me into the family of the gods. Any other man would have died that day in the canyons. I have a destiny to fulfill with which the gods will not interfere."

Aya said, "Enki, you're talking like a fool." And Aya pulled away now.

"Easy, my love, you need not fear for me," Enki said. "I know what I am doing. No one can stop me. I've felt it. Such confidence has welled up in me of late that I truly believe that I can reach out and take hold of any destiny I choose."

"You're sounding like Etana now," Aya said. "They say in Lagash that he speaks thus. An arrogant fool of a king, they say he is. And he just may bring Kish down with him when the gods bring judgment upon him."

"That's the priesthood of Lagash speaking, Aya. Don't believe everything they teach you. I don't think Etana is such a fool. He's trying to rally his people to strength once again. I don't blame him for it. And perhaps he thinks he has a destiny to fulfill as well. But I believe our destinies will one day cross, and then it will be clear which is the favorite of the gods."

Aya said, "Enki, have you spoken this way to your father or brothers? Does Gil know your thoughts? I hope that my father does not! You know, Enki, if your enemies overheard you speak this way, they could bring charges of treason against you!"

Enki said, "Aya, you're overreacting. I'm not after your father's throne. Do you think I would try to take that from Gil?" Enki could sense Aya soften a bit now as he continued. "No, I can't wait for the day that Gil is crowned king in Uruk."

"What then, Enki, is it Ur then?"

Enki laughed, "Ha! Ur belongs to my poor unfortunate brother. I wouldn't dream of limiting myself to being ensi of Ur. No, my place is elsewhere. My place is on the battlefield and at the gates of Kish itself."

"Oh, Enki, you scare me. You've changed somehow."

"I've grown, Aya."

"Perhaps. But growing into what? I want the Enki I've been in love with since girlhood."

Enki softened a bit. He said, "That Enki is still here and always will be… for you."

Aya seemed to brighten with hope as she recognized a hint of vulnerability cross over Enki's face.

Enki, silent for a moment, was in hesitant thought as to whether to share something with his beloved. Finally, he began to do so. He looked down at the ground as he haltingly said, "Aya… something happened to me in the canyons… that I've not told anyone but Malki."

Enki paused in silence as he sought to gauge Aya's reaction to his guarded revelation. He looked up and was met with nothing but the look of love and concern in her eyes.

"What Enki? What happened?"

He paused for a few moments before continuing. Then he said slowly, "It was probably nothing… But I thought I heard a voice as I was lying there. I thought I was dying. And I heard this voice…"

"What did it say?" Aya asked. Her eyes were wide with childlike innocence.

Several more moments of silence passed. "*Come away with me*, it said."

Aya, with a sense of wonder asked, "What did it mean?"

"I don't know," he said reflectively.

They were both silent for several seconds as only the breeze through the trees silhouetted against the night sky could be heard.

Aya finally said, "Well, perhaps it was the cry of my heart you were hearing. Enki, I love you. I always have and I always will. I am forever yours. You have conquered me."

And with that, Enki's façade finally completely failed him as he melted once again into boyhood. Taking Aya up into his arms, he kissed her deeply.

***

Later that night, after reluctantly walking Aya back to her rooms, Enki returned to his own quarters hoping to find Gil waiting for him. He entered his upper chambers to find Gil and Malki seated at the far end of the room by the great bay windows immersed in an intense game of zia-fe.

"I thought I might find you two here," Enki said. "Who's winning?"

A frustrated Gil said, "Who do you think? It's quite embarrassing to be beaten time and time again by a slave."

Malki said, "Ah, but I am but humbly serving you through my repeated triumphs – instilling in you humility and respect for the lower class folk such as myself."

Gil then looked up from the game as Enki walked closer. Gil said, "And quite honored are we that you would grace us so with your presence. I must only assume that you treated my sister with the utmost respect and reverence, guarding her virtue with your life and honor?"

Enki slumped down onto the adjacent bed. He said, "Gil, you know as well as I that Aya needs no defending. She's a tease that little sister of yours, and she's going to do me in. I'm weakened every time I'm with her."

Gil said, "You say that every time."

Enki said, "Well it's true every time."

"It's your move," Malki interrupted.

"I know it's my move!" Gil said.

Malki said, "Easy, My Lord, recall that I am but serving you."

Gil said, "Truly? Then I suppose you won't demand the 20 dils we wagered once you've done me in?"

Malki said, "I would dearly want to withdraw such a demand, but it would defeat the purpose to which I am serving you."

Just then Shulpae barged in. He said, "Gilgamesh! Are you going to let that slave who's forgotten his place in life speak thus to you?"

Before Gil could reply, Malki said, "Sit down old man.

You're next!"

Enki said, "Ah, what complicated times we live in. I defeat a desert warrior, but I'm beaten down by a ninety pound girl. You, Gil, are the heir to the greatest throne in all of Sumer, will one day be the most powerful man in the land between the rivers, and yet you must persistently submit to my slave. And Shulpae, the aged counselor and teacher, who will most certainly face death any day now, is respected by no one…"

Shulpae had walked up to the gang by now and proceeded to whack both Enki and Malki across their heads with some scrolls he'd brought with him.

Shulpae said, "Why I allow you to continue to pollute the young master's mind here is beyond me."

"Is it because of your love and affection for us?" Enki asked sarcastically.

Gil said, "Speaking of love and affection, maybe Shulpae could fill us in on how to defeat the charms of woman. Enki needs some counsel."

Shulpae then slumped down on a nearby chair and suddenly looked very tired. He sighed and then said, "'Woman is the only undefeatable foe.' That's from a stanza from Jubul himself, so ancient is the knowledge of our demise."

"What scrolls are these?" Enki asked picking up one of the parchments he'd just been clobbered with.

"Oh, just some light reading," Shulpae said.

"Lite reading?" Malki said. He was still rubbing his head.

Shulpae ignoring Malki, picked up the scrolls Enki was

holding. He said, "After your father's performance tonight, I thought I'd refresh my knowledge of the Old Forest and the Great Cedar. You know I made a pilgrimage of sorts there once in my youth."

"You were young once?" said Malki who would not be ignored.

"Yes," said Shulpae. And he gave a hard stern look at Malki. Then turning to Enki he said, "And believe it or not I too have been overthrown by the charms of many a woman in my day. I'm afraid I have no answers for you there."

Enki, sitting up alert now with genuine interest said, "Tell us about the Great Cedar. What is it like?"

"It's a really, really big tree," Shulpae said.

Malki then turning to Gil asked, "How much does your father pay him?"

"Seriously Shulpae," Enki said. "I really want to know."

The old man sat back down gratified that he might actually have an audience. He said, "Well, it was back in the days when I was still actively searching for Utnapishtim, survivor of the Great Cleansing. I had stumbled upon some footnotes in an old manuscript I found in Umma. The notes seemed to allude to there being some kind of gathering place near the Great Cedar where the Ancients used to gather for counsel."

"The Annunaki?" Gil asked in wonderment.

Shulpae said, "Well, it didn't actually use the word *Annunaki*, but this was my suspicion. So I set off, nearly losing my head on a couple of run-ins with various mountain tribes as I sought my way in from the rear through the mountain pass – you still could make it through in those days.

"I'll never forget my first sight of it. Rounding a final pass on my way down the mountain and into the valley I had my first glimpse of the Old Forest and of the Great Cedar rising far above the forest ceiling. The thing had of course the look of ancientness that you'd expect, but it had something else as well. It's almost as though you could sense the thing thinking – watching you.

"Well, one encounter with that massive, ancient thing and I could understand why it gave Kish so much ferocious courage over the years of its imperialism before its fall. And I understand why Etana values it so. It's more than a symbol. There's something deeper there. It's like something from a forgotten age, which of course it is, but I mean it in a way that goes beyond time. There's a power in that monstrous tree that I can't explain."

"So… what are you saying?" Enki asked after a brief pause. "Are you saying you believe the old legends about Humbaba and the magic axe and the indestructible tree?"

Shulpae said, "Enki, at my age I've finally learned to discount no legend. In every legend is a shred of truth. There is very little that is completely made up. Most legends began as fact and drifted into myth. If there's one thing I've learned, its discount no fairy tale."

Enki asked, "Is that why you've wasted all those years searching for the mythical Utnapishtim, sole survivor of the Cleansing?"

Shulpae said, "No myth, Enki. Utnapishtim lived and I believe he lives still, though I never found him."

Enki said, "And this great tree… are you saying you really believe that if an army of us descended upon the tree, that we would be unable to fell it?"

Shulpae said, "That I do not know, Enki. It is sometimes difficult to discern in a legend at which points fact bows to man's creative fears and genius. But I'll tell you two things I believe to be true. That tree is the oldest living thing I've ever seen and looks of no tree I know of in this world. It belongs to the world before the Cleansing. It has a power that is not of this realm. And second, Humbaba, or the Bull of Heaven as the Hurrians call him, is also no fairy tale. There's something lurking in that forest, jealously guarding that Tree. He – or it – is not called *guardian of the forest* for nothing. Why, I understand Kish, even now, after retaking the forest from the Hurrians, still won't even go near the tree at night. All their little religious ceremonies they do around it, they do during the day and then scurry off out of sight of the Tree before dusk. I don't know what or who Humbaba is, but many an unfortunate Kishite has found out the hard way of late, so I hear.

"I nearly did as well. I ventured as close as I dared that day long ago, and still was a hundred yards away. Dusk had been approaching and I'd wager half of Eridu that I saw the eyes of that thing pouncing through the forest on its way to ward off any intruders. I wasn't about to be one of the intruders the thing was looking for, so I scurried off myself into the hills and found a cave to hide in for the night. The next morning I was driven away by a small band of Hurrians and never did get my chance to see the Tree up close. But even at a hundred yards away I've still the memory of it etched into my mind like it was yesterday."

All were silent for several minutes. It was indeed late and fatigue was setting in, but something had been stirred in Enki's heart. Enki in those moments made a decision that years later he would look back upon as the moment that changed his life forever.

After Shulpae and Malki had left and Gil and Enki were together by themselves, Enki unveiled his plan.

"Gil?"

"What?"

Enki said, "While Shulpae was going on tonight about the Cedar, the gods spoke to me."

Gil said, "Excuse me? O I'm sorry, which ones? Enlil? Ea? Maybe An himself? There were so many talking at the same time that I couldn't make out which one of the gods was speaking to you…"

Enki said, "Oh you poor unfortunate unbeliever." Enki rose dramatically from his couch and walked to the room's great windows. Looking out and up into the night sky he said, "Nanna speaks to me, Gil. I sense her voice in my heart. She has given me a destiny to fulfill. It's your destiny too Gil. You and I are both destined for greatness. Sargon – curse his name forever – will be a forgotten sideshow when we're through."

Gil said, "What the shadowland are you talking about?"

Enki said, "Gil, it's like I can see the future. I know exactly what we must do. You and I are going to leave next month on our previously planned trip to the marshes…"

"…and?" Gil asked.

Enki said, "Not *and… but. But* we won't actually go south. We'll be heading north to the Old Forest. It's what no one would expect. They've already had their big Sargonist Rite thing or whatever they call it, so the Cedar is bound to be less guarded, especially a month from now when we go."

Gil said, "Enki, you're starting to get a little too religious for me. You want to do pilgrimage to the Cedar when it's controlled by a rege or two that would kill you on sight if they recognized who you were?"

Enki said, "Correction. I want *us* to do pilgrimage, and they would be far more likely to recognize and kill you than me."

Gil said, "O thank you, that clears away my objections…"

Enki said, "Hold off on your objections until I'm finished. We're not actually going to do pilgrimage."

Gil asked, "Then what? You want to climb the thing? Or maybe we could just go ahead and cut it down?"

"Oh, so Nanna spoke to you too?" Enki asked.

"Spoke what to me?" Gil asked.

"To cut down the Cedar," Enki said.

Gil said, "I was joking! Cut down the Cedar, are you completely mad?!"

Enki said, "Not mad... Inspired. Anointed. In a really good mood. Call it what you will…"

"No way," Gil said.

Enki said, "Oh come on, Gil, do you want to live your whole life in safety?"

"I'd like to live!"

"Gil, you're going to be the High King someday. You want to just ease into it like you would a new pair of breeches? Or do you want to come into the crown having won the hearts of the people? We'd be heroes!"

Gil said, "We'd be flayed alive, first by my father and then by the Shamashites and then by that Old Forest Cedar cult whatever they call themselves, you know they're still pretty strong in Uruk!"

Enki said, "Your father would be the first to congratulate us… I think. At any rate, even if he's upset at first, he'll see the wisdom in it. Kish must be made to see that we would not simply roll over and allow a second Sargon to annex the realm. They need to know we would fight and ultimately destroy them should they attack. It's part of my destiny to make them see that. Our people need me."

Gil said, "That's really it, Enki, isn't it? This is all about you winning the hearts of the people. The great *abram teshua* strikes again. That's what you want to hear, isn't it? You know there's already talk amongst the nobles. Many of the lords are already second guessing your motives…"

"Gil, that's nonsense and you know it," Enki said. "I'm as loyal to New Sumer and to the Union as my dull and dreary older brother Haran. In fact, I'm more loyal. I would see Sumer rise to an even greater place than it was in the days before Sargon. Gil, you and I can make that happen – you as the High King, and me as the High Commander of the armed forces."

"This is nonsense," Gil said. "You heard Shulpae. The

tree can't be destroyed. You know the legend of Ki. If a band of thirty couldn't destroy the tree what makes you think we could?"

Enki said, "Apparently you weren't listening close enough to Shulpae. The Legend of Ki is a myth. Sure there must have been some truth in there as Shulpae said. A small band attempts to enter the forest to destroy the tree and get slain by the Hurrians controlling the forest. Over the years that grew into the Tree itself bringing poor Ki and his band to an untimely end. Shulpae was correct with the first thing he said to us about it. 'It's a really, really big tree.' That's all. We'll just need a couple really, really big axe's and a better plan than Ki had."

"And if I refuse to go with you?" Gil asked.

"I'll go alone of course," said Enki.

Gil asked, "And how do you suppose to even get close to the tree with Kish in control of the forest?"

Enki answered, "Ah… that's where legend works to our advantage. You heard Shulpae. Kish is scared to death of this Humbaba creature, which is probably no more than an oversized owl flying about the forest at night, but apparently big enough to spook a bunch of illiterate Kishite mercenaries. The tree is unguarded at night! So all we need to do is to sneak into the forest, preferably during daylight, which again would be least expected, perhaps disguised as Kishite soldiers, and find a safe hiding place to wait for nightfall. Then, once the patrols have vacated for the night, we start swinging a couple axes. We'll be out of that forest before dawn and racing for the River and a hero's welcome back in Uruk.

Gil sat there inwardly fuming, more from exasperation with himself than with Enki.

Finally Gil said, "Why do I allow you to talk me into these things!? It's just like when we were kids!"

"Then it's settled?"

"I'm going to live to regret this."

"Unless you're killed or maimed or something," Enki replied easily.

Gil let out a final groan.

CHAPTER 6 – THE FOREST JOURNEY

The next day for Enki was highly anti-climactic. Lugulbanda, for all his high talk of the Great Convention and quick action, was definitely playing it safe, which seemed to Enki to further justify his pending expedition. He sat in on most of the sessions with the high nobility, but soon tired of it all wishing he had spent more time with Aya before her quick departure back to Lagash to finish off her studies. But evenings were now full of high adventure as he and Gil plotted together their coming excursion. Gil was finally, as Enki had known he would be, starting to enjoy the notion of their journey north. By week's end, as Lugulbanda and the party from Uruk were preparing to head home, Enki and Gil had laid out their entire course of travel along with various contingency plans and a pretext for their long absence. They would both meet up in the Blue Hills at their old childhood meeting place and from there would head deeper east across the meadowlands. Supposedly they would be hunting wild gazelle and bear in the eastern reaches south of Lagash. However, once beyond the populated areas of the foothills, they would head northeast cutting across the wooded terrain and then traversing the plains until the Great Central Road was in sight. Avoiding that heavily traveled trade route they would keep to the fields of the outer estates. Once passed these they would move through wilderness till the River presented itself. Then an even more wild and unsettled country on the other side until the Zargos Mountains came into view. Then, on to Amanus.

After Gil left, Enki spent several dreary weeks waiting for the final day of departure. He debated with himself whether or not he should let Malki in on the secret. Malki already knew of course that something was up, but Enki decided against it in the end. He simply couldn't risk it. Malki confronted him once concerning the mystery. Enki repeatedly changed the topic until he eventually gave up. Everyone else was oblivious. His father and brothers were immersed in plans for strengthening Ur's defenses and securing greater economic allegiance from the northern guilds. Enki considered that Uruk's ruling family was doing the same, leaving no one time to guess their plans.

When the determined day finally arrived, Enki could hardly contain himself. He had had Malki pack all his things for a hunting expedition in the East. The additional items needed for the true journey he was able to secure while Malki was busy attending to Larzo who needed a servant for a quick day trip to Eridu. And so awaking before dawn, he simply threw on his traveling clothes and grabbed his ready supplies and headed off through Ur's main square and out the northern lane.

He considered the normalcy of it all. He simply was strolling along the deserted streets of Ur's main thorough way as the city slept, as if he were going for an enjoyable early morning walk. And yet his destination was one of tremendous danger and great risk. He was setting off once again to do the unthinkable. He smiled inwardly. Yes, that is what he wanted his life to be marked by. To be known as one who is unpredictable. To forever keep friend and foe alike on edge, always wondering what his next move would be. Surely, if successful, this venture would solidify the image. Coupled with his victory against the Amorites, he would be forever known as the creator of destiny, the maker of history.

As he reached the stables and mounted his steed, Shamash was beginning to rise above the northeastern hills. It was a crisp morning and the breath escaping the horses' nostrils rose like a Hurrian smoke signal. But there was not a cloud in the sky and it would prove to be a beautiful day. Preceding Shamash, Nanna hung overhead, beaming down her blessings of light upon his journey. The silence of the early morning was beginning to give way to various song birds as he led his horse into a trot and then a gallop. The breath from the horses' nostrils soon lost visibility as his speed increased.

He was soon pushing the mare to her limits. Raising

himself up and leaning forward, he extended his speed even further. He breathed in deeply, enjoying the rush of blood and increased heart beat rising from the precariousness of his pace. He looked behind him and already could see the cities walls shrink behind another wall of trees. He followed the road until he reached Farduk's farm and then veered off the road across the old man's fields. Reaching the fields limits he made for a lower portion of the farms eastern fence, and led his mare to leap into the air, easily clearing the barrier. Now he was speeding into the woods, a straight but narrow forest path that shut out most of the early morning's light. Emerging from the cave of trees on the other side, a vast plain opened up before him. The sun now had escaped the horizon of the hills and cast upon him a spell of radiance that sent a warm shiver throughout his body. Enki let out a yell as he stood in his saddle, only slightly decreasing his great speed, and lifting his arms into the air, he cried, "I claim you forest and field! I am your father, your deliverer! *Abram teshua* is my name and Sumer is my child, my destiny!!"

***

By the time he had reached the rendezvous point, it was already late afternoon. Gil was waiting for him, having arrived ahead by only an hour or so. Given that they had left their cities about the same time, and how much closer the Blue Hills are to Uruk than to Ur, Gil was amazed that Enki had arrived so quickly. As Enki rode up, Gil grabbed the reigns of his horse.

Gil said, "What? You couldn't sleep last night and decided to ride with Nanna's company instead of Shamash's?"

"I left same time as you," Enki said. "You're just slow."

"You cut through Farduk's fields, didn't you?" Gil asked.

Enki said, "And you stuck to the road, no doubt."

Gil said, "Well, at least one of us has got to keep his head about him on this foolish journey of ours. Honestly, Enki, I've been cursing myself all morning. You're certain you won't reconsider?"

"Oh come now, Gil, we go through this every time we launch out on an adventure."

"Perhaps, but this is no adventure. This is suicide."

"Gil, you're not going to enjoy life if you go about worrying about every little thing that could happen. We'll be fine."

"We'll be dead." Gil murmured the last comment as he walked back to the fire he'd started.

Enki dismounted and unpacked his sack and set up his tent. They both shared in the preparations for supper. They would save their arrows for later on in their journey. Rather than hunting for meat, they enjoyed a simple meal of fruits and nuts and the last bit of fresh bread that they would have for some time. After they had had their fill, they sprawled out on their mats under the stars, gazing upwards as dusk turned into night. Gil finally broke the silence.

"You know, sometimes I wish I were more like you, Enki, foolish as that sounds, I know."

"Not foolishness, Gil, but emerging wisdom," Enki said.

"No seriously, Enki. I mean, sure, you're impetuous, impulsive, unthinking, self-centered, self-absorbed and highly critical of others, but there's strength in you that I don't think I'll ever have."

"Uh… thanks… I think," Enki said.

Gil said, "I just don't know how you do it, Enki – first luring hundreds of blood-thirsty desert Semites into a trap, and now coming up with this crazy scheme of cutting down the Great Cedar…" Gil paused before continuing. "I think if it wasn't for you, Enki, I'd be content to waste my life away in comfortable ease, never attempting anything risky, but also never accomplishing much of anything of real significance."

Enki allowed several minutes of silence to pass before responding. "Oh, I don't know, Gil. I think you underestimate your own strength. Sure, we're different. Maybe I've been good for you, luring you over and over again to move beyond what you think you can or should be capable of doing… but… you've definitely been good for me too. I know I'm impulsive. But a couple of years ago I could never have pulled off what I did to the Amorites. I learned careful planning from your cautious nature. The more I thought about what I was doing, the more I'd hear your predictable objections in my mind. Those objections helped me to think through what I was doing. Sure, I still took some huge risks, but they were calculated, whereas a couple of years ago they would just have been blind leaps. You've been good for me, Gil. I think there's strength in both of us and that we've rubbed off on each other."

"Perhaps," Gil said.

Eventually, their conversation began to trail off as sleep overcame their need for reflection. They both slept sound and the morning came quickly. The moisture left by the mornings dew made them accelerate their breakage of camp. After a quick breakfast they mounted their steeds and were off on another one of their boyhood adventures. At least it felt that way for them at first. They commented on this as they rode, how much like children they still felt, and yet they were heading into a hundred dangers and would end up taking some huge risks before this journey was complete. From time to time Gil would begin to talk fatalistically. He must have repeated his last will and testament ten times in the first couple of days of their travels. Each time Enki wouldn't let him finish. Instead, Enki sought to keep the conversation light. They talked of hunting boar and of wooing women and of a thousand tales.

The first day was an easy one, involving the trek through the Blue Hills and the meadowlands. The roads were still good and they met little resistance from the weather. It was a bright, crisp day for the most part. At one point, darkened clouds covered Shamash and a brief torrent of rain fell. But the storm quickly passed and it was crisp and sunny once again. This was beautiful country – land they loved from their childhood. It was a safe land, tamed by the prosperous city-states of Uruk and Ur and Eridu. It was a common wilderland, filled with tiny streams, green forests, and the occasional bluff rising above the hills. Small forest creatures scurried about fearlessly, accustomed to travelers on this popular trail of the unhurried tradesmen on their way to Lagash or beyond. Affluent members of society also enjoyed the hills, having the funds to allow them the leisure of hiking and exploring the terrain for no other reason than the pure delight of Enlil's handiwork.

Despite their leisurely pace that first day, Enki and Gil made it through the broad valley of the meadowlands and were heading down the gentle slope on the other side by the time night fell. Throwing just a little bit of caution to the wind, they risked a few arrows and brought down a brown stag. Only one arrow was lost in the endeavor and the result was a midnight feast. They stayed up late curing the meat and preparing it to keep through the coming days of their travels. The stag was large enough to nourish them for about half a week, but the extra weight was not welcome to their steeds. Still, they managed to break camp the next morning and to maintain a healthy speed down the eastern slopes of the Blue Hills. About half-way down, they veered off the main trail and headed north-east, being careful to keep the northern bluffs in sight as a reference point. It wasn't long before they stumbled upon the Old North Road, greatly narrowed by years of the forest growth swallowing up its width and turning it into a trail. Another few years and the trail would disappear as well. Gil, light-hearted once again and no longer thinking of wills and cruel deaths, decreed that as High King he would one day restore the Old North Road which made its way across some of the most beautiful parts of the foothills.

It was mid-afternoon of the second day when they actually began to leave the hills and emerge upon the great open plains of the land between the Rivers. These lands were held mostly by farmers and herdsmen, but even now there were still to be found tracks of land unclaimed and untilled. But mostly the land they saw was of great fields with extensive crops of barley and wheat. Cattle ranged across several of the fields over which they now traveled, but they ran into very few plainsmen. The ones they did come across were mostly indentured servants with very little care or concern for the business of strange travelers crossing their masters' lands.

They maintained their easy pace throughout the remaining hours of daylight. Their conversation now turned to the playful dreams of their youths. Those dreams, however, took on new color as the reality of the potential for their fulfillment began to come clearer into focus.

"So tell me Gil," Enki began. "What will be your greatest achievement as High King of all Sumer?"

"Marrying you off to my sister and seeing to it that you settle down to a quiet lifestyle as an over-fed lord," Gil said quickly.

Enki said, "No, seriously, Gil. I'll, of course be off fighting your wars. What will you build with the peace and prosperity I'll win for you as your favorite general?"

Gil said, "Now, there's an idea. I'll send you off to look for Dilmun or something. By the time you find it, conquer it, and return to me, I'll be a happy old man."

Enki said, "Ah, but if ever I found and conquered Dilmun, I think I'd settle down in that paradise of the gods and take my deserved seat next to Nanna. I'd of course send for you and allow you to serve me in my court…"

Gil said, "There you go again, Enki, blaspheming the gods!"

Enki said, "Not blasphemy. Figuratively gracing them with my presence…"

Gil said, "Well, the real thing will never happen. And even if you did find and conquer Dilmun, you know you couldn't abide by the life of a god. You'd need to find something else to conquer. The land of the dead no doubt would be your next victim."

"Ah, now there is an attractive idea," said Enki. "Perhaps someday I will set off to find those lands and bring them under my sway. But I think I'll start with Kish. And so I come back to my query. Once I've disabled our northern nemesis, to what will you devote our kingdom to?"

"You know, believe it or not Enki, I've actually given that some thought," Gil said.

Enki said, "Oh? Pray-tell! Do you mean to say there be a hint of ambition in you after all?"

Gil said, "My ambition is this: To create a university in Uruk that will one day rival the one in Lagash. No… not rival… far surpass it. To bring to it the best minds in all Sumer. To bring them together, not for the propagation of dead history, but to put their minds to the task of making Sumer the greatest of all the lands once again. Greatest in art and science and medicine. Greatest in agriculture and mechanics. Greatest in the languages of all the realms and so become a land sought for by all peoples. To be a kingdom looked upon by all peoples as a higher realm than their own.

To be a kingdom that other peoples are drawn to. To be a kingdom where those drawn to it are enlightened and are drawn into a new culture, a new community of peoples. Uruk, Ur, Eridu – all will be words that will mean less and less. Instead, Sumer will be the word that stirs the heart, at first in our own people alone, but one day in the hearts of the men of Lagash and Umma and even of Susa and beyond, and, dare I even say it, Kish…"

Gil, finally taking notice of the drama in his voice, trailed off into silence. He bowed his head almost ashamedly for speaking so fervently. He seemed to be awaiting Enki's sarcastic reply, but it never came. Instead, Enki just stared at him in wonderment and shock for a few moments before speaking.

Enki said, "Gil, I've never heard you talk that way before. Perhaps I'm not the only one with a destiny to fulfill. Indeed, your dream seems greater than my own. If I'm to be Sumer's *abram teshua*, father of deliverance, then you are certainly what I'm saving Sumer for. If I am *abram teshua*, then you are *abram miqvah* – father of what we long for, father of hope. That too is an ancient title Larzo had told me about. It's as ancient as *abram teshua*. I was never sure why Larzo had explained it to me that day in Roeth, but now I know. You, Gil, are the *miqvah* and I the *teshua*."

Gil laughed, not disrespectfully, but more from embarrassment. Speaking then he said, "Well, my friend, *abram teshua*, if we ever come back from this little misadventure of ours alive, then we sure will have our work cut out for us."

"Oh we'll come back alive," Enki said, seemingly awakened from his generous mood and back again to his old obnoxious self. "But speaking of work cut out for us, Shamash is disappearing and I don't want to camp out here in the open. I'll race you to those woods over there."

And without waiting for reply, Enki was off at a reckless speed, with Gil forced to follow as swiftly as he dared. They sped along across several fields before the forest Enki had spotted began to take on shape and size. They soon discovered that it was both farther away and larger than Enki had thought when he had made his characteristically impulsive decision to make for its shelter before nightfall. Darkness descended well before the time they reached its borders and a cloud cover shielded them from the lights of the heavens so that it was quite dark indeed. In fact, the darkness became such that there arose a couple hours of precarious travel before they finally reached the forest's edge. During that time, they were forced to repeatedly call out to each other to keep from losing each other. And they found themselves losing their bearings more than once as they attempted to keep as straight a line as possible toward the woods. What saved them was the wind. A few times they were forced to stop and listen as quietly as possible until they could make out the distant rustle of the wind through the trees of the forest.

When they finally did make it to the woods, they were exhausted from the extended travel and cold from the chill of the wind. Glad to be out of the open fields and into the shelter of the great trees of the forest, they ventured in a short ways and then collapsed upon their mats for the night without even bothering to prepare a hasty supper.

The arrival of morning hit them with the dripping of a light rain which somehow made its way through the forest ceiling. They didn't even trouble themselves trying to make a fire as the forest floor was quickly becoming dampened by the building storm overhead. Instead they hastily gulped down the last of their bread, ate a few chunks of uncooked meat and sped on their way. At first they clung to the edge of the forest as it led them northward, but when the forest began to trail off to the east, they broke with the forest and continued northward across the open fields once again.

They knew now that they would come across very few wooded areas. They were now truly heading into the heart of the great *Land Between the Rivers* as it was unimaginatively called. Here were great endless stretches of fields and rolling hills expanding as far as the eye could see. Owned mostly by wealthy land owners who lived that life of lordly ease in the various cities by the Rivers, the land itself was leased to numerous farmers and herdsmen who knew nothing of ease and very little of the cities. Various farm houses could be seen spotting the countryside at regular intervals. Many had quite the homey look to them and Enki and Gil both noted more than once their desire for a warm bed and a hot meal prepared by one of these common but certainly hospitable country folk. But they, of course, could not risk being recognized for who they were and so risk news of their travels preceding them to their destination.

For this same reason they made certain to veer well

westward of the outskirts of Umma. It was at this renegade city that Enki was perhaps most well known outside of Ur and Uruk, not for his princely status as much as for his skill at the games. Often in the past he would steal away to Umma to take part in the competition of the great sword-hun matches and very often he would win. He always attempted to conceal his identity, but he suspected that the act was not convincing to the wizened folk of Umma. Since everyone within fifty miles of Umma bet on the games, they made sure to veer off at least fifty miles west of that great town of prostitutes, scoundrels and intrigue.

And so they kept to the less interesting but safer rural areas during the dreary days that followed. It rained most of the time and being in a land overly domesticated, there was very little to hunt. They once caught a hare, but it was so starved that it provided very little real nourishment. They met with no other travelers and the field workers that they came across were content to stare without speaking.

After several days of this had past, the steady storm cover began to finally break. They were now approaching the heavily populated towns surrounding the central trade route. Indeed the Great Central Road was only half a day's journey away. They debated whether they should risk an overnight stay in Nippur. That ancient city full of old ruins and strange inhabitants had its hospitable quarters as well. It might not be a Lagash or an Umma, but there would be a quiet inn with a warm bed and a hot meal waiting for them. Both agreed it would be wiser to continue northward crossing the road well west of Nippur and far east of Babylon. But both also agreed that some hot stew and a pint of ale would be worth the risk. And so they spun off to the northeast, meeting up with the Central Road just a few miles west of Nippur. They were almost to that ancient center's gates when they noted a party leaving the city bearing the emblem of Kish. It certainly had to have been a simple trade caravan, but they cautiously decided not to risk the trek into the city after all. Quickly, they scurried off the road to the north, mourning the loss of the hoped for bed and hot meal, but grateful the party from Kish had not spotted them.

They spent that night in a small wooded area a few hours north of Nippur. Fortunately the weather was now more agreeable and they were able to build a fire and roast the last bit of their meat supply. It was then, lying on their mats and gazing up at the stars through an opening in the trees overhead that they began to discuss their pending engagement with greater precision. The next day would see them reach the Tigris and from then on they would be in Kish's territory. They were now wishing more than ever for that warm bed, but Enki soon snapped them out of their lethargy by bringing up once again his desire to enter right into the sacred forest via the main forest gate.

Gil responded by nursing a now old argument. He said, "You still think we should simply enter the forest through the front door and stroll up to the Tree like we own the place?"

"It's what they would least expect," said Enki. "And the first rule of the academy is 'the unexpected thing is always the safest thing.' There will be fewer guards along the road. Most of their concern is with the Hurrian tribes of the mountains. They won't be too concerned about the road leading up from Kish."

Gil said, "Perhaps. But I still feel very uneasy about trying to pass ourselves off as Kishite infantry. Are you sure the uniforms you got from Larzo are up to date with what their soldiers are wearing?"

Enki said, "Hey… trust me. Remember, I've done this before. Four days in the desert, remember? If I could survive in disguise in a sacred desert land, then surely we can survive in a sacred forest. It worked before, it can work again."

Gil said, "What are you talking about!? You were almost killed in the desert!"

"Well… maybe," Enki said. "Perhaps there were a few kinks in my plan then." Enki spoke now embarrassingly as he recalled the ridiculous way he had worn the desert headband and the look of spite in the eyes of the tribesman who had almost ended his promising career. Enki felt a twinge of pain cross his chest as he recalled the deepness of that fearsome wound that day. "But I've learned a lot since then," he continued, regaining his arrogance. "And besides, it all turned out fine then – it will now as well."

Gil said, "I wish to the gods I had your confidence."

"No you don't," said Enki. "You're content as a doubter. It's the one thing you do better than me."

Gil said, "You know, we could do as Shulpae did, and rediscover the back road over the pass. It would drop us down right in sight of the Cedar."

"Sure it would," said Enki. "And we'd be escorted by a

Hurrian contingent."

"Well, I'd rather take my chances with Hurrians than with Kishites," said Gil.

"Don't be too sure about that," Enki said. "Have you heard what the Hurrians do to their prisoners?"

Gil said, "No… and I don't want to know. I'm going to be a nervous wreck as it is."

Enki said, "So it's the front road through the main 'Illvesti Gate then?"

"Let me sleep on it," said Gil. "Maybe the gods will speak to you tonight, as they so often do, and dissuade you from this ridiculous plan of yours."

Enki knew he had him at this point and allowed the conversation to die away. The embers of the fire soon did likewise as did their own alertness and they soon gave way to sleep. Enki and Gil slept so sound that it was well past nine when they finally arose. Scouting the forest looking for wood for a fire, they stumbled upon some berry bushes well stocked and perfectly ripened. Enki in his usual way of careless blasphemy, took it at as a sign of the god's intimate affection for one of their equals. Gil simply ignored him and ate the berries.

Mounting their horses once again, they set off due north. The terrain was now becoming slightly more rugged, and the open fields less numerous. Pockets of forest sprang up all over the countryside and rolling hills soon replaced the flat plains. The land was vastly different than the lands around Uruk and Ur and it gave Enki an increased passion to see and explore the world beyond Sumer's borders.

They were pushing their steeds rather hard as they both desired to reach the River before nightfall. Enki was even hoping for some fish for supper, though Gil was not so optimistic. The day was uneventful, but beautiful. Various shades of green pocketed the landscape in the form of hill, tree and vale. One ridge off to the east even boasted a small but impressive looking waterfall. The mist from its spray drifted casually over the trail and soaked them as they came near its base. The bright sun quickly dried them, unhindered by the puffy white clouds strewn across the horizon.

Finally, around mid-afternoon they lessened their pace and were happily struck by the distant sound of the River. They had run their horses harder than they had thought and had achieved a great distance in half a day. They now contented themselves with a slower speed, which if their steeds could speak would have been greeted with great adulation. They talked again of life and love and of the great stories of old, seeking to distract themselves from the dangers they would soon be entering.

About an hour before nightfall, they reached the top of the ridge overlooking the Great River Valley. They gaped in wonder at the sight. Lush, rich foliage extended down a steep hillside arriving at last upon a silver and white band called the River Tigris. The parts of the river now in sight revealed numerous rapids and extended lengths of great width, but also a few promising curves which appeared crossable, at least from where they now stood.

With a leap of his horse, Enki led them in a gallop down the hill leading into the valleys depths. A few times their horses almost stumbled upon the uneven terrain, but both were skilled horsemen and handled the descent with relative ease. It was now approaching dusk and Enki was mourning the loss of the daylight hours and thereby the loss of any chance for a dinner of roasted salmon. They resigned themselves to their fate of a meal of berries they'd collected and saved from that morning. They would seek to camp that night on the edge of the river by a warm fire and wait for the mornings light.

The sound of the River was now full in their ears as they made their approach to the final ridge blocking their view of the mighty torrent. Arriving at that ridge they gazed down at the River, now only a hundred yards away. The sun had descended and darkness was quickly approaching. And so, it was that they caught a glimpse downstream of a company of men being warmed by a fire. They were taken aback by the sight, for a company of travelers was the last thing they expected to see this side of the River in this wilderness land. They backed away again into the forest to conceal themselves before ascertaining the identity of the jovial band below. Quietly, they inched their way through the forest along the edge of the ridge looking down on the River until they were directly above the strange contingent. Gil was the first to recognize the mark of Kish on some of the men's shields. There were not many of them, but certainly enough to be wary of being noticed. One appeared to be a Kishite nobleman, and the others, eight or so armed men, appeared to be his traveling guard. But there were no goods anywhere to be seen, lowering the likelihood that the nobleman's expedition was for the purpose of trade. And in any case, this was no trade route. There was, to be sure, a narrow path along the edge of the River, but this was far from being a common and well-traveled road. Rather, it was a simple path for traders who took their goods by River, but needing at times to land and bypass the various rapids by land. But these travelers had no barge or boat but were traveling solely by land. And the nobleman's contingent was small indeed. Often a nobleman would travel the populated lands with fifty or so guards, but here was one in the dangers of the wilderness with only a handful to protect him from the unexpected.

Enki and Gil, having tied their horses a ways back, inched their way through the foliage until they were able to get a better look at the faces of these men.

"What do you make of them?" Enki said in a whispered tone.

"They're not traders," Gil whispered back. "They're heading downstream, but by land not River… strange indeed."

Enki said, "Only eight… or is that nine guards the Barron has with him?"

"I count ten," said Gil. "Look over there, by that turn in the path."

Enki said, "I see him. Okay, ten guards and one nobleman. Heading to Lagash?"

Gil said, "Not likely. Why take this route to Lagash from Kish and encounter a hundred dangers via a slower and less direct route?"

"So, what do you think?" Enki asked.

"I'm not sure," Gil said. "Kish has just retaken the Old Forest, giving them greater control over the wilderness to its south and north here of the River. Perhaps they're scouting the terrain and seeking to gauge how far to extend their control."

Enki asked, "But a nobleman engaged at such a task?"

Gil said, "I know… it doesn't seem likely… but I don't like the alternative…"

"Which is?" asked Enki.

"Susa," they both said together.

Enki and Gil just stared at one another for a few moments and then backed away again to where they'd left their horses. There they were able to continue their conversation with greater freedom.

Gil said, "Shulpae confided in me his suspicions that, despite what the common consent of the court was, that Susa was not at the Lagash summit to seek an expansion of trade."

"Scouts for war, then?" Enki asked.

"Maybe not for an immediate war," Gil said. "But Shulpae believes they're expansionist, this new ruling house in Susa. He recognized their dialect as being that of Media, a fearsome warlike people if the old tales are true."

Enki asked, "Why wasn't this discussed more at court? I'm certain my father suspects none of this. Lord Salzarto seemed to discount them as a threat. Does the High King?"

Gil said, "I don't know. As you know, my father is a hard one to read. And he conceals much, even from those closest to him. It's possible he's ignoring Susa for now, and focusing his full attention on Kish. But if this is indeed a Kishite emissary to Susa…"

"Then Sumer may one day soon find itself at war on two sides!" Enki said.

Gil said, "Perhaps."

Several more moments passed before Enki decided for them their course of action. He said, "Well, whatever this Kishite duke is up to, we're not going to find out hanging around here by our horses. And that old nobleman had fresh fish on his fire. I'm determined to get some."

And with that, Enki began unstrapping his sword and checking his person for any insignia of Sumer. Gil did nothing but stare blankly until he could stand it no longer. Finally he said, "And what is it that you're proposing? What is your plan for getting us killed this time?"

Enki said, "We're going to sneak right up to their fire and steal some of their fish, listen in on their conversation and head on back to our horses full of fresh salmon and information."

Gil said nothing but simply stared at Enki, not budging from his spot.

Enki this time was compelled to speak. He said, "Don't just sit there. If we're going to sneak into the Kishite infested Old Forest, we may as well get used to their foul stench now. And I'm not about to just eat some berries for supper when there's fish to be had."

Gil said, "I prefer berries to eating the dirt that's poured over us as we're laid into our graves."

"Don't be foolish," Enki said. "If we're killed, the crows

will eat our rotting flesh. There'll be no graves."

"You have a great gift for comfort." It was Gil's turn now for sarcasm.

Enki said, "Why, thank you Gil. It is indeed a gift. I don't like to talk about it."

Gil said, "Give me one good reason why I should go along with yet one more of your impulsive plans!"

Enki said, "Because if that Kishite nobleman is indeed heading to Susa, then we need to know why. This is for Sumer! And don't think it's impulsive. Recall that I am the indispensable instrument of the gods. It's their plan working its way through me. We can't be harmed."

Gil said, "Enki, the gods will judge you one day soon for all your impiety! And something in me dreads that I'll be caught in the middle somehow. Unfortunately, I know you're right on this one. I'll do this for Sumer, but you're doing it for the fish and don't you deny it."

Enki did not deny it, though he knew it was really the novelty of eating ones enemies' supper that moved him. Realizing that they could not take on the ten armed Kishite soldiers in a fight, they left their weapons with their horses, and removed any garb that would give away their country or status. Together then they slithered down the hillside until they were once again in full sight of the company of Kish. Gil pleaded with Enki not to do anything foolish. He insisted that it would be enough to overhear their conversation from within the foliage closest their fire. Gil hoped beyond hope he was not serious about the fish.

To further position themselves, they crawled carefully

across the forest floor until they were in the closest possible position to the fire without actually emerging from the brush. The fire was now perhaps only ten yards away from their hiding place amidst the trees and thick bushes of the untended riverside growth. The loud rumble of the River kept their audience from hearing the unavoidable snap of a twig here or a branch there as they had made their way to their current location. They were now close enough to overhear the conversation by the fire. Several soldiers were warming themselves. A tent on the far side of the fire must now have housed the nobleman who was nowhere to be seen. A couple guards appeared to be positioned on either end of the beach connecting the small landing with the riverside path. The remaining soldiers by the fire were chatting amongst themselves.

"How much farther do you suspect we'll go before crossing?" It was a big burly fellow who spoke nervously.

"Ha! Nervous are ye of being swept away, you rock?!" A tall slender guard had made the reply and set the others to laughter.

The big one defended himself. He said, "I'm not nervous of the River, you clod! Well… perhaps just a bit. I just ain't never swam is all."

The tall one then spoke in a kinder voice. He said, "Ah friend Belgor, 'tis not at your expense we laugh. Just an irony of the gods that you so fearless in battle should shy away from the water."

Another one spoke now. He said, "Belgor, you just keep your thoughts focused on Susa."

Enki and Gil gave each other a quick glance as the guard continued.

The guard said, "They say the women of that city give of themselves freely, and that their menfolk care little. Or at least so say the men I know who were on the first expedition there last year. There's great reward awaiting you my friend if you can brave a little water."

The others laughed once again. Then a smaller fellow spoke. He said, "I've heard that the men of that town have several lasses each. Scantily clad they say they are, even those of noble birth."

Just then the nobleman emerged from his tent, and the conversation around the fire died away. The nobleman said, "You men must constrain yourselves in Susa. I'll not have any of you impacting our relations with that land because a foreign lass catches your eye. But constrain yourselves and I'll see you're rewarded with what you desire. I'm certain that Lord Amon of Susa will supply us… with all our needs."

The nobleman spoke those last words with a lightness that lifted the men's spirits and set them once again to laughter. The nobleman was then about to head back to his tent when something caught his attention. To Gil's utter dismay, Enki had snuck out of the cover of the bushes while the distracted soldiers had engaged in their exchange with the nobleman. Somehow he had managed to snatch a roasting fish from the fire. He almost made it back to the cover of the forest amidst the shadows when the nobleman caught sight of him.

"Ho there!" The nobleman shouted in Enki's direction.

His men turned just in time to see Enki disappear into the forest.

Enki, as he sped past Gil shouted a whisper, "Split up." And with that Gil and Enki were off in different directions. But the soldiers saw only Enki at this point and did not pick up on Gil's trail. Gil headed back to the horses, but Enki sped on through the forest to the east along the river, his heart racing like never before. Not all the guards had apparently joined the chase. Some stayed back to guard the camp. But at least four or five were in close pursuit of Enki. Enki, free from his sword and light armor that he'd worn through most of the trip, had the advantage of freedom of movement. He sped on downstream and the distance between him and the Kishite soldiers seemed to be growing. Another few clever turns around a grove here and a rock formation there and Enki would have been safe. But the gods finally let Enki down at this point and he tripped over the roots of a great oak. Down he fell lying silent in hope that his pursuers would pass him by. They didn't. One almost ran right on top of him and soon all were gathered round him. Enki felt strong, brutal hands lift him roughly to his feet. He was shoved forcefully into a tree only to be grabbed once again and shoved to the ground face first. His hands were then tied behind his back and his body searched for concealed weapons.

"What do you make of him, Roden?" one of them asked. "A spy or just some local urchin?"

Roden said, "Ah… look at him, the poor bastard. Just some woodsman's son I'd gather, but Lord Morgan might have a different take on him, he's so jumpy about this mission of his."

The first man said, "No doubt, no doubt. Well, let's get him back to his *royalness*."

The one tying him finished his job, pulled Enki to his feet and shoved him down the path. He then said, "Come on, boy. The less of a fight you put up the better."

Enki at this point was taking this advice. He knew his only hope was to play the role of the aforementioned woodcutter's son, or something similar. He pretended not to understand their speech, which was in common Akkadian. And in truth, his Akkadian was so poor and their dialect so different that he understood very little of their conversation. Gil would have understood it better. He wondered now if his royal friend had escaped their notice.

Several times it was the pointed jab of one of the soldier's swords that sped Enki along his way. Once it pierced the skin and caused a slow bleeding on his lower right side. Enki winced in pain, trying to show the panic that he suspected a letterless youngster of the wilderlands would be experiencing right now. And with his own fate so precarious, panic was not too difficult an act to pull off.

Finally, they emerged into the open beach of the Kishites camp. Enki was shoved again face first into the sand near the fire. The nobleman queried Enki disdainfully. He asked, "So what have we here? A Hurrian spy, perhaps? Or could you be Sumerian? You have the look it seems to me."

Enki spoke a few words in a dead language he learned at the academy and which he knew would be unintelligible to this man of the north. He spoke it in frightened tones and faked a northeastern accent, "Ebli ocknar! Ebli ocknar wodessi netten!"

One of the soldiers ventured a kindly word. He said, "My Lord, the lad seems to be but an illiterate local. All we found on him was the fish he snatched from our fire."

Lord Morgan said, "Hummph. Poor lad indeed. Look at the meat on the boy. He's not been starving at any rate."

The kindly soldier said, "Ah, sir, I say we just let him go. He's a done us no harm and we've plenty of fish. No spies would know of our mission."

Lord Morgan turned on the guard then. He said, "No spies you say?! You fool! There are those indeed who know of our mission. Do you think that Kish's court is free from men of folly bought off by the highest bidder? No, even Kish is not free from such wretches."

Morgan then grasped Enki's face in one of his great hands, and squeezed so hard that Enki let out a squeal. The pain of course led him to it, but he still had the presence of mind to appear the naive and cowardly boy he hoped they'd conclude he was. And so he squealed and let out a cry and a few more words in that lost and obscure Sumerian dialect he was now grateful he'd been forced to learn. "Erreb adenitheari ic ishin obtolien! Allehii, allehii, allehii…"

The act seemed to be working for Morgan finally shoved Enki's face back into the sand and spoke again spitefully. He said, "There be spies all about in this world, good men. But you are right. This one here likely is not one of them."

Enki tried to conceal his relief, but the relief was short

lived.

Lord Morgan said, "Take the urchin and beat him. Then kill him."

The soldier said, "But sir, he's just a boy!"

Morgan said, "He's a thief and so deserves a beating. And he's seen us passing through and so cannot be allowed to live. If word somehow reached Uruk or Ur that we have an alliance with Susa, it would destroy all our plans. Why even now there is a delegation from Susa heading for Ur. And they will deny having had any contact with Kish whatsoever. They must secure the confidence of Ur if we are to surprise Sumer from two sides. I take plans of the king for that final engagement with Sumer that will forever wipe that land from all memory of the living. We shall take Uruk and Susa shall have Ur."

The nobleman looked deep into Enki's eyes as he spoke this. Then he said, "You can't understand a word I'm saying can you? Or perhaps you really are from Sumer and are playing the fool for our benefit. No, we cannot take the chance. Take him into the forest and do as I say. Then cast him into the River."

Reluctantly the soldier said, "Yes, My Lord."

Enki began to squirm as they grabbed him. He continued to pretend that he did not know what they were saying and so concealed his immediate fear of death. He would hold out the act as long as possible, hoping for escape once they took him into the forest.

They were not in the forest long before they started to carry out their orders. First Enki was flung against a tree and then tied with one end of a rope around his neck and the other to a branch on the tree. They had no whip to beat him with, but took turns with their own fists and with fallen branches. Enki cried out with each blow and was beginning to despair of rescue. He hoped that Gil would be nearby seeking some way to intervene. He'd noted the presence of all the soldiers at that camp and so any sent off to look for any of his potential companions had apparently returned without knowledge of Gil or the horses. And then Enki wondered if Gil was still in hiding back away by the horses, unaware of his fate. He began to despair once again.

A blow to Enki's face now caused a spittle of blood to shoot from his mouth. But he continued to hold back any kind of skilled resistance, knowing that it would inevitably be futile with the armed soldiers standing nearby watching the beating. He continued to cry out in his secret dialect, but half-heartedly so now. Another blow to his ribs brought him to his knees, then to the ground. But the angle of his view gave him a glimpse of a pair of human eyes hiding in the brush nearby. He knew it was Gil, waiting in agony for an opportune moment. But Enki could see none coming and in a rare selfless moment, he wished Gil would leave him, lest they both face certain death. But Enki was helpless to do anything about it. If he tried to communicate this to Gil hiding in the forest, then his oppressor's attention would be drawn to Gil. And if he did nothing, then Gil at the point of his own execution, would emerge from the forest to join him in death. Enki would have to be content with trusting his fate to the gods and hoping for a miracle.

Finally, the beating stopped. Enki was bowled over in agony. Though he could not see himself, his face was black and blue and spattered with blood from his mouth. He didn't believe his ribs were broken, but they were certainly badly bruised and his old wound from the desert had been reopened causing a stream of blood to flow slowly but steadily from his side. Enki raised himself to his knees and allowed the soldiers to see a glimpse of his nobility as he patiently awaited the sword, fearing at the same time what Gil would do in this moment. The designated soldier drew his sword and moved forward to strike as Enki noticed from the corner of his eye Gil in a nearby bush preparing to attack, apparently weaponless.

But the moment did not come. Instead, came the miracle Enki had hoped for. The soldier who'd been given the order from Lord Morgan and who had sought to defend Enki now stepped forward from out of the darkness.

He said, "Hold your hand, Erithon. I'll not have this boy's blood on my hands and so anger the local gods and demons of this foreign forest we travel through now. I've a boy of my own back home his age. I'll not have an offended god of this land seek revenge on my boy back in Kish while Shamash is sleeping."

Erithon hesitantly lowered his sword. Another nameless guard spoke the questions of the others. "But sir, you're not just going to let him go? I'm as fearful as the next of any here of the local gods of these haunted lands, but if Lord Morgan found out he'd have all our necks once back in Kish. We'd never be able to return!"

The chief soldier said, "I said nothing about letting him go. We'll carry out Morgan's orders. We'll throw him into the River and let the gods decide his fate."

This seemed to satisfy the men who all shared the same fear of the local deities as much as they did Lord Morgan. The compromise seemed to appease both fears. Enki noted Gil sink back down to his hiding place and then disappear back further into the brush, probably to position himself downstream to try to pull him out. Enki, with new hope renewed his act with greater vigor. He cried and wailed in his obscure dialect, pretending to call out to some local god to save him. This seemed to speed along their determination to cast him into the River with some life left in him. Soon Enki was flying through the air thanks to a host of strong arms which had hoisted him up and flung him a good ten yards out from shore. To Enki's dismay he quickly realized his hands remained tied behind his back. This knowledge hit him as he was flying through the air, and combined with the shock of the frigid rapids that suddenly enveloped him, sent his spirits sinking to despair once again.

But knowledge that Gil was out there somewhere kept his hopes up enough to put up a fight with the Mighty Tigris. He managed to kick his shoes off which gave him greater thrust as he sought to tread the water. But the point at which he was flung into the River was a section of fast flowing rapids which quickly carried him farther into the center of this wide portion of the Tigris. He was soon a good fifty yards from shore on either side as he sped precariously down the center of the torrent. He kept trying to get a glimpse of the shore and more specifically of Gil, but glances were hard to come by as he was repeatedly pulled below the water's surface by the strong current and then briefly up again to gather in some air before being plunged under once again.

Finally, at one point, a lucky glance landed upon Gil running along the southern shore. He was back a ways and seemed to be progressing at a slower speed than his own. This was confirmed a few minutes later when Enki caught his last glimpse of Gil, now farther still upstream than before. And the River showed no signs of slowing, but instead seemed to be picking up speed. Enki again fell into despair. Instinct kept Enki fighting for air, but no longer was he trying to make for the shore. Instead he let the current carry him along and spent all his exertion on his next breath. The temperature of the River began to numb his body. This lessened the pain of his recent beating, and seemed to stop the flow of blood from his various wounds, but he was aware as well of the other dangers to his person with the drop in temperature.

Enki at this point placed all his hope on the next bend in the River. He knew that a rivers rapids could smooth out as quickly as they emerged and hoped that such would be the case around the next turn. But as he rounded the curve his last bit of hope faded. The River stretched ahead for what seemed many leagues from his brief vantage points as his head occasionally bobbed above the waters ever-changing surface. Then, after those several leagues, the River seemed to drop off and disappear. Perhaps he just couldn't see a bend in the River after that point, but this he knew not to be the case as the sound of the torrent grew stronger and stronger at each point his head rose above the water. There were falls ahead. And though Enki could not have known how great the falls were, he suspected the worst and would have been right.

Enki now lost all hope of being saved. Once again, in the moment of pending death, Enki cast aside his impiety. He resigned himself to the watery grave which would be his own and gave out a final cry to Nanna, Enlil and An, knowing Shamash to be asleep at this hour. As he continued to draw closer to the edge of the falls, he allowed himself to be carried down into the waters depths for the last time. Sinking down, resigned to his fate, he suddenly felt a strong impact which at first he thought to be a large boulder in the water, but soon felt to be a strong arm about his waist. Suddenly, his body was no longer being carried along by the current, but was being pulled against the current with the full force of the rapids hitting his person and flowing violently against his form. The strong arm of his rescuer lifted him briefly above the waters' surface and Enki gasped for air. But he was thrust down again before he could get a look at the body attached to the arm about his waist. The figure seemed to him to be pulling both of them to shore, against the strong current, presumably with a rope fastened to some anchor on the shore. Several minutes passed involving a few more gasps of air as Enki did nothing but allow his wearied body to be dragged along. Finally, the current lessened and strong hands lifted him out of the water and onto the north shore of the Tigris. Half expecting Gil's familiar form, Enki looked up into the face of Sadiq.

CHAPTER 7 – THE DEATH OF A GOD

Enki awoke as if in a dream. He was once again lying underneath a tree. Nanna was once again overhead shining down on his warm alive body. And Sadiq was once again preparing a meal over a nearby fire. One key aspect was different though. They were not alone this time. Across the fire, huddled in a blanket, drying and warming himself by the fire, sat an exhausted looking Gil. Enki allowed a sudden wave of relief to wash over him as the reality of resolution fully struck him. Gil was safe. He was safe. Food was being prepared. At the moment he didn't care how it all happened. He didn't care to wonder why or how this same Sadiq could and would once again be his rescuer here in an obscure part of the northeast wilderland. Here he simply was and Enki cared not for asking questions just yet.

Enki sat up and looked over the fire toward Sadiq. "So

what are we eating, Sadiq? Smells good."

"Oh… just something I threw together," Sadiq said. "A few herbs here, a few roots there, and the fresh flesh of a quail roasting and awaiting its immersion into the mix. How are you feeling?"

"Never been better," Enki said. "Thanks for asking."

Gil just sat with a blank stare on his face as he listened to the exchange.

"How are the boys?" Enki asked.

"Oh, doing fine," said Sadiq. "I left them in Babylon with the assignment of establishing more trade connections. You know that little town I wager has a very promising future."

"That dirty old hovel? Not a chance," said Enki.

Sadiq just smiled and continued his cooking.

Gil finally could contain himself no longer. He asked, "Would someone please explain to me what is going on? No offense to our mutual rescuer here… but who the shadowland are you?! And how do you both know each other?!"

"Relax, Gil, relax," said Enki. "We're in good hands here with Sadiq. He's the one who rescued me in the desert. Back again for a repeat performance."

Gil then addressed Sadiq. He asked, "And… you have nothing better to do than to follow Enki around and bail him out of his stupidity?"

"Oh… I was just passing through is all," said Sadiq. "I happened to be in the right place at the right time once again. Surely not by chance – the One you call Anu has been gracious to you two."

"I see." Gil was almost ready to give up but not quite. "And I suppose Anu speaks to you like Nanna speaks to Enki?"

Turning then to Enki, Sadiq asked, "Nanna speaks to you? How has she been?"

"Oh, doing quite well," said Enki. "She sends her regards."

"Ah, that's nice," said Sadiq.

Gil gave up.

Later that night over supper, Sadiq explained that he was passing through the northern reaches, hunting for fur to bring back to the aforementioned Babylonian connections his two servants were seeking to secure. He had overheard the commotion in the Kishite camp from his own camp on the other side of the river. It had been too far away to make out exactly who was being tossed in the River, but Sadiq had been able to track the bobbing head as he rode downstream along the northern shore to a point at which he was able to jump in and overtake Lord Morgan's victim. What Enki then learned was that Gil had jumped in as well. Once Gil had seen that he would not be able to overtake Enki by land, he had jumped in hoping to be carried along by a faster strain of the current. But the current had proved too much for Gil and the falls would have taken him as well had Sadiq not intervened shortly after pulling Enki to shore. And so here they both were, Gil's debt to Sadiq now added to Enki's.

Sadiq then listened patiently to Enki and Gil give a full

account of their adventure. Enki did most of the talking and even ventured to disclose to Sadiq their full intentions. Sadiq only nodded from time to time and looked annoyingly thoughtful. Finally, when they had finished their tale he responded.

"So you two are just going to stroll into the Amanus and chop down the Tree?" Sadiq asked blandly.

Gil suddenly brightened up. "Yes, that's Enki's ridiculous plan, or lack thereof," he said hopeful that Sadiq would take his side now and dissuade Enki from his scheme. "The whole thing is just foolhardy."

Enki said, "I'll admit going after that fish was foolish. But don't you see the gods hand in all this? The gods spared us so that we could complete the task we've set out to do. Sadiq here is evidence that the blessings of the gods are upon our mission."

Sadiq then said, "Don't bring me into this. My rescuing you two I'll admit is somewhat extraordinary and may indeed have some greater significance, but I'm personally troubled by your casualness in what you've set out to do. Amanus is no ordinary forest and the Great Cedar is no ordinary tree. And I've yet to hear you even mention the Guardian of the Forest."

Enki asked, "You mean you believe those stories too about Humbaba and the magic Axe, Sadiq?"

Sadiq said, "I do more than believe it. The one you call Humbaba is indeed alive and well in the forest. I've spoken with him. And the Axe is real too."

Both Enki and Gil now with eyes wide said at the same

time, "You've spoken with Humbaba!?"

Sadiq said, "On several occasions. And Humbaba is only one of many names given him by legend. His real name in the ancient tongue is Kreon, one of the fathers, from before the Cleansing. For long centuries he has been bound to that Tree, a slave to its fruit for a great evil he committed long ago. You would do well to consider carefully his reaction to your attempt to destroy the very thing that gives him his power and long life."

Enki said, "So you think we should just turn around and go home?" There was obvious dismay in Enki's eyes at the thought, and a matched amount of hope in Gil's.

"I didn't say that," Sadiq said to the surprise of Enki and the dismay of Gil. "All things must come to an end. Even Kreon."

Gil then seemed to lighten up inside as if remembering something he'd long forgotten. He asked excitedly, "The prophesy?"

Sadiq said, "Yes, Gil, the prophesy. Perhaps Anu's hand was indeed in this rescue after all. But if you're to be the ones to fulfill it, it won't happen by your marching into Amanus through the front door."

Gil was now getting more excited. He said, "The Axe! You know where the Axe is, don't you!?"

"It is no secret where the Axe is. Every Sumerian would know it if he'd only recall the songs of old."

Enki felt a bit of a jab at that for he'd neglected all study of the songs. But Gil had not and now seemed to take on new life. Gil didn't quite sing the words, but there was the rhythm in his voice that characterized one of the ancient songs of old. He then gave the translation.

The great Axe, Might of Heroes, in chambers old and gray,
The seat of the gods under Silver mountain lay.

Sadiq looked a bit surprised at Gil's perfect recitation of the Old Sumerian. And there was also a bit of sadness in his eyes, as if he could see something that they could not.

"Well done, Gil," Sadiq said. "Well done. You will be a great aid to Enki on this quest."

"Oh yes, I can surely see Gil's usefulness now," Enki said sarcastically. "*Seat of the gods* really gives it all away, doesn't it?"

Neither Gil, nor Sadiq, looked particularly amused. They ignored Enki's remarks as Sadiq continued. "So what else, Gil, do you recall from the ancient songs?"

"Quite a bit," Gil said. "I memorized all the standard fragments and some lesser known favorites of my teacher Shulpae. He's fanatical about the old songs. And he grieves that they all seem so incomplete."

"They are indeed," said Sadiq. "Sadness it is that the lore of the Benel have faded out of reach, for great use it would be in many matters. Now only fragments remain of the great songs of old. But not all is lost. Much could probably be pieced together from what you've memorized, but I will tell you what I know. The great Axe forged in the mountains roots long ago is awaiting the *called one* to lift it from its ancient resting place and bring an end to a great age.

"If you intend to pursue this end, then take my counsel and abandon all plans of sneaking in through the front door.

Under the mountain and through the ancient chamber of the Annunaki, great citadel of the Benel lords is the route you should take. Long ago did I venture into its depths. The seats of Madai and Javan, of Kros and Gaylen and Avilah and all the rest are there and still intact. And in the midst of those seats of wisdom and counsel is the sacred Axe *Might of Heroes.* Wield that weapon against the Tree swiftly, for Kreon will know of it at the first stroke. There is a power infused into that Axe similar to the power that's wedded to the Tree. Three strokes of that Axe will bring the Great Tree down, so the legend goes. Fail to cast the tree down before Kreon reaches you and he will cut you down in its stead. The Bull of Heaven lives my young friends. Do not underestimate his power. But you need not fear it either. His power is completely wedded to the Great Tree. At its fall, he will be broken."

Silence followed as Enki and Gil allowed Sadiq's words to sink in. Later they would wonder at how quickly they accepted Sadiq's testimony, still knowing so little about this mysterious traveler. After they finished dinner, several hours passed as Sadiq gave them instructions on finding the southern entrance into the intricate system of tunnels long ago carved into the depths of the Silver Mountains. An old leather patch became their makeshift map. Using the edge of a knife, Sadiq drew a map of the tunnels and of the route to the chamber of the Annunaki. He also jotted down several other pertinent pieces of information that they would need on their quest.

"Who were the Annunaki really?" Gil asked at one point.

"That my young friend is a long story indeed," said Sadiq. "In brief, they were the Benel lords of the various realms in the world before the Great Cleansing. Together they comprised a great council that ruled in terrible matters in those now distant years. Kreon was one of them once, until his crime forever banished him. In the early ages of the world, the First Ones were themselves members of the council. That was when the Annunaki were great indeed. But alas, nothing lasts forever, and even the grace and power of the Annunaki faded into shadow and suspicion. Eventually, the ancient meeting places were abandoned as each of the Benel lords left each other to fend for themselves. They retreated, inwardly concerned only for their own land. It is a sad but common tale."

"And what was Kreon's crime?"

Sadiq paused painfully as if remembering some old personal wound. At last he said, "That I will not tell you now. Perhaps you will have a chance to ask him 'ere this is all over."

Gil and Enki queried further, but Sadiq's story was at an end for the night and he spoke no more. Rather, in thoughtful silence Sadiq patched Enki up, applying various ointments to his wounds and bandaging up his abdominal gash now for the second time. That night Gil and Enki slept long and hard. When they awoke, Sadiq was gone. He'd left some provisions for them and some needed supplies, and a much needed new pair of shoes for Enki, but he himself was nowhere to be seen. As Enki and Gil prepared breakfast they reflected on their mysterious friend.

"So what do you make of Sadiq? Do you trust him?" Gil asked honestly.

Enki did not answer right away. When he did, he spoke slowly and thoughtfully. "I'm not sure how to answer that. I guess I'd have to say, 'yes, I trust him' but I honestly can't tell you why. Well, I suppose the fact that he saved my life twice now might have something to do with it." Enki smiled at that thought and then continued. "No Gil, I don't know what to make of Sadiq. It must be more than chance that led him to cross our paths again. I know I'm somewhat irreligious…"

"Blasphemous is the word I'd use," Gil said.

"Okay… blasphemous then. I've never really put much stock in the gods and yet I suppose I can't help but believe in them as well. My life seems to testify to their intervention… and…"

Enki paused for a moment as if deciding whether he should continue his thought.

"And what?" Gil asked.

Enki quietly then said, "I think I heard one of them speak to me once."

Gil just looked suspiciously at Enki expecting another launch into blasphemy but it never came. Gil saw that Enki was serious and softened a bit. "Well… what did this god say?" Gil asked.

Enki said, "It was when I'd killed the desert Semite and lay dying in a pool of his blood mixed with mine. I knew I was done for. I was just waiting for death to come when I heard this voice. It was sweet, soft, warm, terrifying and intoxicating all at the same time. It said simply, *come away with me*."

Neither spoke for several minutes. Gil finally broke the silence. He said, "I hear you speak those words, Enki, and there's a burning in my heart that I can't explain."

Enki lighted up at the thought that someone might actually understand his experience. He said, "Yes, Gil, that's exactly how I'd put it too. And I do believe I sense a bit of that when I'm with Sadiq. It's as if he's a faint echo of that voice I heard."

Gil just nodded and thought on that. Finally he said, "You're going to think I'm out of my mind for saying this, but do you think Sadiq could be one of the Benel lords of old, one of the Annunaki? They say they never age. What if he survived somehow the Great Cleansing? This Kreon we're setting off to threaten apparently did. And how else would he know the exact location of this underground council chamber?"

"That thought crossed my mind as well," said Enki. "And then, at the same time, it seems like we must be out of our minds to even be talking this way. Can we really believe that all the old songs we grew up on are really true? I mean, I guess I've always believed them, but never to the point of testing them."

"Well… there's one way we can know for sure," said Gil. He was smiling now as he arose and picked up Sadiq's makeshift map.

Enki smiled as well, knowing that Gil was now with him to the end.

Enki said, “Well, what are we waiting for? Let’s go kill an immortal!”

Still feeling somewhat foolish, but caught up in the excitement of the possibility that this all might really be true, they broke camp quickly and headed off in the direction of the Silver Mountains. Their original course was to head directly northwest skirting the mountains southern tip and entering the forest of Amanus from the west. They now instead headed due north and eventually veered a bit northeast as they followed the landmarks Sadiq had laid out for them on the map. They were now on foot, but the terrain was such that a couple horses would not have increased their time by much. They were in the true wilderness. Deep gullies stretched out to endless reaches as they looked about. Rolling hills covered with forest and shrubs surrounded them. Occasionally they traversed old trails laid out by traders and sometimes even older paths laid out by ancient dwellers of this now abandoned realm. Once they came across a great stone pillar, covered in vines from endless years of unchecked growth. It was one of the landmarks Sadiq had told them to look for. Spotting it, their faith in Sadiq’s stories increased. They spent some time examining the ancient runes. Sadiq had noted that it was a road marker from before the Great Cleansing. Apparently, this entire wilderness realm had in that ancient time been peopled with cities and great roads, even more advanced than their own modern era. The language written on the pillar was of a kind unlike any they had ever seen. Gil jotted down some of the writings on the back of their leather map hoping to one day be alive enough to show it to Shulpae.

Departing from that ancient crossroad, they headed northeast again. They now made with all haste, hoping to reach by nightfall the final valley that would lead them into the foothills of the Silver Mountains. However, they were forced to stop shy of their goal, defeated by the downing of the sun and a gathering storm. They quickly made a makeshift shelter amidst the trees and huddled close to keep warm. They had risen in altitude over the course of the day, and the winds of the oncoming storm brought on a deathly chill. Finally the rain came and its onslaught made them think that a second Cleansing had begun. But by morning the rain had subsided and Shamash was able to break through the clouds and dry their weary bodies. They ate a soggy meal and headed off again toward the approaching valley's entrance. Arriving there, they now headed northwest into the shadows of the foothills rising on either side of them and continuing on toward the base of the mountain till each side rose to meet the Silver Mountains growing height.

Their clothes were still damp and their bodies were weary from a poor night's sleep, but their spirits were high and their conversation light as they made their way to do the unimaginable. Shamash was now out in all his glory and the dampness of the valleys forest floor was drying fast. The trees surrounding them were ancient looking things and seemed to grow older with each passing league. The valley was narrowing as they progressed and grew ever steeper on each side as they neared its collision with the mountains. A stream flowed down the center of the valley. It was this brook they now followed upstream. They would lose sight of it at times due to the thickness of the brush below them, but it would reappear in time to mark their continued course.

As they progressed, the valley quickly transformed itself into a deep gorge, with themselves near its depths and the mountains walls rising all about them, blocking them off from the light of Shamash. Suddenly, they were struck by the sound of a distant rumble. It grew louder as each half hour passed and they knew it to be the falls of which Sadiq had spoken, another one of their landmarks. It was well passed midday when the falls came in sight. A beautiful stream of color springing from the Silver Mountains side, it gushed in a brilliance of white, silver, blues and greens. The falls height from the floor of the gorge was well over three hundred feet. As the water neared the ground, it lost some of its form as the fringes of the falling water frayed into a white mesh of spray gently watering the ferns and moss below. Rolling off the rocks, the divided droplets of water reunited giving birth to the spring they'd been following. It was a beautiful sight, and Gil and Enki paused to rest a while to take in the majestic scene. Here was Enlil's handiwork at its best, Gil said, and Enki agreed. Each took in the sight with wonder that they were among the few who had ever ventured so far into the wild to view such a wondrous sight. Sadiq had said that a Hurrian tribe had at one time occupied this hidden valley, but had left it vacant long ago for reasons unknown to even Sadiq. Sadiq had come upon the valley long ago, he had said, and dwelt there one whole summer enjoying the spray of the falls and the coolness of the cliffs shadows.

When they had fully rested, they sought out the hidden crevice spoken of by Sadiq. He had told them of a thick forest to the left of the falls, hugging the mountain and cutting off all sight of the cliffs surface up to a height of one hundred feet. There, great trees grew – greater than any Enki had ever seen. Tall pines rose on that narrow strip between the falls and the cliffs as if in an attempt to reach the heavens and escape the shadowed covering of the rock wall and embrace the warmth of Shamash. They made their way through this narrow forest and found that the wall of trees they'd come under blocked off the sound of the falls. It seemed as if they were now in a different world, though the falls were only a hundred yards away.

Finally, they emerged through the forest and found its end. The trees indeed did grow right up to the edge of the cliffs. Certain ones of the greatest trees seemed to grow right into the mountains rock surface itself. So mingled together were these trees with the stone wall of the mountains side that they almost missed the crack in its surface. Lying to the right of one great trunk of a tree merged into the rock, was a slit no more than ten feet across, but stretching up thirty or so yards until it narrowed to a close just above the tops of the trees. A debate then ensued as to whether they should embark now upon this entrance into the unknown or to wait out the day and night and attempt the feat in the morning. Sadiq had not told them how deep this crevice went, nor when and how it stumbled into the entrance of the tunnels. Should the tunnels come quickly then it mattered not how much daylight remained. But the sun was sinking fast and the light was fading quicker still into the shadows of these cliffs. Finally, caution gave way to adventure, and they decided to take the plunge into the mountain's side. They would proceed only so far and would attempt to back out should the light fade completely before finding their mark.

Into the darkness of the mountains crack they crept, trying hard not to think of the small creeping creatures that might be lurking just beyond the next rock. Soon, all light was gone and they were truly groping in the dark. They felt their way in and were forced to climb several large boulders and then down again the other side. Then their feet were touching solid earth, but only briefly before they were once again suspended over rock and crevice. They found themselves crawling between great stones, squeezing through the narrowness of the cracks and occasionally hoisting themselves up over a barrier by wedging their bodies against either side of the tunnels walls. Fearing they would soon be forced to spend the night in this narrow slit, they were about to turn back when they noted a glimmer of faint light far ahead through the maze of stone and rock. They ventured on toward this goal, squeezing through a tight spot here, wedging themselves up and over a barrier there, until they finally emerged into what was left of daylight.

They found themselves in a small enclosure. All around them were high cliffs reaching up to the sky a good fifty yards on every side. Straight above them they could see a small portion of the early evening sky. The open space they had emerged into was but twenty or so yards in diameter, with no sign of any continuing route save the slit in the mountain from whence they had come. There was no vegetation in this natural rock chamber, but a small pool of water, ten or so feet across, graced its center.

In despair, they collapsed upon the surface of the rock floor. Had they gone through the correct crevice? They had seen no other, but perhaps they had missed it. Or perhaps the narrow passageway through the cliffs Sadiq had spoken of had collapsed long ago. Not wanting to think of alternatives just now, they laid down in silence gazing up at the faint specks in the sky emerging into stars as the night blackened. Finally, Gil spoke.

"Well now what?" he asked.

"I don't know," said Enki.

"What do you mean, 'I don't know?' Why don't you ask one of your god friends to tell us what to do?"

"Oh now look who's lapsing into blasphemy."

"Well I get it from hanging around with you. Honestly, Enki, why did I ever let you talk me into this crazy scheme?"

"Hey, you were the one so excited about going the route of the *ancient chamber of the Annunaki* and finding the mysterious *Magic Axe.* Tell me Gil, are we not both fools for buying into these old fables? Have you ever heard of anything so ridiculous as a magical axe called *Might of Heroes*?"

Gil did not respond for he was nursing his own doubts now. Finally, he spoke again having softened a bit.

"Okay, we're hungry and tired and probably shouldn't take it out on each other," he said. "I guess I started it. Let's have a good meal and get some rest here and then figure out what to do in the morning. At least we're probably safe from wild beasts in here."

And so they set up camp, wishing there was at least some vegetation from which to gather wood for a fire. There being none, they contented themselves with a cold meal of grains and fruit Sadiq had provisioned them with. After eating they drank deep from their water supply. They didn't dare drink from the still pool of water at their feet, but they knew that they'd be able to fill up again at the falls the next day on their way out of the valley. Readied for sleep they gazed up at the now brilliant display of stars in the small portion of the sky they could glimpse.

Gil finally broke the silence. "Sorry about blaming you for all this. It's as much my fault as yours."

Enki said, "No… you were right the first time. I did kind of drag you into all this. I knew what it would take to get you to go along."

"Well, I'm going to kick myself for saying this, but I'm glad you did. Look at us, Enki – lying here on some hidden rock cleft in the interior of the Silver Mountains! We're probably not more than fifteen leagues from the Amanus and a Kishite squad of armed mercenaries. And my father thinks we're out hunting stag off near Lagash …"

Gil laughed softly, but with an increasing nervousness. Enki could tell that thoughts of Gil's father were infiltrating his mind and so he engineered a quick change of subject.

"So, Gil… sing me one of those ancient songs you so impressed Sadiq with."

"Since when are you interested in the old songs?" Gil

asked.

"I'm not, really. But it will kill time and I like to hear you try to use that old Sumerian dialect accent thing you do."

"Okay. I suppose that was a compliment. Let's see…"

Gil remained silent for several more minutes. Then in a crisp clear voice he began to sing in a sad tone a song older than he or Enki could even imagine. He'd learned it by rote, and had never thought much about its meaning or background. But he knew it was ancient and this gave it its enchanting quality. As he sang, Enki felt as if one of the kings of old had come back to life and was speaking to them now. Gil sang most of it in the common tongue, but for some of it he lapsed into Old Sumerian. Part of it ran thus:

As darkened days invaded all
We sought retreat in council hall
For we didst know that evil now
Would run its fateful course

At first we gasped in wonderment
But then as wizened ones we sent
To each to gather for repose
And languish in the hall

Through rock and water we did pass
Into the depths of earth and grass
And found our seats prepared for us
By ones more ancient still

We sat, we prayed, though knew not how
We spoke of enemies profound
Until at last we delved the deep
And struck the thundering sound

We fashioned in the depths that day
A stone to break the evil way
Until the sacred branch be wed
It would in underhill remain

Gil's voice trailed into silence and both reflected for a time upon the words. Finally, Gil spoke. He said, "There's more but that's all I remember by heart. Much of this one fades from my memory, but I believe it's a reference to the forging of the Axe."

Enki did not respond right away. His mind was lost in reflection upon certain words that Gil had sung in the song.

Gil continued his commentary. "Shulpae used to love to recite this one. It's not the most elegant of the songs, but it's one of the oldest. The original language has been long since lost. Even the Old Sumerian version is but a distant translation. You can never truly judge the quality of the older songs. So much has been lost in translation. It's the newer songs that truly stir me, but still the ancient themes of these older songs haunt you in a way the new songs fail to."

At some point while Gil was expounding on the song, Enki had gotten up off his sleeping mat and was gazing strangely into the pool of water at their feet.

"So you say this song is about the forging of the Axe and its placement in the chamber of the Annunaki, deep under the Silver Mountains?" Enki asked.

"Yes, that's what Shulpae told me."

Enki continued to walk about staring at the pool.

"Are you okay, Enki?" Gil asked.

"What?" Enki responded distantly. "Uh… yes… I'm fine."

"What is it you're looking at?" Gil asked.

Enki didn't answer.

"Enki?"

Then a smile crept across Enki's face and with one great leap, he dove head first into the pool of water and disappeared.

Gil simply sat there in disbelief. He didn't speak a word or give out any yell. He just gazed into the pool in shock. Finally, he snapped out of it and frantically began searching the pool for signs of his impulsive friend. Several anxious minutes passed before Enki reemerged from the water gasping for air.

As Gil helped him out of the water, Enki said, "Gil, you're a genious!"

"And you're a fool! Enki, what possessed you to do that?" Gil asked.

"Why, your song, of course – third stanza, first line. *Through rock and water we did pass, Into the depths of earth and grass…*"

"You jumped in head first based on that one line? And you called *me* foolish for believing in a magic axe," Gil said dryly.

"Yes, Gil, I did. I guess your faith in the gods and the ancient songs are rubbing off on me."

"Well, what did you find in your swim?" Gil asked.

Enki said, "I didn't go for a swim. That pool is the ancient portal into the caverns beneath the mountain. It took some groping around in the dark down there, but I found an obvious opening near the bottom. The pools pretty deep – twenty feet or so. You'd never guess that from looking at it, and to be honest I didn't expect it to go down that far, but near the bottom is an underwater passageway big enough for two or three astride to swim through. I didn't have enough air to try it out – I'd spent too much air swimming to the bottom and groping around the sides looking for the entrance – but I found it!"

Gil asked, "Enki, how do we know where it leads? It could just lead to an underwater dead end, and our underwater grave."

"Perhaps," said Enki. "Care to join me in finding out?"

Gil's disapproving frown finally gave way to the break of a smile as Gil allowed all his good sense to melt away in the face of adventure. "Let's do it!" he said.

They tied what food and supplies they could to their backs, eating first the last of the bread Sadiq had given them – they did not relish soggy bread and so disposed of it now. They also tied their shoes and shirts about their waists and prepared for a swim the length of which they knew not. Taking deep breaths, they dived in before they could allow themselves to second guess their endeavor.

Down they swam, Enki first followed by Gil. Gil noted how dark it was in the depths. They groped around together searching for the aquatic passage, but did not find it right away. It was Gil this time who stumbled upon it. Together they excitedly swam through. Had darkness remained for long, their hearts would have given way to panic, but a soft glow soon began to be seen throughout this underwater tunnel. The glow was greenish-blue and lighted up more and more of the water as they progressed. Feeling their air start to run out, they swam with greater and greater haste, trying not to panic. Finally, when it seemed they could hold their breaths no longer, the tunnel emerged into an underwater cavern. Up they swam desperately hoping the surface to be close at hand. To their great relief it was and they both emerged gasping for air.

They found themselves in a large cavernous room. Nothing was in the room save the pool of water from which they now surfaced and some kind of ancient looking stones giving off the bluish-green light they had sensed from under the water. These *glow stones* as they would eventually call them were fastened to each of the walls and seemed to trail off down several passageways exiting the room.

Dripping with water they surveyed the length and width of the room, not yet verbalizing their mutual excitement. They felt the surface of the walls about them, noting their smoothness. Gil traced with his finger the outline of an embossed mural on one wall. Enki came over to examine the ancient work with him. The markings and the style were unlike anything they had ever seen. They considered that these must be writings and sketches from before the Great Cleansing. But to their amazement, these ancient carvings in the wall looked anything but primitive, but spoke of a great civilization forgotten in the selectiveness of history.

Enki was ready to move on and follow Sadiq's map to their goal, but Gil's wisdom prevailed. It was already quite late, and they had been traveling on foot all day. Enki really did not need much persuading. In exhaustion, they both collapsed in fatigue upon the solid ground. They slept sound all through what they later considered was left of the night and perhaps part of the way into the next day – though they had no way of knowing what was day and what was night.

Gil awoke first. While Enki still slept, he surveyed some more of the wall carvings. He noted that one wall contained what looked to be a map of the system of tunnels extending from their current location. He compared it with Sadiq's map and thought he was able to discern where the two maps intersected. The wall map was incomplete. Much of it had been washed away by years of erosion. But enough was left intact to be discernable and Gil believed he was able to make out markings highlighting the chamber of the Annunaki.

When Enki arose, they ate breakfast in silence, as much from awe and wonder as from fatigue. There was something extraordinary about being in the depths of a mountain in tunnels once walked by the ancients. When they did speak, their voices sounded strange and awkward, as if they were intruding upon some sacred conversation. In hushed whispers they spoke admiringly of the ancient architecture. It was clear that these were no mere caves. The walls, floors and ceilings were either as smooth as marble, or hewed with some ancient art form. Here and there, hints of color remained, alluding to a once ornate interior.

Finally, Gil showed Enki some of his findings resulting from his comparison of the chambers map with Sadiq's. From these discoveries they were able to discern which passageway to take first. They quickly put on their still damp clothing and shoes and headed off down a presumably eastward passage. The glow stones amazed them the most during this first part of their journey into the mountains heart. They were unlike any gem or rock they'd ever seen. They considered that these beautifully chiseled rocks had kept their translucence for hundreds and hundreds of years. They did seem rather faint now and they guessed that once they had given off a far more brilliant illumination. But even now, they still granted more than enough light to make out intricate details carved into the tunnel walls.

Several times they passed by doorways opening into side rooms. Some of these they took the time to explore and found thereby an odd assemblage of various items, none of them very useful. The unforgiving centuries had left little to salvage. Still, they did come by a few items worthy of note. One room contained a majestic looking candelabrum. Another contained a large store of ancient and decaying books. A couple of these they tried to open but each crumbled at their softest touch. Another room contained a collection of beautiful, but rusted and ruined weaponry. From these artifacts they began to discern the magnificence of the civilization undone by the Cleansing. Some legends spoke of a great history in those years from the distant past, but most in Enki's day regarded these as but fables conjured up as a critique of contemporary decadence. But now they began to believe the possibility that some of these legends might be true. Gil, holding up one great double-sided sword and admiring the tremendous detail worked into the metal, commented upon the pity that such a people that had reached such heights were doomed to perish. What great secrets of the universe discovered in those ancient times had long since been forgotten? What great deeds of men and women, of kings and armies, of ladies and lords had been forever lost to the modern man? These and other similar thoughts Enki and Gil confessed as they made their way down the intricate tapestry of tunnels.

For the remainder of the day they traveled down this main *roadway into the mountains heart* as Sadiq had called it. They dared not venture too far afield for fear of getting lost in one of the many side passages and never finding their way back to the main trek. Twice they were stopped at a fork, unsure which tunnel to take. Once they nearly fell through a gaping hole in the tunnels floor revealing a deeper level far below and giving them a small glimpse at the extent of these ancient caverns. When they grew hungry they sat down and ate. When they grew weary, they lay down and slept. For two days this went on. Deeper and deeper into the mountains roots they went. It was a slow downward slope that they tread, occasioned at times by stairs facilitating a quicker descent. At one point, the glow stones no longer lined the wall. The path simply continued onward into complete darkness. Enki and Gil managed to break off a couple of the stones from the wall and they used these to light their path through the darkness. Eventually, the stones lined and brightened the tunnel once again. Why there was this discontinuity in the trail of the stones was a question they never had answered.

On the third day of their journey, the tunnel began to widen substantially. They were no longer going down, but had leveled off into what appeared to have once been a populated subterranean village of sorts. They were coming across various larger chambers dotted with debris from a forgotten age. Some of the ruins were of items for which Gil and Enki could not fathom their purpose or use. Going forward was much slower as they continually had to make certain they were heading out of the various larger chambers down the correct exiting passageway. More than once they were forced to back track a bit to correct a wrong decision.

It was toward what must have been the evening of the third day that they finally came upon what they were looking for. They had just emerged into a vast chamber the top of which they could not see. Flowing down the center of the chamber was a great chasm along with a corresponding underground river being fed by a waterfall the top of which could not be discerned. The sound of the falls crashing into the rocks below and of the swiftly flowing subterranean river was eerie after three days of relative silence. It was both welcomed and disconcerting. But excitement overcame all emotions as they knew this to be the great Rock Field spoken of in legends and noted on Sadiq's map as the portal to the Chamber of the Annunaki. The cavern itself was so vast that not only could they not discern the top, they also could not see where to the left or to the right the room had an end. However, straight ahead, perhaps a hundred yards away, a great cliff rose high into the enveloping darkness above. It was out of this cliff that the falls came tumbling down. To the left of the falls and a good ninety feet above the ground, an opening could be seen. Mostly darkness greeted the searching eye, but a soft goldish hue throbbed from somewhere within its depths. This opening high above them, according to Sadiq's drawing, was the chamber they sought. But how to reach it Sadiq had not said. Exhausted, but excited, they sat down and decided to ponder the situation over a meal and perhaps another nights rest.

"Well, there it is," Enki said. "There's your magic axe. Somewhere up there in that room. See any magic ladders around?"

Gil didn't bother to respond. He just nibbled away at their dwindling supply of nuts that they were growing weary of eating.

Enki then said, "So, I think it's your turn to take a leap of faith and dive into some water or something."

Gil looked up exasperated. Then something caught his eye and his face brightened. He said, "Okay, whatever you say." And then to Enki's amazement, he suddenly stood up, started walking and soon vanished behind the falls. Enki followed his friend to the location of his disappearance, and found that as he got closer to the falls, that a thin ledge, behind the falls, trailed off connecting the two sides of the chasm. Connected to the center of this ledge, mostly hidden from view by the waterfall, was a ladder with Gil now nearly at the top. The ladder, certainly not a part of any original design, connected the bottom ledge with one winding back and forth across the chasm wall until it reached the high ledge leading into the opening of the council chamber. The lower portion of this winding trail apparently had long since collapsed and some later adventurer had constructed a ladder to traverse the fallen portion of the trail.

Excitedly, Enki ascended the ladder and soon the two were standing side by side on the high ledge leading into the council chamber. Both their hearts were pounding with anticipation for what they might, or might not find.

Into the ancient meeting place of the Annunaki they crept. As they did, the brightness of the glow stones increased in luminescence. But these glow stones, unlike every other they had come across, were of a burning, fiery gold color. After three days of blue, the golden light created a surge of warmth to flow through them. And indeed perhaps this was the desired effect. This chamber, apparently set apart from every other, was itself the very place the First Ones once sat to discuss the great matters of their own times.

Enki recalled just then his own great-grandfather Ur-Nammu and how the war chamber back in Ur had been built to convey a sense of warmth so as to lend aid to minds and hearts weighed down with the heavy and stressful matters of state. This room apparently served a similar purpose. Whereas all the chambers, halls and passageways they had traveled through up to this point had given off an austere, yet beautiful impression, this room now gave off a sense of warmth and rest. It was not a cavernous room, but large enough for a healthy sized gathering. As Sadiq had said, a circle of ten great stone thrones faced each other in the center of the room. In the center of these, a stone slab rose to a man's height and on this was an axe, a bow and a book.

Enki and Gil just stood there staring at each other. Neither dared to move for several minutes. They would later both agree that it was as if they had fallen into a dream. None of what they were experiencing seemed real. It was as if they were living in one of the fables of old. Finally, they began to move about the room. The room was spherical with perfectly curved walls highlighted by ten evenly spaced statues behind each of the ten thrones. These statues almost seemed to take on real life the more they looked at them. Being nothing like the statue work Enki and Gil were familiar with, these had a realness to them that conveyed a sense that if you pricked them, blood would pour forth. They were carved right into the wall, but with a sense of movement such that it appeared that the figures were ready to leap out of the lifeless stone into a body of flesh and a mind of steel. Of the ten figures, nine were male and one was a woman of such dignity and beauty as Enki and Gil had never imagined possible. The men too were of a form beyond description. Most wore regal looking beards and each wore a crown. One statue was incomplete, the body formed, but the face left flat and smooth. Inscriptions were written above each in a script and language that neither Enki nor Gil had ever seen, nor could they decipher.

Approaching the ten thrones and the stone pedestal in their midst, they caught their first good glimpse of the axe. *Might of Heroes* legend had called it and it fit this description. The axe head looked as though it had been forged out of diamonds. This was connected to a handle of smoothly polished cedar. The handle was inlaid with gold and bore on one side an emblem from a distant age. Next to the axe was a simple looking bow and then a book which to their amazement was intact and unspoiled. Gil was about to reach for the book when Enki let out a yell. Gil froze. Then, looking down to where Enki was pointing he saw the skeletal remains of some unfortunate adventurer, probably he who had secured for them the aforementioned ladder. They looked for some sign of how he perished but could find none. Presumably, the stone table was trapped by some kind of deadly mechanism to protect against vandals. They began to give the room a more thorough search as they sought for some means to avoid triggering the deadly trap.

Gil was the one that found it. Fastened behind one of the stone thrones was a small indentation. Presumably it was simply part of the larger design intricately carved into the backs and sides of each of the thrones. But this one was just different enough to catch Gil's careful observation. He triggered it and at first it seemed that nothing happened. Then a sound came from the center table and an onyx stone emerged from the table's side nearest the skeletal remains. Proceeding to the stone they found on it an inscription in some unknown language. There was also a series of symbols below the inscription. One appeared to be of a bull's horn. A second was that of a wild beast of some kind. A third was a head of a man. And finally a fourth was that of a great bird.

"So what does this mean?" Enki said voicing his confusion.

Gil however had a bright grin on his face. He said, "Ah, my friend Enki, remind me to give old Shulpae a kiss when we get back. All that meaningless lore he used to force-feed me is finally finding a most unusual use. These are symbols of the Four Worlds!"

"Oh, I see," said Enki. "Four worlds. That certainly makes sense. I'm not sure why our skeletal friend here didn't see it…"

"Quiet down Enki and listen," Gil said. "It's one of the oldest legends but it's not commonly known. Shulpae only knew it from his own unique research during the days of his search for Utnapishtim. He found some ancient writings buried away in some dark archive in Shurrapak. In the writings was something about there being four worlds before ours and that ours was to be the fifth and final world. According to this legend each of these four races from each of these four different worlds have lived out a great and glorious history each in their own times and now these various beings are mostly agents of some great god called Aél. Supposedly, they helped Aél in the creation of our own world."

Enki said, "Aél. Sadiq used that name back in the desert to refer to a god. He said it was Aél's favor that I survived. I just assumed he was referring to some local god of those badlands."

"No, I don't think so," said Gil. "Aél is an ancient god. His name is not much known. And Shulpae thought that Aél is really Anu, but who can say?"

"So… I repeat my first question," Enki said. "What does this mean?"

Enki was about to touch the stone panel but Gil excitedly stopped him. He said, "Don't! It's probably what our friend here did. There are four symbols each representing the four previous races. If you didn't know the legend, the temptation would be to touch one of them. I don't think that's what we're supposed to do. Enki, we are the fifth race. That must be the key. Look! The symbols aren't centered. They're a bit lined up more to the left of center. It's as if there's been left room for one more symbol… here."

Gil didn't touch the surface, but he placed his finger near the blank area to the right of the bird-like symbol. As he did so, the faint outline of a circle began to emerge. As Gil drew his hand away from the stone panel the circle faded once again into the smoothness of the surface.

Gil said, "It's hard to say if were supposed to touch it or not supposed to touch it. What do you think, Enki?"

Enki didn't think, but in his usual impulsive way, he stretched out his hand quickly and touched the flat of the barren portion of the onyx stone. The reddish circle reemerged in greater brightness than before. As Enki pulled his hand away a new symbol had appeared making the set of five complete. The new symbol was apparently some kind of a merging together of the previous four symbols into one. It looked something akin to looking down upon the previous four beings from above each with their backs facing each other. At least this was as best as Enki would later be able to describe it to Shulpae. They didn't study it long for in the seconds that followed, a noise from above broke off their attention. Breaking forth from somewhere in the smooth marble ceiling above came a stream of bluish-green light shining down and landing upon the top of the great center table.

Taking this as a sign of permission, Gil proceeded cautiously to lift the great book from the stone table. As if under a spell the book still had its bindings intact and showed no sign of decay. Even dust seemed to elude its grasp. The book opened to about its center. It was written in the same ancient script inscribed upon the statues and upon the stone panel. This was an unknown language to them that they had stumbled upon in these underground places. But set in the center of the book was a loose page. Gil lifted this out of the book and then in amazement realized that it was written in an archaic form of Old Sumerian! After the shock subsided, Gil spoke the translation, slowly and reverently:

Greetings Axe Bearer,

If reading this you be, then favored are you among the holy Benel.

I am a Benudim, of the line of Setharon, but chosen was I to walk among the Benel and learn their ways and acquire some of their powers and knowledge. Their language I learned at great cost to myself and my kin, such that I was given up by my foes to be one of the despised Nephilim. But persevered did I in spite of my fellow Benudim's persecutions. An outcast from my clan, I wandered the world and learned of its ills and, finally, at long last, of its ultimate cure. Forbidden am I to write of these great mysteries now, but you, Axe Bearer, are a part of that healing plan, should you decide to embrace the task given you. Take up this axe and strike down the Great Tree. In doing so you will set our race upon a new course, even as you bring an end to the path of the Benel whom I so love. Yes, indeed, you will be giving our outcast people the place of greatest favor in Aél*'s sacred Plan. I smile to myself at the thought that we, an outcast race, should be the ones to fill the fifth and final role. Indeed, not the holy Benel, but we the cursed Benudim will take the highest place! Ah, but alas, such is the ways of* Aél.

So take up this weapon, forged by the Ancients, but fastened to the Cedars branch by myself in this my own dark age. Only beware that your own heart not deceive you.

Consider well the end to which you strike. May malice and pride not be found in your heart. For while ye hold the Axe, it will draw into itself the virtues and the vice of your heart. Upon the third strike it will thereby release blessing or deadly poison into he who strikes the final blow.

Fare thee well, Axe Bearer!

Servant of the Benel, Enoch of the West,
Madain Seeker and Keeper of Avilah's Flame,

Orion

Gil closed the book softly and placed it gently back in its place. Then he seemed to sink into deep thought.

"Well, that's an odd letter," Enki said abruptly and with an annoying degree of irreverence.

Gil just stared at Enki. Then he said, "We stand here, the first to hear words written by one of the greats of a long forgotten age, words of great mystery and prophesy, and all you can say is 'well, that's an odd letter'?!"

Enki, in casual response to the challenge, strolled over to the stone pedestal, and picked up the axe in an overtly carefree manner. He said, "Gil, my naïve friend, I know my place in history. This letter comes as no surprise to me. I am a favorite of the gods and this merely confirms it. Now, ease up on the spooky reverence and let's go chop down a tree."

Gil, at first angered, allowed this offense to melt away into laughter. He knew his friend only too well. He would not be coaxed again into frustration. Enki was Enki and that said it all. Still laughing he said, "Okay, oh great *Axe Bearer*. I surrender to your vanity. Let's not waste any more time."

"Now, that's more like it," Enki said.

Enki picked up the bow and tossed it to Gil. "Know of any legend that speaks of a plain and dull looking bow?" Enki asked.

"No, but perhaps Shulpae does. If nothing else, it will be a good peace offering to present to the old man who will no doubt be outraged that we even undertook this crazy scheme."

"Ah, he'll be envious. Maybe next we can really irk him and go find his elusive *Utnapishtim*."

Before long they were off again – Enki clinging to the axe and Gil with the newly acquired bow. A quiver of arrows was also found hanging to one of the chambers walls. This he took without question, but Gil was almost inclined to leave the book out of a sense of reverence. However, Enki convinced him to take it along to show to Shulpae. Perhaps, he had argued, Shulpae might have some knowledge of the ancient tongue. Gil gratefully allowed himself to be convinced. Down the trail behind the falls and down the ladder to the chasm bottom they once again descended. A quick reference to Sadiq's map led them to exit the great chamber through a northwest passageway. They sped on now in great haste.

Enki, for all his carefree façade had not been left unmoved by the Chamber of the Annunaki, or the letter Gil had read. He seemed now possessed with determination to destroy the tree as never before. Whereas initially the drive had been an impulsive attempt to create a name for himself, added to this was now a fierce passion that came from someplace foreign to him. Gil felt it too, but not to the same extent Enki did. He never told Gil, but his quick departure from the council room and his flippant attitude had been in part a quick and easy means for dealing with something that terrified him. He could not explain it, but it was as if in that moment of hearing the words of the letter and taking the axe, that he had truly been transported to the presence of that ancient author and that his words poured into him an icy chill that seemed to leave his very soul naked and exposed. It was the most uncomfortable feeling he'd ever encountered and he was glad to be rid of it now that they were speeding along the now familiar passageways of this underworld. But the overwhelming passion to destroy the Tree remained and moved him to keep a fast, steady pace that Gil was forced to keep up with. Many times Gil pleaded with him to slow down so that they could rest, but to no avail. With great haste they proceeded to make the ascent along upward sloping tunnels leading them to the surface of what they expected to be the northwestern slope of the Silver Mountains.

Two very irritable days passed for Gil, as Enki seemed to be getting more and more agitated. It was all that Gil could do to keep up with him. There seemed to be no hope of shaking him from his present mindset. There was a growing intensity in Enki's eyes – a frightening resoluteness. Once in a while a glimmer of the old irreverent and flippant Enki broke through, but it was a veiled lightness that sprang forth, not unbounded ease as was usually the case. Gil noted that at times he clung so tightly to the great axe that his knuckles became pure white with strain.

They made no side-adventures on this exit route from the mountains depths. Numerous rooms and caverns jutted off from the main tunnel of their path, but they stopped to explore none of them. Gil's eye caught glimmers of some of them and he noted, in a few, a wild extravagance of décor and decaying art that he was sorely grieved to leave unstudied.

Toward the end of the second day since their finding the

axe they emerged into a large cavern lighted by faint sunlight invading through some crack in the ceiling far above. Exiting this large chamber through what would be the final stretch of their underground route, they noted that the glow stones no longer shone. Soon they were traveling in utter darkness and were forced to slow their pace, which Gil accepted with gratefulness and Enki with anger. After about an hour of this slow groping ahead in the dark, faint bits of sunlight began to add just enough light to keep them from bumping into any walls or archways. This light grew steadily until at last they emerged into a small round chamber. It was a simple room without any décor of any kind. It was lit faintly by sunlight, the source of which came from a gaping hole in the floor. Peering over the side they saw that the hole was their final exit. Apparently this room had been built as a one way exit from the tunnels of the Silver Mountains and into the Amanus forest. Presumably, somewhere there existed a separate one-way entrance. However, they would have no way of knowing where this was to be found and it was no doubt placed to keep it that way. This would be their final departure from the relative safety of these mines. What awaited them through the hole and into the Amanus forest Anu only knew.

Enki went first. They had no rope to lower each other with, but the ground appeared to be close enough to risk the drop. They first each dropped their supplies. Then Enki took the plunge as impulsively as he had when he'd discovered the tunnels through the pool on the other side of the Silver Mountains. Gil could see Enki brushing himself off apparently unhurt. Gil dropped down as well and both found themselves at the end of a small cave. The entrance to the cave was but a few feet away and revealed their first glimpse of the outside world in five days. The sun was setting over a distant range of hills and trees. It was the Amanus forest, lush and green and old. Rising up out of the forest, only a couple hundred yards away, was the Great Cedar. There was no mistaking it and no discussion whether it was indeed the right tree. There was no other like it. Even from this distance it seemed ominous and strangely foreign. And it rose a good hundred feet above any other tree around it.

"Well, we made it. I can't believe we're actually here," said Gil. He was rubbing his eyes as he said this, the sunlight causing a brief wave of pain to surge through his brain.

"Yes, I suppose we have." Enki just stared, unblinking, into the forest and toward the Tree seen through the cave exit.

"What now?" Gil asked.

"We wait for darkness," said Enki. Any Kishite forces will be fleeing the area of the Tree for fear of this Humbaba creature."

"And are we fearing this Humbaba creature?" asked Gil.

Enki didn't respond.

Gil said, "Okay, Enki, I don't know what magic from this axe has done to you, but I'm becoming more of a believer than ever. Are you sure you are up for this? It's like we're in a dream. I really can't believe any of this is happening, but… here we are."

Enki sat down, wearily, and seemed to be briefly awoken from his spell. He shook his head, blinked his eyes and finally gave Gil his attention. He said, "I'm sorry, Gil. I don't know what's come over me. Ever since you read that letter and I first grabbed this accursed axe… I know I'm obsessed with this…"

Enki didn't finish his thought. He just gripped the axe tighter and stared at it, falling once again under its power. Then, with no warning, Enki sprang forth through the cave opening into the open air and disappeared into the thick forest brush. A pang of fear swept through Gil, but he set it aside and lunged after his impulsive, now apparently obsessed, friend. Gil was able to stay within eyesight of Enki, but the sunlight was almost all gone and darkness was descending quickly. The terrain was uneven and Gil stumbled several times. He would have completely lost Enki had he not had the towering Tree as a guide. It grew larger with each passing second. Every glance at the Tree ahead of him sent shivers throughout his body. Looking at the Tree was like looking at a god. It gave off the sense of something thinking and alive. By the time Gil reached the Tree it was completely dark. He arrived just in time to see Enki lifting the great Axe over his head. Enki swung it around and around and then let it strike its target. Contact of the axe with the Great Tree sent a jolt through Enki's body and he fell down backwards. Looking up at the Tree it appeared as though a surge of power was sent flowing through every vein of the Great Cedar. The Tree shook and even gave out a momentary glowing sensation before fading again into its relative *treeness.*

In the distance a great and terrible cry was heard. The distant hills seemed to shake with the horrified call. The cry continued and seemed to be growing stronger as Enki slowly rose again to his feet. Whatever it was that was crying out was heading this way and doing so fast. Enki shook the sting of the sensation off and sought again for the fallen axe.

Gil kept watch in the direction of the fast approaching cry as Enki reassembled himself. Gil had lost his sword in the Tigris, but now had the ancient bow strung with arrow ready to fly. He was a master bowman and marveled at the ancient weapon he now held in his hand. Though seemingly simple, it was indeed a far more advanced bow than any his own people had been able to produce. Truly, this was a great civilization they had just plundered, Gil thought.

Enki, with axe in hand once again approached the Tree this time with greater fear and respect. And he braced himself this time for the full impact of the blow. High into the air he lifted the axe. Then he swung it further back and down and finally forward into the Great Tree. This time a greater jolt followed and an even more terrifying scream of pain from the not so distant direction of the oncoming creature. The Tree once again pulsated and gave off another momentary glow that lit the darkened forest all about. Enki was flung backward this time several yards hitting his head and drawing some blood. Gil came to his aid, helping him up and directing him to the resting place of the axe. Enki, in haste, took the axe in hand again and poised himself for the third and final blow. Again, raising the axe up and back, he readied himself for the final impact with the Tree.

But it never came. As he prepared to swing, the Bull of Heaven flew out of the forest with a great leap through the air and down in front of Enki. Humbaba was a massive creature, of a manish form in every respect, but on a grandeur scale. His hair came down to the middle of his back, but he wore no beard. Golden brown was his skin and his body was a mountain of muscle and flesh. No clothes did he wear but a simple cloth about his waist and a great sword at his side.

In that brief moment, Enki and Gil, frozen in fright, got a glimpse of his face. It was the oddest sensation looking into the face of Humbaba, or this ancient Kreon as Sadiq had called him. He had the initial look of a savage, but peering deeply into his eyes revealed an imprisoned and pained intelligence. It was as if they were staring into the eyes of a god. Enki, in that moment, suddenly had his fright melt away to be replaced by an intense sadness for the tortured being, for that was what his look revealed.

It lasted only a moment though, for in that instance the creature grabbed the axe from Enki's hand. As he did so he screamed with such pain at the touch of it that he flung the axe indiscriminately into the forest brush and then in anger swung his hand back toward Enki sending him flying in the opposite direction. Humbaba turned then to finish Enki off but was intercepted by a barrage of arrows launched from Gil's bow. The arrows did nothing. They bounced off the creature as if he was made of stone. He turned toward Gil in annoyance and with one brush of his arm sent Gil flying head first into the forest. Enki saw Gil fly toward a tree. He heard a thump and then silence.

Humbaba then turned again to pursue the Axe-Bearer. Enki no longer had the axe but he drew the sword Sadiq had left for him and rose to face his fate. Blood was streaming down Enki's face now and his left arm was badly bruised. But he mustered enough courage to stand and raise his sword in answer to the Bull of Heaven's confidently slow approach. As Humbaba drew near, he spoke to his victim in the common tongue. His voice was rich and deep and terrifying.

"So… Axe-Bearer," he said. "You would destroy immortal ferocious Humbaba? Bull of Heaven? Is that not what you and your people call me? A despised and wretched people you are – destined for death. Your fate is locked with mine. We are all imprisoned. There is no escape. My hell I endure even now. Yours I now send you to."

And with that he drew a mighty sword, greater than any Enki had ever seen. As he drew near to Enki to release a final blow, Enki lunged with a desperate strike. Humbaba allowed Enki's sword to strike his flesh, but the sword merely rolled off his body leaving not even a mark. Humbaba then let out a great and terrible laugh.

Humbaba said, "Did you think that Benudim weapons could destroy the greatest of the Benel? Ha! You pitiful creature! Cursed one! I am Benel! I am greater than Benel, for I hold the Mark. Even the Cleansing could not destroy me. The Tree has seen to that. And now Axe-Bearer, with your death dies the prophesy. The Tree will now survive for all time and so will I. It is my blessing and my curse, but I embrace it!"

Enki lowered his sword in despair and awaited Humbaba's fatal blow. The great god of a man lifted his mighty sword above his head and prepared to swing round to his victim. Down and around came the sword with a great swish, but just prior to it reaching its target, Humbaba lunged to one side in agony, letting out a scream. The jolt of the creature caused his sword to miss Enki by a foot or so. Both then spun around to see Gil being thrust away from the Great Cedar. Gil had just swung the third and final blow and as he did so the Axe fell from Gil's hand and exploded into a hundred pieces. The Tree grew suddenly dark as if losing all its color. Then light seemed to pour into it from above in all directions. It was as if a thousand bolts of lightning began striking the Tree repeatedly. A look of horror came over Humbaba's face. He cried out in agony and the earth itself began to shake. Enki was knocked to the ground and from there he saw the Tree suddenly grow to an intense brightness before being enveloped into a mighty flame of fire. The light of the great blaze revealed Gil lying unconscious twenty or so yards away from the flame enveloped Tree. Humbaba, in a final rage, turned toward Gil to avenge his fall, but was overtaken by Enki who lunged quickly forward, driving his sword into Humbaba's side.

Humbaba's rage suddenly ceased. The creature turned around to face Enki as Enki withdrew his sword from Humbaba's pierced side. The creature just looked down at his wound and the blood flowing from his side. He said nothing nor did he respond with attack. As if in shock, he reached down and placed his hand on his wound and drew it back covered with his own blood. He just stared at his own bloodied hand in wonderment and awe. A silent moment passed. Then he fell to his knees and hunched over. He gave out a brief yell of pain, but this subsided and was replaced by a gradually increasing laughter.

There the creature Humbaba lay, bleeding to death and overcome by laughter. Enki knew not what to do. He simply watched the poor immortal embrace his new found mortality. The laughter began to subside. Something within Enki compelled him to move closer toward Humbaba. Enki reached out his hand, placed it on the creature's great head and spoke a simple word.

"Kreon."

The soft remaining laughter now completely ceased and Kreon looked up in surprise. Something in that moment passed over Kreon's face. It was as if deep emotions denied for two thousand years surfaced in that instance. He looked up at Enki with a look of terror and hope.

Enki said, "I know not what great sin bound you to this Tree and to this fate, but it's over now. Be freed from your suffering…" Enki faltered then as if not sure what to say next, but knowing he should speak something more. Kreon just continued to look up into his slayer's eyes with suddenly child-like simplicity. Suddenly Enki knew what he was to say. He said slowly, "You… are… forgiven."

Enki didn't know why he said it. It was as if a remaining effect of the Axe's magic lingered in his head giving him these final words to speak. But whoever or whatever it was that aimed at Kreon with these words, they hit their mark. Kreon bent over once again and a quiet weeping overtook him which soon gave way to loud wailing. He flung himself to the ground and began crying out through his incessant sobbing:

"Dellan! Dellan! Eberethi onitoni! Ori, ori, ori, oben er torenti! O Dellan! Dellan! Dellan! Mis ontari, mis ontari, mis ontari, Dellan, mis ontari!"

Enki found himself in tears as well.

He sat down in quietness and sadness as he watched the last of the Benel lords die.

CHAPTER 8 – THE BIRTH OF A LEGEND

Gil regained consciousness just in time to see the last bit of the smoldering Tree collapse into a heap of ashes. He limped over to where Enki sat and observed the dead form of Kreon. Both then saw the cause of Gil's limp – a fragment of the exploding Axe had fastened itself into Gil's lower leg. Carefully Enki pulled the metal piece from Gil's leg. Gil winced in pain. The wound looked clean and Enki quickly dressed the wound and wrapped it in a clean bandage. Enki described to Gil the scene of Kreon's death and both then sat in reflective silence. Overhead, Nanna shone adding her soft moonlight to the golden light of the Great Tree's burning embers. The night was calm and still. An owl could be heard nearby offering a lament for the fallen god. At long last Enki spoke slowly, still staring at the lifeless form of Kreon.

"Gil, I've been a fool. I've been a prideful fool. All this talk of building a great name for myself, of controlling armies and conquering distant peoples all in the name of Sumer..." He paused reflectively. "No… in my name. All of it in my name."

Gil offered no response.

Enki continued. "Kreon was one of the First Ones. An immortal. A real immortal. And who am I? A spoiled son of a minor kingdom. What hope is there for any of us? If the life of an immortal who has lived thousands of years finally at long last ends in death and despair – what can be said for us? Our lives are but a vapor compared to his. And yet we all end in dust."

Gil finally was stirred to speak. "I don't know, Enki. I didn't see him die, but from what you told me, it sounds more like Kreon was given hope at the very end. At long last, after all these years, he was freed from the curse of life under which he carried the burden of guilt and shame. I don't know who this *Dellan* was that he spoke of at the end, but he was perhaps the one against whom Kreon had sinned. Just think of it, Enki – harboring that guilt and shame and bitterness for thousands of years, alone here in the wilderness. He must not have always been as we see him now – half savage and half god. He must have been at one time something of great glory and beauty."

They sat again in silence for several more minutes.

"So… do we bury him?" Gil asked at last.

Enki looked up at Gil and then over to the body of Kreon. He said, "No telling what the filthy Kishites would do to him. Yes, let's bury him. But let's find a place hidden from view lest his grave be defiled."

Together they spent the next hour digging a sufficient tomb for the fallen Benel lord. They laid him in the grave and placed his mighty sword upon his chest. Then Enki also laid upon him fragments of the magic axe that had been obliterated with Gil's final stroke. They also took bits of the Tree's ashes and laid it around the body. Finally they covered him over with the dust of the earth.

"So I suppose we should say something," Enki said. "What kind of a funeral do you give a Benel lord do you think?"

Neither said anything at first. Then Gil softly began to sing a song of his own making.

Away great lord of ancient lore
From wind and wave and stone
Your bondage to the guilt and shame
Forevermore is shorn

At peace, great lord of yester year
Your last great cry is felt
When burning embers of thy Mark
Didst melt thine hardened heart

New hope, great lord of ages past
Your glory is renewed
For the Maker of the earth and sky
Forgives and heals and sooths

To Hall of Thrones, great Benel lord
Your banishment is through
So take thy seat prepared for thee
When first the earth was new

As Gil finished his song, Enki rose and approached the mound.

"Kreon, I don't know your sin, but I did see the faint look of hope in your eyes. May there be hope for us as well. May there be hope for me. In a fierce obsession of pride and greed, I approached the task of felling this Great Tree, but in humble obeisance I now lay you to rest…"

Enki broke off his concluding thoughts as he considered something. Something about what he had just said troubled him.

"Gil, you still have the book don't you?"

"Yes".

"And the note inside? The note to the Axe Bearer?"

"Yes, it's here."

"Read it again. Not the whole thing. Just the last paragraph. The part about the warning. I faintly remember a warning."

Gil fumbled through his pack until he reverently dispatched the Book and opened it to reveal again the note. He moved his thumb down through the letter until he found the part Enki was referring to. He read it again.

…So take up this weapon, forged by the Ancients, but fastened

to the Cedars branch by myself in this my own dark age. Only beware that your own heart not deceive you.

Consider well the end to which you strike. May malice and pride not be found in your heart. For while ye hold the Axe, it will draw into itself the virtues and the vice of your heart. Upon the third strike it will thereby release blessing or deadly poison into he who strikes the final blow.

Fare thee well, Axe Bearer!

"Gil! I'm the axe bearer! And pride and malice was indeed in my heart as I clung to the Axe these last two days! But it was you who struck the third and final blow!"

"Enki, what are you getting at?"

"It says it will send 'deadly poison into he who strikes the final blow'. That is, *if* the axe bearer harbors malice and pride in his heart. I did Gil, I know I did. But you struck the final blow!"

"But I'm fine, Enki. I feel no 'deadly poison'. And the wound in my leg here is clean. It will heal. It's difficult to interpret many of these ancient writings and songs. Often they mean more than one thing. It's best to not try and be a theologian. Perhaps Shulpae will have greater insight into the meaning of the note and who the writer was and what he meant by all this."

Enki wasn't fully convinced, but he allowed Gil's reasoning to quiet him for the moment. Enki was lost in thought when Gil directed their attention to less philosophical matters.

Gil said, "Well, the darkness won't last forever. At

daybreak we'll find ourselves in the company of an outraged Kishite erst or two. We've done what we set out to do. How do we make our escape? I'd kind of like to make it back alive if possible."

Enki was stirred as if from a dream. His glazed over look suddenly disappeared and a new resolve came over him. He said, "We'll make it back alive, Gil – you and me both. I promise you that. Come on. Let's go."

Enki walked one last time over to Kreon's grave and spoke a final word of farewell. Gil did likewise and then they were off. They began by following the old forest path, now restored by the Kishites for their sacred rites performed in sight of the Great Cedar. It was the only charted road in these parts. Occasionally, they came upon trails created by trappers that veered off from the main road. But for the moment they stayed on the road, always on the lookout for some Kishite outpost guarding the approach to the Great Tree. Enki and Gil discussed the likelihood that the nearest outpost was still some distance away because no scouting parties had as yet descended upon them. Surely, a nearby outpost would have heard the noise from the powerful felling of the Tree. But there was no sign anywhere of anyone. They continued on, resolving to stick to the road as long as they were able to without being spotted. It provided the quickest and most direct exit from the forest. They travelled on for an hour in the darkness without speaking. It was a steady descent most of that time but finally the slope leveled off.

"Well, we have to be nearing some Kishite outpost by

now. What's our plan?" Gil asked at last, without much hope that Enki had actually thought of a good plan.

"The plan will present itself to us soon enough my worrisome friend," Enki said easily which served to justify Gil's suspicions. Enki seemed back to his old self, but Gil noted there was a slight edge to his usual flippant attitude. There was that new intensity in his eyes that the flippant response seemed to attempt to mask. Gil was about to ask Enki about this when through the trees emerged the view of a wooden tower rising into the sky and reflecting the light of the moon. They immediately fell back off the trail and into the forest brush. Peering through the leaves of the trees they discussed their options.

"What we need, of course, is a good horse," Enki said matter-of-factly.

"That shouldn't be a problem," said Gil sarcastically. "You've already shown how easy it is to steal away fish from a Kishite camp."

Enki declined to respond to this jab and instead continued on with his forming plan.

Enki said, "Suppose we get close enough to the camp such that we locate some of their sentries. There must be a guard or two stationed outside the tower. If we get close enough we can take him out with your magic bow and arrow there and steal his clothes, slip into the tower, jump on a horse or two and ride like we never have before!"

Gil just stared at Enki blankly for a minute. Then he said, "That's your plan? That's the best you could come up with?"

Enki looked slightly embarrassed. "You have a better

idea?"

"How about we just turn ourselves in and be done with it?"

Without a better option, they decided to proceed with Enki's plan – or at least the first part. Slowly they crept closer to the tower, keeping away from the trail. They slithered through the thick brush until they came within a bows shot of the tower – still no sign of any sentries. They crept closer but still no sign of life. They were now within fifty feet of the towers walls. It was not a large structure – perhaps a hundred feet wide and a hundred feet deep. A central tower rose up above the forts walls. It was perhaps fifty feet high. They were now close enough to see any guards that would be on lookout duty, but they could see no one.

"Well, this is odd," Gil whispered. "Perhaps most are out on patrol."

Enki had a curious look on his face. Then he said, "There's no one here."

Gil was still staring up at the tower when Enki leapt out of the forest brush and into the open. The sun had not yet risen, but dawn was fast approaching and it was now light enough for any guards on the watchtower to clearly see Enki's Sumerian form. Enki said nothing as he leapt out, but cautiously strolled around the tower walls to the opposite side where a large gate presented itself as the entrance. Gil simply cringed, uncertain what to do. He strung an arrow into his bow and waited for a target to present itself. But the target never came. Enki had disappeared around the other side of the tower now and Gil decided to throw his fate in with his impulsive friend. Out he leapt and ran to catch up with Enki just in time to see him entering the Kishite stronghold. The gate had been left ajar. There was still no sign of life as Gil passed into the fort and scurried over to Enki's side.

The interior of the fort revealed a simple and functional layout. In the center of the courtyard, the main tower rose to the sky. Around the perimeter was a two story structure which apparently housed the men of the squad. Out in the open below one of the far walls was a kitchen area with some adjacent tables and chairs made from the rough wood of the surrounding forest. The fort appeared to have been completely abandoned sometime during the night. Gil noted that some of the cooking pots were still slightly warm revealing an evening meal that very night. Something had forced the Kishite men to leave in a hurry. Enki and Gil speculated that the noise of the Trees destruction had somehow reached to this distance and created a fright that sent the Kishites fleeing deeper into their own territory. This didn't seem likely, but it was their best explanation.

Enki and Gil searched most of the premises and became satisfied that they were the only inhabitants. Gil discovered some food left over in a few of the pots in the cooking area and a famished Enki and Gil sat down to a relative feast. Exhausted, they ate but did not speak. Finishing their hasty meal they were just about to vacate the fort and tempt their fate no further when they heard the sound of horse hoofs and the rabble of a half-dozen men speaking in the common tongue. They both quickly slipped into one of the side rooms just before the first of the returning Kishite men entered the fort. There were only a handful of men in this returning contingent. They dismounted their horses and entered the fort closing the gate behind them.

"It was the demon queen and her clan I still say," a voice said. "Why, I still feel a chill when I think of it."

Another voice said, "Oolog, there no such thing as a demon queen, you clod. And, in any case, this is the land of Shamash."

"Shamash is no match for the demon queen," Oolog said.

"Blasphemy. And foolishness too. A Hurrian tribe is all it was and Gordal will catch 'em before nightfall I bet."

A big burly man interrupted them both. "Enough of this, now. Both of you. It was enough that we had to endure your debate all the way back to camp. I'll not suffer to hear any more while trapped in the compound with you two. Now, get to work on cleaning this place up. The others will be back by morning no doubt. I want everything back in place or the both of you will be strung to the tower wall when Gordal returns."

That silenced them and they each set to work on cleaning up the kitchen and eating area. Enki and Gil, through a crack in the nearby door, looked on in the hopes that their service of finishing up the leftovers would go unnoticed. It apparently did, but it was only a matter of time before one of the six men needed to enter into the storage area which was their hiding place. They knew they would need to either make a break for it or stand and fight. Gil readied his bow and arrow and Enki drew his sword. Just then one of the Kishites cleaning the kitchen area let out a yell. It was Oolog.

"The demon! She's come here when we was gone and eat my soup! I set it aside before we left and look here – it's all eaten up!"

"Calm yourself, Oolog. You probably just ate it before we run off."

"No time! You know in what a frightful hurry we left to chase that invisible prey. It was no Hurrian clan. It was the demon queen! She lured us away from the fort so she and her minions could eat our sup!"

"Utter foolishness. What would a demon queen want with our pathetic meals?"

"She'd a eatin it nonetheless!"

"Quiet down now or Yrtahn will have us strung to the tower like he said. Now, go fetch us some soap from storage."

Oolog had settled down a bit but he entered the storage area clearly shaken and out of sorts. Enki sprang quietly out of the darkness, firmly clasped his mouth and then choked him until he fell silently to the floor unconscious. Enki now wanted to spring out and attack immediately, but Gil convinced him that he could get a good shot at the guard climbing the tower reducing their foes to only four before the heat of battle fell upon them. Slowly Gil opened the door. It pained him to shoot at an unsuspecting victim and to bring a man down without a fight, but they had no choice. Gil strung his bow and launched a perfect shot that entered into his Kishite opponent through the rib cage and directly into the heart. Killed instantly, the unfortunate Kishite fell to the ground without a yell. The others ran out to see what had happened, suspecting at first that he had simply fallen. But Oolog's friend, who was cleaning the kitchen area, heard the twang of the bow and the wiz of the arrow. He yelled out a warning to the others even as he turned and saw Enki emerge from the storage area. Enki came running directly for him with sword drawn. The Kishite drew his own sword just in time to block Enki's fierce attack. He blocked two strokes of Enki's sword, but was no match for the *abram teshua.* Enki's third thrust caught his wrist and the Kishite dropped his sword writhing in pain. The pain was short-lived as Enki sent the next thrust into his chest. He dropped to the ground in silent finality.

Gil, during Enki's attack, had positioned himself such that he was able to let fly another arrow into one of the remaining three Kishite warriors. The arrow hit his target in the leg and the Kishite recipient dropped to the ground with a cry of agony. The two remaining Kishites each fell upon Enki. Gil, fearing he would hit Enki, dropped his bow and ran to one of his fallen foes. Grabbing a sword from the first victim that had fallen from the tower, Gil turned to come to Enki's aid. But it was unneeded. Enki with one swift move thrust his sword into one of the guards and then swung immediately around slashing the other across the chest. The first fell to the ground dead, the second fell wounded and bleeding. Enki was about to strike the fatal blow, but the Kishite pleaded for mercy and Enki gave it to him.

Both Enki and Gil relaxed for a moment. Then they

heard a grunt followed by the sound of metal sinking into flesh. It was the Kishite Gil had wounded in the leg. He returned the favor now by flinging a dagger through the air. It landed upon Gil's leg right where the axe fragment had wounded him. The blade did not go deep, but it reopened the wound and Gil yelled out in agony. Gil fell to the ground as he watched Enki, with lightning speed, fall upon the wounded Kishite.

Enki checked each of the fallen Kishites confirming their fallen state. Each was dead but the one Enki had slashed across the chest. Also, Oolog could be heard struggling out of unconsciousness in the storage room. The wounded Kishite was bleeding freely and Enki could tell he wouldn't make it. Not wanting any surprises while he tended to Gil's wound, Enki first fell upon Oolog in the storage area, grabbed some rope and tied him fast. Then he moved back to the wounded Kishite but he was now dead, so Enki left him and leapt over to Gil's side.

Gil had already pulled the knife from his leg and was placing pressure upon the reopened wound to stop the bleeding. Enki re-bandaged Gil's leg and the flow of blood was stopped. Gil allowed himself to be hoisted over to a nearby cot. Enki raised his leg above his body and left him there to rest while he hurriedly gathered some needed supplies for their forthcoming escape.

"Do you think you can ride?" Enki asked.

"I think so. The pain is lessoning." Gil sat up cringing in pain. He spun his legs slowly around and rose to his feet. He placed a bit of pressure on the wounded leg and it seemed to hold up well enough. He limped over to the horse Enki was preparing for their journey home.

"So do we do anything with this one?" Gil asked. He was pointing to Oolog who was tied up just outside the storage room.

Enki walked over to Oolog. "This one we let live," Enki said. "He's our signature." Then speaking to Oolog, "Kishite, do you know who we are?"

Oolog cried out, "You're servants of the Demon Queen, aren't you? Come to finish us off!"

"We have nothing to do with this Demon Queen of yours. I am Enkidu, son of Terah, lord and ensi of Ur. And this is Gilgamesh, heir to Lugulbanda's throne in Uruk. We have slain the Bull of Heaven and we have destroyed your sacred Tree. Take this message back to Etana. Sumer rises again and Kish dare not stand in her way. Sargon is forever dead. The age of New Sumer has begun!"

Oolog gave out a fearful groan as Enki finished his little speech. How the cowardly Kishite had survived so long in the service of an army known for its brutality Enki could not say, nor did he care. He hoisted Gil up on the horse and then hopped up himself. Together they sped off through the gate just as the noise of galloping horses reached their ears from the north. The returning battalion was fast approaching. Enki led his own horse into a gallop. They sped on west along a trail that soon met up with a trail going north and south. This second trail they took as they set their sights on the south and on Uruk and Ur.

It was only a few minutes before they heard the sound of

a horn blast. The Kishite squad had reached the fort and after hearing of their exploits from Oolog, they set out in all haste to overtake the princes of New Sumer. Neither Enki nor Gil spoke of Enki's foolishness in relaying to Oolog their deed. Enki, however, knew it was what Gil was thinking. They sped on in silence. Dawn had turned into mid-morning, but an emerging thick fog clouded any view of the enemy behind them. However, they could hear the thundering beat of the Kishite's horses as they galloped on in search of revenge. Continuous horn blasts were apparently sending an alarm out to neighboring Kishite outposts, calling all squads to participate in the chase. Had Gil not been wounded and had they each been able to ride their own horses, their freedom might have been more easily secured. As it was, they were greatly slowed by over burdening their steed and the Kishites were gaining ground fast. Adding to their plight was the sound of shouts and horses coming now from several other directions. The entire Kishite rege was after them.

Enki considered heading off the path and moving across country, but thought better of this. They would be surely done for if they came upon an uncrossable portion of the Tigris. Surely this path would lead them to a bridge or some shallow portion of the River. They would need to stick to the path at least until they crossed.

And so, they sped on. The enemy was gaining but they still had a strong enough lead to lend them hope that they would arrive at the Tigris first. But it would be close and once past the River it would only be a matter of time before they were overtaken. But Enki resolved to worry about that after they were on its southern shores.

An hour passed. Twice an arrow whizzed past them from behind. Once their horse almost lost his footing ending the chase in an unfortunate conclusion. But soon the distant rumble of the River was heard. They were much farther upstream than the portion they had crossed on the northward journey. The River from their previous crossing point turned sharply north and west such that they were now much closer to the River than if they had returned the same way they had come. Enki urged on his horse even faster now. His only thought was making it to the other side of the Tigris. Once across the enemy would be on their heels and their horse spent. But he would deal with that problem when it came.

Another arrow whizzed past. Then another. And another. The fog still prevented them from seeing the Kishites behind them, but fortunately, it also prevented the Kishites from seeing them. However, they were close enough now that they could make out their voices and certain captains calling out orders. Suddenly, the terrain shifted. It had been relatively flat up to this point, though it was covered in trees.

The path now took a steep downward turn as it made its way toward the River valley. They still could not see the Tigris, but the sound of the water was clear and produced a loud rumble causing a pang of fear to creep across Enki's heart that the River might not be crossable at this point after all. Too late to second guess his decision to stick to the path. He sped on at a dangerous speed.

It was all that Gil could do to hang on. The bleeding from his wound had stopped, but every now and then a sudden turn in the road caused his leg to strike the side of the horse sending a fresh wave of pain through his body.

As they descended into the valley, they left the fog behind and above them. The Tigris emerged suddenly into sight. They were only a couple hundred yards away, and this was a good thing, for a quick glance behind them revealed the Kishites emerging out of the fog trailing by only fifty yards or so.

Enki's heart fell as his fears were realized. The River, at this point, was full of rapids and rocks and far too wide to cross by horse. But the path disappeared into some trees as it turned west and north to follow the River upstream. Another couple of arrows shot past them, closer than before now that they were no longer an invisible target. Gil somehow managed to turn himself around on the fast moving horse and returned their shots with shots of his own. Enki kept his attention on the River and the path ahead. All hope rested on what they would see once they turned that sharp corner at the River's shore. Just then, that hope became surer as Enki caught a faint glimpse of a bridge through the trees.

"Gil! Turn yourself back around and ready your bow! There's a bridge!"

Gil obeyed hurriedly as their horse finally emerged from the forest with the River visibly before them. The bridge, stretching across the mighty torrent of the Tigris rapids, presented itself just a few hundred feet away. Also, presenting themselves were two guards on the bridge, alerted to the chase by the trumpets of the Kishites behind them.

Gil readied his bow as Enki sped on. Their horse was exhausted after carrying the weight of two for so long and fast a ride, but he gave his new masters his all in these last few minutes. Gil, with great pain to his wound, lifted himself up above Enki and aimed his bow at one of the guards. The guards had bows as well and let their arrows fly toward the oncoming Sumerians. Gil was, however, by far the better shot, and just as they neared the bridge he let his arrow fly directly into the heart of one of the guards.

Seconds later, they were on the bridge. Enki sped on toward the other guard with sword drawn. The guard fired an arrow at Enki, who ducked just in time. Another second passed and Enki was upon the guard with a slash of his sword. He didn't kill him, but he left a scar that would be with him to the end of his days. The guard fell back as Enki and Gil sped over the bridge. The guard lay there in the center of the bridge and inadvertently acted as an obstacle for the trailing Kishite battalion. Each horse crossing the bridge refused to trample the fallen guard, and this gave Enki and Gil just enough breathing room to hope again as they emerged on the other side of the River and began heading upward to exit the Tigris river valley.

It had been steadily growing darker as the chase had gone on throughout the morning. Thick rain clouds had been slowly gaining on them during the course of the race. These now overhead let loose their supplies and down came water from the sky. Thunder and lightning began to accompany the rain as Enki and Gil sped on up out of the River valley. The narrowness of the bridge had sufficiently delayed the Kishite army such that they now had a marginal lead again. However, with the rain and the great fatigue of their steed, this lead was once again diminishing and all hope with it. The path began to become muddied due to the rain and their horse began to falter. Enki and Gil had just repositioned themselves when their horse suddenly fell head first launching Enki and Gil into the air.

They came crashing down on the west side of the path. Into the brush they landed only to find that they were now rolling down a steep slope. As they slid through the wet foliage and slippery mud of the hillside they could hear their horse above them back on his feet, apparently with leg unbroken, and racing once again along the road. Why the horse would continue without his cargo urging him on, they could not tell, but it temporarily worked to their advantage. They had slid to a stop now some fifty yards below the road. Above them, they could glimpse faintly the Kishite army pass them by, chasing their riderless steed. Surely, they would catch up with the horse in the next few minutes and return to search the area for them. Quickly, they raced off on foot to the west grateful now for the hard rain eliminating their tracks.

They ran for over an hour through the thick brush, expecting at any moment that they would be overtaken by their pursuers. But the sound of the Kishites was not heard from again. They sat down to rest and check Gil's wound which, though painful, had not prohibited their flight on foot. They now considered their dilemma.

"So, why do you suppose they haven't followed us?" Gil asked.

"I don't know, Gil. I can only guess that upon catching up with our horse they figured we must have jumped off and headed on foot toward Uruk. That would logically lead them to pursue us on the east side of the road which would lead most directly to some neutral territory in Nippur or one of the other central towns. By the looks of our course, I'd say we're making straight for Babylon – not a logical choice for a couple of Sumerians fleeing Sargon's heirs."

Gil said, "Strange, though, that they haven't split up and pursued us on both sides of the road."

"Perhaps they have," said Enki. "But there's a lot of ground to cover if they are canvassing all the southern routes. We may yet make it after all."

Gil considered this. "So what's next?"

"We continue with the unexpected. We make for Babylon."

The next few days were miserable ones. It rained the entire time of their travels. Gil's wound seemed to be healing, but it caused him to limp most of the way. Several times they lost their bearings due to the thick cloud cover and had to backtrack. Once they almost were blown down an adjacent gorge due to a fierce wind. The only good thing about the trek was that they were still alive, for which they were both grateful.

They finally arrived in Babylon on the third day after their fall from their horse. Had they taken the road all the way they would have arrived in Babylon in a day's time, but traveling through the hinterland proved slow going. Babylon was an ugly town, but one that was bustling with activity. Built as a small agricultural village along the banks of the Euphrates, it was quickly being transformed into a center of trade. But the infrastructure of the place could not keep up with its growth. The result was a small city of shacks and dirty hovels packed to the limit. Because of the population explosion in the town, it had become a favorite center for scoundrels of every type. The unruly populace seemed to welcome the riffraff of the four winds and so give aid to Babylon's growing reputation as a place of corruption and disorder.

Enki and Gil, at first, were paranoid that they would be discovered for who they were. But the streets were filled with so many strange sorts that two more seemed not to matter. At the Kishite fort, Enki had secured a few gold coins from the fallen squad leader so they found a small inn and paid for a night's rest in a real bed. Well, some would call them real beds. Enki and Gil were grateful for the dirty cushioned wood planks nonetheless. In the morning, they ventured into the dining area. Already, the place was filling up with townsfolk. Surprised at such a gathering at this hour of the day, Enki inquired of the innkeeper what the commotion was about.

"Seems those two filthy Sumerian princes somehow snuck in to the Amanus forest and cut down the Great Cedar several nights ago. Words just reaching us here about it, but the news is spreading fast."

"Those bastards!" Enki said quickly. "Who do those Sumerians think they are? Well, they'll get theirs once Etana gathers his forces."

"No doubt, no doubt," said the innkeeper. "But I fear our Babylon here will get caught in the middle of it all if there's a war between Kish and Uruk."

Just then the innkeeper was called away by another customer across the way.

Enki whispered to Gil, "Let's get out of here."

"Right behind you."

They soon found a traveling tradesman about to head for Lagash and paid him to smuggle them out in the back of his cart. It cost them the remaining gold that Enki had but they made good time this way and they were out of sight. The rain still had not stopped and all travelers were making haste in fear that the flood season would come upon them early this year. Their escort did not say much, and they didn't volunteer any conversation. Content to just lay there and rest in complete exhaustion, Enki and Gil soaked up the rain and dreamed of a warm real bed and a hot meal.

When the tradesman turned off toward the east for Lagash, Enki and Gil rolled out of the cart and bid their ride farewell. The man acknowledged their thankfulness and continued on his way without a word. He knew better than to ask any questions and he had made a good profit on this cargo. Enki and Gil then turned to face south.

"Well, I can't believe we've made it this far," Gil said as they walked on toward Uruk. "A few more hours and we'll be in my father's realm."

"Oh, I believe it, Gil. I believe it." Enki let flow an easy laugh of elation. He allowed a tremendous wave of relief to flow over him as he now considered that their dangerous mission was near its conclusion. He had set out to do the unthinkable once again and he was now returning victorious… once again.

"Gil, don't you see it? I know I've said it before, but we have a destiny to fulfil. The gods really do favor us! Even an immortal dies at our hand. We're invincible. Nothing can stop me!"

Gil was less impressed. "Have you learned nothing from all this?! Enki, we almost died! Several times! You still think this is all about you, don't you? What happened to your little 'I was a fool for having such pride' speech?"

"Gil, I've had a lot of time to think on this journey home. I've concluded that I was a fool for thinking I was fool," Enki said light-heartedly.

Gil just stared at him.

Enki said, "Look, we've witnessed some amazing things on this journey. Not all of it makes sense to me yet, but one thing is for certain. Our survival was miraculous. You can't deny that. The favor of the gods is upon us. Doesn't that give you some kind of sense of destiny like it does me?"

"No, Enki, it doesn't," Gil said.

"Well, then bask in my own destiny if you don't have one of your own. Look, Gil, I'll not have you ruin this for me. We've done an amazing thing! Something totally unfathomable. I won't let your pessimism destroy this victory. The stage is being set, Gil."

Gil did not respond but allowed the awkward silence to permeate the walk on. They settled into silence for several minutes till Enki suddenly released some inner frustration and lashed out. He said heatedly, "Listen, Gil, isn't there an ambitious bone somewhere in your body?! I need you to be a powerful king if I'm going to fulfil my destiny as a conquering general! If you can't do that, then just tell me now!"

"Or what, Enkidu? Gil asked. "Will you go find yourself another crown prince to exploit? Who do you think you are?"

"I am Enkidu of New Sumer, favored one of the gods, chosen axe bearer, slayer of Humbaba! And you are to be the king of my empire!"

"Your empire!? And what if I order you to withhold your conquering armies?! What if I tell you to stop at the gates of Kish and return to Uruk? What will you do then?"

Enki was filled with rage and frustration at that but held his response. Neither spoke further for several minutes. They simply walked on in silence. The rain had finally stopped and it was becoming a beautiful day. The sun was beginning to appear through the clouds. The sound of birds singing rose up all around them in the trees along their current path. Perhaps it was the sun beginning to dry out Enki's clothes that suddenly softened him. With difficulty he turned to Gil and said, "I'm sorry Gil. You didn't deserve all that. I'm acting like a fool again, I know."

"On that we're agreed," said Gil. Then he thought better of it. He said, "Well… I'm sorry too for being such the pessimist. Maybe we do have a destiny to fulfill. I don't know. Everything that's happened just makes me more fearful than confident. It's like, we've witnessed these amazing things that it seems no mortal should witness. Who are we to be involved in the affairs of gods or of the Great Ones from before the Cleansing? It's unthinkable. And it's not what I want. Enki, I'm not like you. I don't want to be involved in such great affairs that I don't understand. Crown prince of Sumer or not, it's not my place. So don't try making me into something I'm not."

Enki just considered those words in silence. The anger began to return, but then subsided as some internal unspoken resolve played itself across Enki's soul and mind. Enki kept his inner thoughts hidden and simply said, "Okay, Gil… okay."

Gil then said, "And I don't want to make this whole affair into a big deal, okay? My father is going to be furious with us when he finds out. I was hoping he wouldn't find out it was us who felled the Tree, but of course you made sure that wouldn't happen back with good old Oolog or whatever his name was. But please, Enki, let's keep this whole thing as quiet as possible, okay?"

"Okay, Gil. Fine," Enki said unconvincingly. Still, Gil accepted his assurance as the best he knew he would get and simply hoped for the best. Conflicting emotions seemed to be dancing within Enki until he looked down and was suddenly distracted by Gil's leg.

"Gil, your wound – it's bleeding again…"

Gil looked down and suddenly became aware of the

throbbing pain of the wound. The wound indeed had reopened and was slowly bleeding through his clothing. They stopped then and Enki helped Gil redress the wound and stop the bleeding. The exercise helped break the tension further and they gave their full attention once again to simply getting home to Uruk and to thoughts of a hot meal and that warm bed that so frequented their minds in the last few days.

Several hours later, as dusk was beginning to settle, the great city of Uruk came within sight. Enki had been there many times, but still the sight impressed him. Its great walls were far greater than those at Ur and though Ur's temple was perhaps greater than Uruk's, it was Egalmah, that great palace of Uruk, that was Uruk's chief wonder and by far bested the palace at Ur. It rose high above the city walls and all surrounding edifices and was to all who saw it a beacon of the power and prestige of this great city of the New Sumer that was emerging. Pride welled up in Enki at his first sight of the city and of the palace. He turned a beaming glance aside to Gil but noted that the sight to Gil only brought on a deeper melancholy. He considered shaking his friend out of it, but resigned himself to remain in silence lest their previous debate ensue and thrust them once again into an uncomfortable tension. Still, Enki resolved to not allow Gil's own issues to keep him from enjoyment of the sight or of his own dreams and visions of the future and how he knew his destiny was wrapped up in this great city as representative of all his aims and ambitions. Deep down inside he knew that he was to be the true father of this nation. He was the *abram teshua*, the 'great father of deliverance' and he would deliver New Sumer from the hand of Kish and from the hand of Susa just as he had delivered her from the hand of Zoreth and the desert Amorites.

He knew he had begun this work already in the slaying of Kreon and in the destruction of the Great Cedar. Kish would now be on notice. He was conflicted as he considered Gil's desire to keep all their exploits quiet. How could he possibly do so? Wasn't the whole point of the venture to create a name for themselves and to give Kish a warning? And they had indeed given Kish that warning. Surely, they would already be discussing the destruction of their sacred tree in the streets of Kish at this very hour. They would even now be considering what bad omen this meant for them as a people. They would be trembling with new fear and respect for Enkidu of Ur and Gilgamesh of Uruk, fearsome princes of New Sumer. Surely, Etana would even now be questioning his own destiny in the face of Enki's own. It wouldn't stop him from seeking to further his ambitions of course, but it would cause him to question his confidence and more importantly, it would cause his people to question the wisdom of his planned exploits.

Enki considered all these things as they walked on, trying to hide from Gil his inner conflict and his frustration with Gil for not embracing their destiny together. How, indeed, could they keep silent! But as they approached the gates of Uruk, something began to happen that eased Enki's concern. Watchmen had spotted them approaching Uruk along the north road. Soon a throng of the populace emerged from the north gate and was moving toward them. Both Enki and Gil were so exhausted by this point that their own weariness almost made it seem like a dream. For Enki it would be remembered with delight, but Gil reflected on it as a nightmare. Word had preceded them. Enki was correct. They spoke now of their great deeds on the streets of Kish. But they also spoke of them on the streets of Uruk for news travels fast up and down the Euphrates flowing through both Kish and Uruk. Indeed, the people of Uruk had only recently heard the news and as one had gathered to welcome the warriors return who it was rumored had slain the mighty Bull of Heaven and had destroyed Kish's sacred Tree and who it was also rumored had escaped the grasp of an entire Kishite rege. They swept around Gil and Enki and bore them up carrying them jubilantly back into the city. At first, one could hear the chants of "Gilgamesh!" and "Enkidu!" but soon these gave way to a single word repeated in greater and greater volume, passion and unison. Soon all that could be heard was the crowds shouting, "Abram!"

CHAPTER 9 – HOMECOMING

Enki awoke to the sound of birds and the feel of the sun on his face. But he wasn't ready yet to open his eyes. He tried to remember what had happened. Great crowds had been carrying him and Gil into the city. They were shouting his new name – *abram.* He recalled being in something of a joyful daze through it all. He also recalled catching sight of the King on the palace balcony watching the procession as he was paraded into the main city square and then into the palace grounds. He wasn't smiling. But then again, the stern king rarely smiled and few could ever guess what he was thinking at any given time. Enki would hold off his speculation – they would no doubt find out soon enough. Then what had happened? He couldn't remember. Had he fainted? He must have… for here he was now lying in a soft warm bed. And where was Gil… and Aya? He opened his eyes and had one of his questions answered. Aya was sitting at his side and now he noticed she held his hand in hers. Her eyes were closed and he wondered if she'd been like this at his side all night.

"Good morning," Enki casually said.

Aya opened her eyes and a great smile enveloped her face.

"Enki!" she cried. "Are you alright!?"

"How could I not be alright? I'm alive and I'm in your presence." He tried not to sound cocky but failed as usual.

Aya's demeanor then changed and she gave him her best womanly glare. She then said, "Well, you'll not be alright once I'm through with you! How could you do it?! How could you risk getting yourself foolishly killed like that over a ridiculous tree? Do you have any idea what you would have done to me if you had gotten both yourself and Gil killed? Did the thought even enter your head?"

She had meant to scold him playfully, but there was some force in the words which she hadn't planned on. Enki was taken aback at first but recovered quickly.

"Hey now, Aya, everything's okay," he said soothingly, as he sat up and pulled her into his arms.

Her surprised anger relented with the release of her words and she accepted his embrace.

Enki continued, "I'm sorry, Aya. I guess there were a few times when something could have happened to us, but nothing did." Enki was about to say more but wisely chose to remain silent and just hold her close.

After a few moments Aya spoke again softly. She said, "So… are the rumors true… did you really slay this demon of the forest… this Humbaba creature?"

Enki paused before continuing. Then he said, "It's true, but he was no demon, though what exactly I'm still not sure."

Just then Shulpae barged in with Gil at his side, bandaged up and limping, but apparently otherwise healthy and rested. "Oh no, you don't," Shulpae said. "Don't start off on your tale without me. Gil won't tell me a thing and I'm of course dying to know all about this little adventure of yours."

"You mean 'dying' more than usual, old man?" Enki said out of force of habit.

Shulpae just glared and then said, "So, apparently killing an immortal hasn't affected your respect for your elders." Shulpae plumped himself down on a nearby couch and just sent the command, "Talk!"

Enki gave a questioning glance to Gil who finally spoke. He said, "It's okay, Enki. You can tell him everything. I just don't want to talk about it myself and word is out so you might as well fill in the gaps."

Enki did more than just fill in the gaps. He told the whole tale from start to finish with his usual flare for self-aggrandizing detail. Shulpae seemed impatient throughout much of the first part of the tale, but then became hunched over in amazed fascination as Enki spoke of their discovery of the tunnels beneath the Silver Mountains and then of the entrance into the chamber of the Annunaki. Shulpae and Aya were both now in awe as Enki described the chamber and the thrones and the table in the center with the book, the axe and the bow. And then as Enki spoke of what was written in the book, Shulpae became visibly moved.

"Orion wrote those words?" Shulpae said suddenly interrupting the tale. "So it was he who took the forged axe head and wedded it to the branch of the Tree!"

"Who is Orion?" Enki asked.

"Our legends do not record much of Orion, he is remembered more among the western peoples, but he was one of the greatest of those who lived before the Great Cleansing. In his letter you read he says he was only a Benudim, but in truth he really was a Nephilim, though he never fully identified himself as such."

"He was one of the wizards?" Aya said in sudden distaste.

"He was indeed, though not all the wizards were evil in those very early days. In fact, most were good until Addlaan became corrupted by Methus. But, I don't know much really of those days – only that Orion was used to rescue Taran, the first 'adam, and that he exhibited some strange and awful powers that none could fully explain. Apparently they pointed to some prophesy regarding a Seed. My findings in my research over the years are all sketchy and incomplete I'm afraid. It was for this reason that I spent so much time searching for Utnapishtim. If Utnapishtim still lives, then he would have all the answers to my many questions about the world before the Cleansing."

Enki continued his tale, downplaying the next few days of their journey when he was so obsessed and controlled by the power of the Axe. But he spoke in great detail about their coming to the Tree and about the battle with Humbaba, whom Sadiq had called Kreon. And then after Enki finished speaking of Kreon's death, all fell into a long silence.

Enki finally asked, "Shulpae, I couldn't understand anything Kreon said, but he did cry out one word, which sounded like a name – a name he seemed to cry out in affection and despair and remorse. He cried out repeatedly the name of 'Dellan'. Do you know who that was?"

Shulpae answered, "Dellan was one of the First Ones, as was Kreon. Indeed, they were brothers, Kreon the eldest and Dellan the youngest son of Taran. I've heard their names spoken together in some of the more ancient songs that I've not been able to translate. There is some great tale involving the two, but I was never able to discover it. But, alas, the best records I found were at Umma and they were far from complete. It's again a question I would bring to Utnapishtim if I had ever the chance."

Gil then spoke up finally for the first time. He asked, "Do you have any idea what Kreon's crime was?"

Shulpae paused thoughtfully and then admitted, "I do not."

They all sat in silence after the long tale, each lost in their own reflections. Finally a knock on the door interrupted the silence and two guards emerged. They addressed Gil.

"My Lord, the king would see you now if you've recovered strength enough. He requests to see the prince of Ur as well."

Gil grimaced. "Very well, tell my father we will come at once." Then to Enki, "Come, let's get this over with, I don't think he'll have many kind words for us."

"What do you mean?" Enki replied, trying to sound

casual. "We've just won a major victory for Uruk and New Sumer. He should be throwing us a parade!"

"Don't count on it," Shulpae said uneasily. "The king may not see your exploit as you do, nor does he have my fascination with the past. The people may adore you at the moment, but the feeling is quite different in court."

Aya reached for Enki's arm as Gil and Enki rose to follow the guards. "Oh, Enki, please do be careful with what you say to my father. If he should scold you for what you've done, just accept it humbly. He will soften in time."

"This is nonsense," Enki said with something less than confidence. "We've done something great that no other man has ever done. How could what we've done not be received with anything but joy in the court of Uruk?"

"Just try not to say much," Gil implored futilely. And with that, the two guards led them out the door and down the hallway toward the palaces central quadrant. They passed many wide hallways and passageways which gave way to expansive chambers beyond each. As they passed, palace administrators and guards stopped what they were doing and turned to watch with some reverence the two brash young men who had done the unthinkable. Whatever awaited them in the court, it was clear that among the people and even among those with palace credentials, that they were heroes.

The walk to the central chamber of the king and his court was a long one in this great palace known as Egalmah. It had been built in the days of Old Sumer and was one of the crowning accomplishments of that ancient people. Half destroyed during the terrible days of Sargon, it had been rebuilt in the past two generations to become once again a powerful symbol of authority, beauty and culture. Massive tapestries lined the walls stretching up to the high ceilings above. Works of art lined the hallways. The statues particularly caught Enki's attention. Among some of the busts were those of his own people from Ur. Several paintings included historic scenes involving Rue and Serug and Nahor I. Enki couldn't help but feel a tremendous sense of pride that he was following in the footsteps of his grandfather. He thought again of the great destiny that he had been given and of the profound sense of confidence that continued to surge through his being. Lost in these thoughts, he and Gil emerged into the chamber hall of the king.

A high ceiling rose above the largest table Enki had ever seen. It was a great round table which Enki suspected could sit twelve dozen comfortably. Around the table sat nobles of the realm with Lugulbanda at one end in an only slightly raised throne. Lugulbanda rose as Gil and Enki entered.

The great king strode around the table toward the two adventurers as the conversations among the nobles fell to a silence. The stern king wore his crown with dignity. His gray beard and piercing eyes added to his mystique. His footsteps were all that could be heard as he slowly walked closer.

"I am pleased that you are well, my son, and you also prince of Ur", he said slowly and calmly. "But it is all I am pleased about."

Gil and Enki stood at attention trying not to slouch. Both felt helpless because both were. King Lugulbanda was controlling events now. "They say you have destroyed the

Great Cedar. Is it true?"

Neither Gil nor Enki spoke right away. When he could see Enki preparing to answer Gil jumped in ahead. "Yes, father, it is true."

"And under whose orders, and by what authority, did you take on this task?"

"Father, no one gave us the order. We acted on our own."

The king circled the two in silence as all waited the next exchange.

"And what did you achieve by this mission?"

Enki could hold back no longer. "My Lord, we acted for the glory of Uruk and New Sumer. We struck first before Kish could strike us. Etana will now be wary of us. He will not likely be able to motivate his forces as speedily now that this great motivating icon of theirs has been destroyed."

"So, you know King Etana then? You are able to interpret his thoughts? His reactions to events? When did you acquire such intimate knowledge of our northern rival?"

"Um… your majesty, no, I have never met him, I do not know him, but we all know of him, we know of his drive to regain the glory of Sargon, to surpass it, we know he believes he can move sooner rather than later. By destroying the Cedar we have given him a great set back in his plans."

"You have done no such thing!" The king's wrath finally let loose. "You have given him a greater cause for rallying his forces than that solitary Tree ever could. He will have no trouble rallying his nobles and tribal fringe peoples together now that there is a clear threat to the south. You have single-handedly given Etana the greatest weapon a sovereign vying for greater power could hope for – you've given his people a cause that will further his own aims! You are a fool Enkidu of Ur. Your brash action has lost us precious time. Instead of five to ten years I now foresee two or three before the conflict between our peoples is fully engaged. It is to you and to my wayward son that we have to thank for this!"

Enki was steaming with rage at the rebuke, but Gil merely lowered his head in shame.

Enki said, "Then I say let the conflict come! We will be ready for them."

Lugulbanda then, "We are not ready for them! The armies of Kish are nothing like that barbaric tribe you mollified. These are real armies we are talking about, armies with the power to destroy Uruk and Ur and our entire civilization!"

A noble from across the room now rose to speak. He addressed Enki since Gil was unwilling to resist the verbal barrage. "Prince of Ur, the king is correct. No one here doubts the courage of you or Prince Gilgamesh, but the stakes are far too high to ignore what you have done. You have placed us now solidly on a war footing. Our people are soft. Two generations of peace have left us so and we will not be easily able to prepare a soft people for war. We need time. You have taken some of that time away."

Enki was about to respond when Lord Kalat, the noble who had been critical of Enki in Ur after the campaign against Zoreth, came to a surprising defense of the two young warriors. "Lord Galeth," he said. "You speak with the appearance of wisdom as usual, but I must in this case side with the two princes."

All turned a surprised look upon Kalat, not the least of which was the look of the king, who was rarely surprised by anything.

Kalat continued, "It is true that we have grown soft, which is why we need to exert force and reawaken a sense of honor and fire in our people! I welcome what Prince Gilgamesh and Prince Enkidu have achieved. It is the stuff of legends and we are in need of some new legends in our day."

Kalat sat back down just as quickly as he had arisen. Apparently he was not ready for a debate, but merely needed to speak his peace in the matter. Enki was thankful for the defense, even if it did come from one who had so recently wounded his pride in Ur.

"Well spoken, Lord Kalat," Lugulbanda replied regaining control of the exchange. "But I fear your words are dangerous and would lull us into a false confidence."

All knew now to be silent for Lugulbanda controlled a discussion with his tone. All the nobles present knew how to read their king. Debate was being ended before it had a chance to begin. He gave his conclusion slowly and not without some pain and a tinge of sarcasm. He said, "We shall officially apologize to the mighty King Etana of the noble people of Kish, and ask for their forgiveness. We shall tell them the truth – that two of our princes acted independently and that they have been reprimanded for their actions. Prince Enkidu you must return home at once. Etana's spies in our city must not relay the message that we have honored you with a long audience. There will be no banquet in your honor. There will be no parade."

Enki was red with rage and embarrassment, but even he knew enough now to keep silent when the king spoke in such a tone of finality. The king dismissed them and they left. They walked in silence back to their rooms. Upon returning Enki immediately started gathering his pack.

Gil said, "Enki, my father said 'at once', but I'm certain he will allow you to remain one more day to recover strength."

Enki said, "Your father is a strong man, Gil, but so am I. I will leave at once."

Enki was still visibly enraged but he was beginning to bring it under control and to mask it with that deep look of resolve and intensity that Gil had noticed in Enki ever since the felling of the Tree.

"Will you at least say goodbye to my sister?" Gil asked.

Enki considered this as if waking from a dream only to doze off again.

"Send her to me quickly, but I won't wait long."

Gil departed and Aya entered shortly thereafter.

"I'm so sorry, Enki," came Aya's soothing voice as she slipped her arms about Enki's waste. Enki returned the embrace but remained cold and distracted.

"Please Enki, won't you say something?" Aya asked.

"There's nothing to say." Enki said. "Your father is wrong and he will bring ruin upon Sumer through his appeasement of Kish. There's only one way to handle Etana and neither your father, nor your brother are willing to do it."

"Enki, what are you saying?" Aya asked with sudden shock.

Enki said, "I'm saying that someone must take responsibility for this kingdom, and it doesn't seem to be coming from the court of Uruk."

"That's treasonous talk! Please don't say such things again."

"Or what? Or you'll turn me in to your father?"

"Enki, you're not yourself. I know you don't mean this."

"Then you don't know me, Aya. And Gil doesn't know me. And the great High King doesn't know me."

Aya pulled away from Enki at this. "And what about me, Enki?" she asked. "Do you know me? Do you even care?"

"I don't have time or energy for this, Aya. Don't be the little sister again trying to tag along and be noticed."

"How dare you Enki!? Does our love mean nothing to you now?"

"I don't know what love means, Aya. I don't know what anything means anymore. I only know that we're all doomed to death. I only know that we all have only so much time of life. And I only know that I must take, and that nothing is given. I'll not be held back. Not by your father and not by Gil and not even by you. Now, let me go. Your father commands it!"

And with that Enki left the chamber not seeing the tears now flowing freely from the princess.

***

He knew he had been harsh and foolish with Aya. But he also felt somehow helpless to do anything but allow the hurt and bitterness within him to flow out to those around. He hoped he could make it up to Aya later, but for now he needed the strength that the reckless release of anger brought him.

He strode out of the castle compound and headed across the courtyard leading to the outer perimeter of the castle walls and to the gate leading to the rest of the city of Uruk. As he turned to head for the gate, a hooded man approached him.

"A moment of your time," the hooded man said.

A surprised Enki stopped and turned to face the stranger. "Who are you?"

The man leaned forward toward Enki and then slid back a portion of his hood, enough to reveal to Enkidu who he was. It was Lord Kalat, his most recent surprise defender from court.

"Lord Kalat?" Enki asked.

"Yes," Kalat acknowledged in a voice not much louder than a whisper. "Forgive the secrecy but I don't believe the High King would appreciate my coming to see you."

"And why is that?"

"Because of what I'm about to tell you."

"And what is that?"

"Something that could greatly help you on your way toward fulfilling your destiny."

"And what would you know of my destiny?"

"That you are destined to make Sumer great once again," Kalat said with a knowing look in his eyes.

"I, and not the High King you mean, nor the great Prince Gilgamesh!" Enki spoke as though to defend his friend, but something in his manner gave way that his heart was not truly in the defense.

Kalat paused only briefly and then leaned in and whispered, "yes."

The two men stared into each other's eyes for several moments, both of them silent as each read the other. Something passed between the two in that moment. Some unspoken pact was being presented. Both men had felt marginalized in their own realm. Each could use the other to gain the upper footing, Enkidu in Ur and Kalat and his house in Uruk. Enki could see the invitation in his eyes and he did not back away.

Kalat then said, "I have a sealed letter. I would like it hand delivered by you to Ultaro in Ur."

Enki did not need to know what was in the letter. He saw it in the man's eyes. High Priest Ultaro was one other great power that had been marginalized by his father's line. His grandfather had subdued the priesthood and his father had inherited a mollified religious class. Ultaro, as high priest in Ur, had spent his whole life fighting that subjugation and had gained ground, but still the power base leaned unquestionably to the king. But here was a chance to change the political landscape, and Enki could be right at the center of it. The nobleman Kalat, the high priest Ultaro and the warrior-king Enkidu – the *abram teshua*!

Momentarily, Enkidu cringed at the thought of what was being presented to him. He held his hand back as a look of disgust crept across his face. But Kalat remained steady. Enki thought of what this could mean to his father and to his best friend Gil. He thought of what it could mean for him and Aya. This was treason that was being presented.

Still, Kalat held his gaze. Enkidu saw himself then as high king and at the head of armies. And he could see Aya at his side, proud of his great accomplishments – the subjugation of Kish, the conquest of the northern peoples and the stratagem that would fend off the peoples of the east. He could do this and it would protect Aya. It would protect Gil too, for he was not strong enough truly to rule and do what was necessary to protect New Sumer and lead her to greatness once again. Lugulbanda was strong, but old. There was no reason to wait for him to die and pass on his rule when it could be taken. And his brothers – Haran hated him already anyway, and Nahor would be content to contribute to the kingdom as the Great Merchant. His father would understand in time he convinced himself. Enki took the letter.

***

He rode all night, a feverish intensity driving him forward. But as the night wore on, the intensity began to diminish as his thoughts turned toward Aya. He regretted how they had parted and especially the things he had said. She didn't deserve to have him talk to her the way he did.

But what was done was done. One thing he knew – he could not afford now to have anyone hold him back from what he was called upon to do. He had been marked out for something – that much was clear. His thoughts ran back through the recent events. He began to count the times he should have been killed and yet hadn't been. He noted again with uneasy satisfaction the reappearance of Sadiq at just the right time. He thought of the fantastic things he'd witnessed in the last few weeks. He considered the book and the letter from this Orion – this mysterious personage from before the Great Cleansing. He recalled again the death of Kreon and the look in his eyes – that haunting mixture of hope and despair and longing. And the voice he'd heard. The Wonderful Voice. He recalled the warmth of its gentle beckoning to him – *come away with me.* His thinking of it brought a calm upon him he hadn't experienced in recent days.

And then his thoughts turned toward the letter from Kalat he now held in his coat pocket. What was he thinking in accepting the letter? How could he possibly deliver it to his father's great enemy Ultaro? But of course, he didn't know for sure what was in the letter. It could be anything. And Kalat had come to his defense right in front of Lugulbanda. That name sent a quick wave of anxiety through him. Could he really rival Lugulbanda? Was he ready? He shook off the thought with a quick shrug. Of course he was ready. And time might well be running out. Now was his time. The gods were handing him this destiny. He could embrace it or walk away. He would not walk away.

His scattered thoughts continued to torment him in this way as he sped on. He found it hard to focus on any one thought for very long. A deep burning of anxiety suddenly welled up inside. He felt very alone. And then came a wave of despair. Where was this coming from, he thought to himself? He tried to shake himself out of it. He thought again of Aya. Beautiful Aya. Thoughts of her often would calm him. His mind was always racing toward the future, toward his destiny. Aya lived ever in the present. Enki often made fun of her for this. However, at times he secretly envied her capacity for contentment in the midst of the mundane. Enki fled from the mundane. He could not be still. He needed to ever be advancing his position in life. Life to Enki was a race. It was a race against the inevitable day of his dying breath. And there, he realized, was the great irony and frustration. For though he had been greatly advancing in the race of late, he knew that it was a race he would lose. Death comes to all. Who can avoid it? The gods?

Until recently, he'd begun to question the existence of the gods. But so much had happened that he was becoming a believer as in the days of his childhood. Well, a believer of sorts. What he'd grown up with just couldn't be the full truth. The gods stirred feelings of fear and unrest and the gods themselves seemed motivated by subhuman passions most of the time – jealousy, rage, envy. Whatever that Voice was that he heard in the desert came from a different source than anything he'd come in contact with before. The temple ceremonies he'd gone to all his life seemed but a distant and distorted echo of whatever it was he'd heard that day in the desert as he lay bleeding to death. It was a similar feeling to what he felt when around Sadiq, as if Sadiq himself embodied that voice in some way. If ever he came in contact with the mysterious Sadiq again, he determined that he would seek from him any knowledge he had of the gods. For it seemed to Enki now as he reflected on all this, that there must be another god that he had not known of growing up. Perhaps a god of a distant land was calling him. Perhaps Sadiq knew this god and came from that land. Or perhaps there was a god greater than all the other gods – as much greater as that Voice was greater than the gods portrayed in the temple sacrifices of Ur or Uruk.

He wondered then if he should try sharing any of this with Graco, the priest-administrator under Ultaro and friend of his father. He had seemed always different from Ultaro and the rest of the priest-class that served his city. He wondered what Graco would think of his questioning of the gods and of this Voice he'd heard. He knew his questioning would be tantamount to blasphemy in the eyes of Ultaro. And this thought led him again to reflect on the letter he'd just received from Kalat. His thoughts became stilled and a feeling of numbness came over him. What was he doing? Could he really go through with it and pass on this letter to Ultaro? He knew what was implied in the look of Kalat the moment he presented the letter to him. An alliance was being offered. An opportunity was being presented for him to take matters into his own hands and move the kingdoms of Ur and Uruk forward. He knew well enough that Kalat's only motive was to increase the power base of his own house.

His aim was to free himself and the rest of the nobles from the dominance of Lugulbanda and his family. He knew as well that Ultaro wanted the same thing for his priest-class in Ur over against the stifling hold of the House of Eber. Did they think they would be able to control him then? He too was part of the House of Eber. Had they forgotten this? And his best friend was Gilgamesh, heir to the throne of Uruk and of New Sumer. Where was all this leading?

He rode on in silence allowing his thoughts to settle. His emotions and thoughts were now becoming jumbled together again and hard to distinguish. It was as if a lingering effect of the magic, that had so overtaken him in the days leading up to the slaying of Kreon, still had some sway over him. He considered again the letter and what it meant. It meant treason. He considered again his questioning of the gods and of this mysterious Voice he'd heard – a call from a god not of Ur but of some other place, unknown perhaps to his people. Blasphemy. He was on the verge of treason and blasphemy. The Voice he knew had to be good – he had experienced such warmth and peace. If the voice he'd heard was from a more powerful god calling him to abandon Nanna and Shamash and follow him instead, then it was a blasphemy he must embrace. And if this letter, he reasoned, was an offer to free him to become the power and leader he knew was needed at this desperate hour by New Sumer, then this too was a treason he must embrace. He allowed himself a sly smile. With that smile came a decision in his heart to follow this path wherever it would lead. But instead of that warmth and peace he'd hoped for, he experienced something else. He experienced a certain level of renewed strength and determination but mixed with it was a weight and a heaviness and a chill. He considered that it must just be the magnitude of his decision that weighed him so. He shook himself out of it and spoke reassuringly to himself, *I am the abram teshua and I am returning now to Ur to help New Sumer rise again!*

Suddenly, as if in answer to his thoughts, the silhouette of Ur against the night sky came into view through the trees. He sped on with greater haste eager to arrive at the city gates before dawn. He still needed time to formulate a plan and he realized he was over fatigued. He was not quite ready to face the populace or his family or… Ultaro. He needed rest. He needed more thought. He smiled at that. Gil had indeed worn off on him. It was a good thing and with that thought a degree of warmth swept over him. He thought of Gil in these final moments before arriving before the walls of Ur. Whatever happened, he would not abandon or betray his friend. He would rather betray Kalat and turn the tables on whatever he and Ultaro had planned. Gilgamesh would be high king of Uruk. But he, the *Abram*, would be something else, something greater in his mind. No, without Gil and indeed without Aya, all his plans and dreams seemed but an empty shell. Whatever happened, Gil and Aya would be by his side. He was determined that it be so and he would not allow anyone to come in the way of that happening.

He made it to the gates of Ur just as dawn was breaking. It was unavoidable being recognized by the guards, and indeed he would not have been able to enter at this early hour had he not been Enki, Prince of Ur. They allowed him to pass with a respectful nod, and with a certain level of questioning awe. Enki noted this with satisfaction. Had news arrived of his exploits yet? Rumors perhaps, but nothing certain, he guessed. Let them wonder some more. He was tired and needed to rest. He dove down a side street still bathed in darkness. Occasionally he was spotted and recognized by a tradesmen setting up shop or a stable master tending to his early morning duties. All seemed to greet him with the same level of questioning awe afforded him by the guards at the gate. He was being talked about in Ur and he guessed there was a certain level of excitement in those conversations. He grinned at the thought.

Suddenly the temple came into view. He considered again the letter he held for Ultaro. No, not yet. He needed more time to think. He would not pass on this opportunity, but neither would he allow himself to be used as a pawn by Ultaro and Kalat and who knows who else. He turned away from the temple courtyard and down another dark alley. Soon the palace was in view. He headed for the east entrance which he knew would attract the least attention. He arrived and stabled his horse and then ducked inside ignoring the stares of the servants and guards. He could hear them whispering to each other as the side entrance palace doors shut. Inside he headed for a favorite place of solitude from the days of his youth. He was not ready to face anyone and knew that if he went to his main chambers to rest, he would be quickly interrupted by his family, or more likely from Malki his servant. He went to an older wing of the palace that he used to hide in when he was a child. There were some guest rooms with moveable side paneling devised by a previous generation more devious than his fathers. They had been used for spying on foreign dignitaries. He slipped into the secret doorway that led between the walls and then into one that led to an unused guest chamber. The room was somewhat dusty, but there was a high bed fit for a king. He collapsed upon it and was fast asleep.

He awoke hours later. Sun was streaming through a high window. He guessed it must be about midmorning. There was still silence outside the chamber but this was a little used wing of the palace. No doubt the rest of the palace grounds were bustling with activity by now. He rose only to find that he was not alone. Staring at him from a corner chair was Malki.

"Welcome home, my prince," Malki said.

"Malki! You scared me half to death. How long have you been sitting there?"

"Long enough. I thought of leaving for a time but didn't want to risk you slipping off again to confront some other deity."

"So has news arrived of our adventure?"

"Bits and pieces. Care to fill in the details?"

"Not really."

"Need a bigger audience no doubt?"

Enki just gave him a sly grin.

Malki asked, "So did you really do it? Did you actually fell the Great Cedar?"

Enki sat back down on the bed and stretched out with his

hands behind his head. "I wonder how many times I'm going to be telling this tale?" he asked to no one in particular.

"No doubt your exploits get grander with each telling."

"First you tell me your tale," Enki said. "How did you know I was here?"

"I have my spies, My Lord. They noted your arrival."

"And how long have you known about my secret hiding place here?"

"Ever since you talked of it in your sleep. I've learned all kinds of things about you during your unguarded slumber."

Enki gave an uncomfortable smirk at that. "Good thing you're my slave then and are bound to keep all your masters secrets." Enki tried to say this with some force, but it came out sounding somewhat juvenile. For some reason he found it difficult to ever harshly reprimand this servant of his who often seemed more a friend than a slave.

Malki then returned with the real force and with all seriousness, saying firmly, "Your secrets are safe with me My Lord. To the death."

A knowing look passed between them. Enki softened and allowed the weight of the events that had been pressing down on him throughout his ride from Uruk to Ur to be revealed on his face. He let his guard down in the presence of this slave that would keep all secrets.

"Yes, Malki, we cut down the Great Cedar." He said it without his normal boasting and the exploit suddenly sounded empty falling from his lips. But Malki's eyes widened and Enki continued with a recounting of the full tale to his friend-slave. He told of the journey to the River and of his abduction by Lord Morgan of Kish. He told of being pulled from the waters by Sadiq and of their adventure into the underground world beneath the Silver Mountains. Malki listened with awed fascination as Enki told of the finding of the chamber of the Annunaki and of the reading of the ancient letter. He even revealed to Malki the strange power that seemed to overcome him and possess him during the days of the journey from the chamber to the Tree. A tear seemed to well up in Malki's eyes as he learned of the way Kreon died and of his lament for his great sin. Enki sped through much of the journey to Uruk. But he told of Lugulbanda's harsh words and Enki allowed Malki to see the pain and anger that this confrontation had brought out in him. He did not tell him about the letter from Kalat that he still held in his pocket.

"Remarkable," was the only words that Malki could respond with.

Several moments passed.

"So what now, My Lord? What does all this mean and where's it leading?"

Enki wondered if Malki had guessed that there was more he was not telling him.

"Does it all have to lead somewhere, Malki?" he asked.

"Master, I know you. First, Zoreth in the desert. Then the Great Cedar. There's talk at court. People are wondering what you're up to? You are acting as one who has high ambitions and is unwilling to wait for the natural course of events. So, I ask again – where is all this leading?"

Enki just stared at Malki, ever amazed at his slave's

perception. He thought about telling him about Kalat and the letter to Ultaro. But he wasn't quite ready for full disclosure. But he did allow Malki to see some of his inner anguish.

"Malki," he said with a pained look on his face. "What's happening to me? All my life I've felt I've known exactly what I'm supposed to do. I know I have this destiny. I see myself before great armies, pacifying all of New Sumer's enemies and raising us again to our former glory. But now, something has changed. I feel like there are two destinies before me now, but the choice is unclear."

"What do you mean?"

Enki paused in thought a moment, trying to piece together how to put into words the mixed emotions now within him. Finally he said, "I don't know quite how to say it. In many ways the things I've experienced of late just confirm the destiny I've always known I've had. Sadiq saving me first in the desert after I heard that Voice and then again pulling me from the River. The letter from this Orion and the death of Kreon. All of it seems to confirm in me this great sense of purpose. And yet, when I think of those extraordinary events of late, it feels forced to fit it in with the vision I've always had in my head. I feel like I'm missing something now that even the fulfillment of all my dreams won't fill. But this feeling of emptiness is just driving me to ever more desperately pursue the end I've always had in my mind's eye. I find myself considering doing things… I never dreamed I was capable of doing."

"What kind of things?" Malki asked slowly and suddenly concerned.

Enki felt the letter burning against his chest inside his coat pocket. He had within his grasp the opportunity to move his life forward toward his dream, his destiny. Why was he hesitating? Who in his place, of his friends or foes, would hesitate were they in his position. Then something shifted within him. Anger. Frustration. Rage. Pride. Longing. All of it converged in a single moment to produce in him a new power and a renewed sense of certainty. He was being foolish. And why was he entrusting to his slave a window into his soul? He was being tempted, no doubt by the demonic hordes of Kish's deity to throw away the clear call of Nanna and Shamash to raise up his people to new heights. All of these thoughts and emotions poured through Enki in an instant. Then he hid it all with new resolve. He let out a sigh and then allowed a smile to cross his face. "Some things I won't do, Malki," he said. "Others I will. I'll do what needs to be done to free our people and move us forward."

"Okay, My Lord. I'm sure that must mean something."

"It does Malki. It does. It means we've work to do. Where is my father and brothers now?"

"Entertaining an emissary from the East I think."

Enki grew attentive. "What emissary? From where exactly?"

"Susa, I believe. It appears a new family rules in that distant land and that they are looking for trade partners. Your brother Nahor is delighted that they've come to us first rather than Kish."

Enki then recalled all that this Lord Morgan from Kish

had said of Kish's alliance with Susa and the plan to split Sumer between their two peoples.

Enki asked Malki, "So what do they say about Kish? Do they say they've had contact with them?"

"No, actually," Malki said. "In fact, they seemed to go out of their way to make sure your father knew that they'd had no dealings whatsoever with Kish and that they were interested in strengthening Ur's hand against their northern rival."

Enki considered this a moment. "Well then, let's go greet our new friends."

In the Great Hall, an elaborate mid-morning meal had been laid out for the Susa delegation and was now fully consumed. Terah had been sitting at the head of the table with Haran on his right and Nahor on his left. Seated near them around this great banquet table normally reserved for large feasts were three individuals that Enki presumed to be this trade delegation from Susa. Most of the rest of the vast high-ceilinged chamber was vacant of people save those who had been attending to the meal and the guests. As Enki quietly slipped into the hall the meeting was just breaking up. As they rose from the table Enki could hear their conversation come to a close.

"Well then, very good my dear Arius," a jovial Nahor said. "I must say I am very, very pleased with the positions you've presented us and do agree there is a great potential for the mutual aid we could grant one another. We'll retire the discussion for the day and gather again tomorrow for a more substantial talk. And we'll invite some of our key nobles to join us."

"Excellent," this Arius said. "I knew our advisors were correct in directing us to you and not to Kish. We have heard nothing but ill reports from your northern neighbors and are so glad to be able to avoid dealing with them. We look forward to our further discussions tomorrow and hope to be able to come to some substantial agreements."

Just then Enki appeared from out of the shadows.

"Arius is it?" the unpredictable prince said. "Well, you can return home now with your friends here and let your king know that there will be no agreement."

The Susa delegation were stunned by this abrupt greeting from the newcomer but not nearly as dumbfounded as were Nahor, Haran and Terah.

"Enki!" was all Terah could manage.

Haran was immediately red in the face and burst out, "By the gods, where did you suddenly come from?!"

"And what's the meaning of you offending our guests in this way?!" Nahor looked truly enraged which was quite out of character for him but money was at stake of course.

"Settle down brother," Enki replied trying to calm Nahor. "These men are liars. They do not deserve to live. Sending them home will be an act of mercy."

Nahor, always the one to take Enki's side in most things, now abandoned his brother as he turned to the guests from Susa.

"I'm so very sorry about this, Arius." Nahor guided their guests to the door as he tried to cover for his younger brother's impulsive behavior. "My brother here does not speak for Ur. He is obviously sickened and delusional from his recent mysterious travels."

Enki spoke even louder now to recapture the attention of the Susa delegation being scurried away by Nahor. "I am not delusional, but I am sickened by the depth of deceit being demonstrated here! I have a mind to send the lot of you to the torturers. How dare you treat New Sumer with such contempt?!"

All were suddenly silent and aghast by Enki's rash words. Haran then slowly and with force said, "What treasonous sentiments are these. How come you to countermand decrees your own father the King and elder brothers, princes of this land, have made as if you were their overlord!"

Terah interrupted now trying a softer tact. He asked, "Enki my son, are you well? We have been worried to death over your disappearance these last weeks and now most recently there has come these strange rumors of your exploits. Are they true and what truly is the meaning of all this?"

Enki suddenly became hardened both at his brother's accusation of treason, which caused a pain to well up in his chest near where Kalat's letter still rested, but also at being treated by his father as a child. He suddenly launched his attack at the king of Ur. He said, "I have had enough! New Sumer has a destiny to fulfill and here you are being played the fool by these foreigners from the east. I will not stand by and see you toss the kingdom away from me – *from us*!" He had quickly corrected himself, but not before the weight of the words hit their mark. Terah looked hurt and bewildered by the actions and words of his son. The Susa delegation quietly excused themselves in the sudden climatic tension of the moment, being guided by attendants back to their rooms. Nahor, Haran and Terah simply stared in amazement at Enkidu.

Once the Susa delegation was truly gone, Enki continued trying to sound more calm and reasonable now. He said, "I, of course mean our kingdom, not mine, but I do have a destiny to fulfill and I'll not see any of the three of you, including you father, throw away all that our fathers before us and you have built. New Sumer will rise again and I shall lead her to victory over all her enemies. It has been written!"

"It has been written?" Nahor said incredulously. "What the shadowlands are you talking about?"

Enki said, "You would not understand, but it has indeed been written that I have been chosen for greatness. I have seen and done and experienced things that the three of you could never imagine possible. You must now step aside and trust my decrees in these and many other matters. The time has come. I will wait no longer. I will defer no longer. I must act. My choice and destiny is now clear."

Haran and Nahor and Terah dropped their jaws and gapped in astonishment at Enki's words as Haran quietly mouthed the word *treason*.

Haran was about to proceed further in his accusation when suddenly a great commotion was heard outside the chamber walls. The three moved to a balcony of the chamber that overlooked an outer courtyard below. Crowds had assembled and were growing by the throngs. They were chanting Enki's new name *Abram*! News had apparently finally reached the populace with some level of certainty now. The chanting and excitement of the crowd grew louder. Enki turned quietly to his father and brothers and with a feigned look of disinterest calmly said, "My people need me." And with that he turned and stood out on the balcony in full view of the populace. Explosive cheers rose and then subsided as Enki lifted a hand to motion that he would speak. As the noise of the crowd quieted Enki began his monologue.

"Dear people of Ur, I greet you as one who has been commissioned by the gods to fulfill our joint destiny. The time has come to be freed from all convention and commonality and to embrace the greatness and wonderment of what is becoming New Sumer. I, Enkidu, your *abram teshua* will deliver this destiny to you. I come to you as the slayer of Humbaba, guardian of the forest. I come to you as the one who has been blessed and embraced by the Annunaki. I come as he who has felled the Great Cedar and as one who has escaped countless deaths in the course of my travels to deliver this great destiny to you. Let us now rise and…"

Enkidu was suddenly interrupted in his speech by the sound of a trumpet and the galloping of a courier's horse. It was Larzo on his steed and he was racing to the foot of the balcony to deliver an urgent message to the king and his sons. The crowds parted to allow the speeding horse and his rider through. Out of breath from the race through the city, Larzo breathed out his message.

He said, "My lords! Word has come from Uruk. The high prince Gilgamesh… is dying."

CHAPTER 10 – DESTINY'S END

Enki sat in near darkness at Gil's bedside. Gil's breathing was heavy and a feverish sweat enveloped his body. Gil had been in an unconscious daze ever since Enki's arrival earlier that day. After the crushing news that the prince of Uruk was dying, Enki had not waited on anyone. Without a word he had jumped on the nearest horse he could find. He had ignored the crowds continued chorus of admiration as he raced at neck breaking speeds to the same place he had just raced from the day before. Once back in Uruk he had made straight for the palace. He raced passed the guards who allowed him entry without a word – his friendship and love for the dying prince was well known.

He burst into Gil's room to find the room shrouded in darkness and Gil in that unconscious feverish daze that had remained with him all day. Aya had been there at Gil's bedside when he arrived. He and Aya stared at each other at first in awkward silence which soon gave way to a burst of emotion.

"I'm so, so sorry Aya for the things I said to you. I was hurt and angry and I didn't know what I was saying. Please, forgive me," Enki had said.

Aya did forgive him. And yet, something was different. Aya assured him that she had indeed forgiven him, but he could sense that some part of her held him at a distance for some reason. It had not made sense to him. They should be drawing strength from one another at this hour of mutual turmoil. Enki didn't sense that her distance from him was due to the hurtful things he had said. Somehow, he had felt that had been resolved. It was something else.

Enki just stared now at his friend, just as Aya did likewise several feet beside him. Enki could not bring himself to truly believe that Gil was dying. He knew that he would pull through this. He knew that Gil was part of his destiny. And yet, some shred of doubt began to gnaw at him.

What if he did die? What would that mean? What then?

He quickly berated himself for thinking such self-absorbed thoughts while his best friend was lying before him in unconscious suffering. Aya began to weep softly.

Ninsun who had been in the room for much of the day was not now present. She had left an hour or so ago to meet with the king and with his father and brothers who had arrived shortly after he had. Enki had not been invited to attend this meeting, nor did he care. He could not understand why any of this was happening. He could not believe that Gil would truly die. And yet…

Guilt suddenly raced in upon him as it had off and on throughout the day. Gil's wound should have been his own. It was Enki's pride and anger and rage that had filled the axe *Might of Heroes* with its deadly poison that had been released into Gil upon that fatal last swing of the axe. It should be Enki lying here on his deathbed, not Gil.

Aya's gentle weeping finally had stopped. She continued to stare at her brother with eyes reddened from tears that had come and gone throughout the day. She glanced at Enki and then back to Gil. She seemed several times on the verge of speaking but kept pulling back. Enki continued to be bewildered at Aya. Something was wrong. Something was not the same. But he did not know what it was. Certainly her brother in this state must have thrown her emotions into turmoil, and yet it seemed to not be simply her grief over Gil.

Several more moments of silence passed. Then she finally spoke through trembling and quivering lips. She said, "Enki, whatever happens… I will always love you."

Enki looked at her in confusion. What did this mean? What was she saying?

Just then Ninsun reentered the room. She looked at both Aya and Enki first before proceeding to turn to Gil. There was a pained and regretful look in her eyes as she observed them both. Then her gaze landed upon Aya and there was a knowing look that passed between them which seemed to communicate something to Aya. Aya turned her gaze back upon Gil with a look of some kind of passive resignation.

Ninsun then fell upon Gil with the heart wrenching cry of

a mother for her only son.

Several minutes passed before others began to fill the room. King Lugulbanda emerged into the chamber followed by Enki's father Terah and brothers Haran and Nahor. The king inquired of the doctors in the room of the status of Prince Gilgamesh.

"Your Majesty," the chief physician replied, "The prince is not responding to any of the treatments. It is a devilish disease that has suddenly enveloped him. It is beyond our ability to cure. The wound he received during the time of the felling of the Great Cedar has him now in the grip of Uggae."

At the mention of the god of death Enki turned suddenly to the physician in a wave of uncontrolled passion. He said heatedly, "Gil, will not die from this wound!"

"Silence!" Lugulbanda boomed. He looked at Enki but did not address him directly. There was a look of disgust for Enki in his eyes that he did not try to conceal.

Turning then to Terah, Lugulbanda addressed the ensi of Ur with both firmness and respect. He said, "Lord Terah, we must move forward with our plans. You know it is the only course for us."

Ninsun then looked up and pleaded with sudden emotion. She said, "My lords, please, the prince my son is still with us and has not yet passed to the land of the shadows. The gods may yet see fit to restore his life to us. Please, speak no more of this now!"

Ninsun looked briefly to Aya and then to Enki. Aya looked down and would not meet her gaze.

Enki looked up briefly from his grief, perplexed and confused. What was going on? But he decided to ignore their veiled talk as he turned back to the prince. Gil would pull through. Whatever they are talking about didn't matter.

Ninsun caught Terah's glance briefly before she returned her gaze upon her dying son.

Terah then spoke up. He said, "My Lord high king, I do see that your plan may well be the best course for us, but let us respect the plea of the queen and speak no more of this now. It has been a long day for all of us. Let us retire and pray to the gods that the morning will bring us new and better tidings than this day has."

Haran and Nahor said nothing but remained in something of a daze themselves. They had not been particularly close to Gil and so his state of decline would not be the cause for their look of disorientation.

Once again, Enki wondered what was going on and what their secret gathering had been about. But also, once again, Enki shook off the need to solve the mystery just then. Gil would pull through. His destiny would be fulfilled. Gilgamesh would be the high king of all New Sumer and Enki would be his commanding general. Gil would get better and it would happen. The gods had decreed it in his dreams.

***

Prince Gilgamesh died during the night. Enki had been in his guest room sound asleep when Malki came in with the news. At first he thought he was dreaming. Malki assured him as gently as possible that it was not a dream.

"No," Enki said forcefully as he quickly got up and dressed. "You're mistaken. You'll see. Gil will be fine."

Malki did not respond.

Enki raced through the palace halls to Gil's room. He was the last to arrive. Ninsun was clinging to Gil's body as she wept freely. Aya was by her side. Her own tears had subsided now and she at present just stared blankly at nothing in particular. Terah and Haran and Nahor lined the outer wall on the far side of the room. They appeared uneasy as though they were intruding upon a sacred moment. King Lugulbanda was standing between them and the bedside where his dead son lay. Even now, he maintained his stern composure. He appeared impatient as though the grief displayed in the room were some kind of inconvenience that he must let run its course.

Outside, the sound could be heard of the populace who had gathered in the palace courtyard in prayerful vigil. Their prayers had turned to mourning as news of the prince's death spread quickly through the city.

Enki entered the room slowly and with an ever increasing feeling of dread. It did appear to him as though he were in a dream. He knelt beside his friend. He touched his arm. Cold. Death.

Enki backed away shaking his head. He stumbled and fell in numbed silence to the floor not even able to cry.

More minutes of anguish passed. Ninsun's weeping subsided as Aya's tears fell once more. Finally, King Lugulbanda could remain silent no longer.

"My son is dead," he said with finality.

He allowed several moments of awkward silence to pass before proceeding. Ninsun looked down and Aya looked away.

"Our grief must wait. The security of New Sumer is at stake now. We must now proceed with the plans that we have discussed. Kish and our people must know this very night what has been decreed."

Enki looked around at the various faces around him. Was he the only one who did not know what the king was talking about?

Lugulbanda continued to spell out what had apparently already been decided. He said, "Uruk is now without an heir at a point when our Sumerian alliance is particularly vulnerable in the face of the affronts to the Kishite realm by the two wayward princes one of whom has paid the price now with his very life."

Enki began to rise meaning to object to the Kings statement, but he felt the hand of Shulpae on his shoulder from behind holding him back with a plea of caution. He sank back down as Lugulbanda continued.

"Kish will feel encouraged to rally their own alliance against us and strike while we are weak. They will assume that there will be a grab for power among our own nobles. And they will be right. Indeed, as we foresaw, this has already begun. My sources tell me that at this very moment there is a secret meeting of the rival houses of Uruk and several of Ur gathering to discuss how they will attempt to overtake House Anu of Uruk and House Eber of Ur. This must not be! We must quell this dissent before it takes another step and Kish must never hear of it. Etana of Kish must have communicated to him this very night that New Sumer is secure and strong and that the succession is intact.

"And so by united decree of myself and Lord Terah of Ur, we have decided to unite our houses. Prince Haran, you will be betrothed to my daughter Aya and I will adopt you as my heir. Prince Nahor will rise to take Haran's place as heir of Ur."

Enki rose now to his feet, "No! It is I who would be betrothed to Aya!" He stepped forward and looked at Aya but Aya would not return his desperate gaze.

Lugulbanda turned viciously upon the prince. He scornfully said, "You Enkidu can have no part of the kingdom of Uruk. You certainly will not take Prince Gilgamesh's place. Your name is now as blackened as his for your folly. Already the people of Uruk turn upon you. They blame you for the death of the prince and for this new instability of our realm and for the heightened and very real threat now from Kish."

Enki stepped toward the King and pleaded. He said, "No My Lord, I want nothing to do with being your heir. Haran may have it. It's Aya I want. All I want!"

Enki looked desperately toward Aya. Timidly Aya finally looked up to meet Enki's gaze. It was still there – the look of love in her eyes for him. But she quickly smoldered the flame in her eyes and drifted once more to her repose of stoic resignation. She looked away.

In a sudden wave, realization swept Lugulbanda as he

looked first incredulously at Enki and then to Aya and then back to Enki. He reddened in acknowledgement that he was apparently the last to know of Enki's true affection for the princess.

In a spiteful glare of contempt, he slowly but firmly spoke to the prince. He said, "You… will never… have anything to do… with my daughter. You have sealed your doom Enkidu of Ur, great *abram teshua*. You will go back to Ur and live out your days as a lesser lord and will never again set foot in this city."

Enki would have resisted the assault upon him if only he had but a glimmer of encouragement from anyone else in the room. But all were silent. Aya now would not look up. Everyone else looked away in embarrassment. Even Malki and Shulpae averted their eyes. But it was the silence of Aya that crushed him. She had apparently known this was coming. She had already resigned herself to this fate. No doubt Lugulbanda had already convinced her it was for the good of the kingdom, for the sake of New Sumer. Oh, Aya, my love! Oh my dear sweet Aya. He wanted to run. He wanted to cry out in anguish and despair. He wanted to die.

Lugulbanda turned from the dazed Prince Enkidu and spoke to King Terah. "Lord Terah, do I have your agreement in this matter?"

Terah with a brief painful and knowing glance at Ninsun said, "You do, My Lord."

And then Lugulbanda turned to Haran. "And Prince Haran, will you consent to be my heir and to wed my daughter Aya?"

Haran hesitated only a moment as he glanced quickly at Enki with a brief look of regret and sorrow for his brother. But he recovered his composure and stated his affirmation.

Lugulbanda then said, "Very good. Then let us this very moment announce to the populous that the one year betrothal of Haran to Aya has now begun, but that as of this very night Haran has been embraced as my son and as my heir of a united kingdom of New Sumer. A grand wedding day will be set one year from this very day, but Haran will bring the rest of his family immediately to Uruk and will begin to step into his role as heir of the realm. And now I will make announcement of this new joy born out of sorrow to our people awaiting outside, and more importantly to the spies of Kish and also of our rival houses here in Uruk mulling about the crowd."

And with that, Lugulbanda turned and moved toward the balcony and appeared before the crowd. The populous had been wailing in sorrowful mourning for the dead prince and also in anxious trepidation for the future of their realm and the growing threat from the north now perceived. When they saw Lugulbanda emerge, the crowd quickly grew silent to await his news. He proceeded to comfort the people and joined them in mourning for the loss of the prince, but he quickly moved on to speak of the future of the realm. And when he announced the engagement of Haran to Aya and the naming of Haran as his heir the crowd roared in relieved approval. Enki listened to the whole spectacle in a numb daze. He was unable to think – unable to move. He just sat there stunned through it all. Lugulbanda invited Haran and

Aya and the rest of the royal family to join him on the dais and Enki eventually rose as well and silently inched forward to view the scene. Suddenly the crowds roared in disapproval, chanting hateful words at someone they had just noticed. It took Enki several moments to realize it was him they had just spotted and were now berating with their angry words.

"Traitor! Blasphemer of the gods! You led our Prince into folly and to his death!" various voices in the crowd accused.

Lugulbanda glanced back to see Enki behind him now in plain view of the people outside. He did not seem to mind his appearance and in place of his most recent look of spite for Enki now had a feigned look of pity.

"My people," Lugulbanda said. "Pay no heed to the wayward Prince Enkidu. He is to have no place in our realm and is consigned to a lesser role now in his own city."

This seemed to quiet the angry outbursts of this same fickle crowd that had so recently been singing the praises of the Slayer of Humbaba. Now however they saw the death of Gilgamesh as the curse of the gods for his impious assault upon this sacred Tree of a foreign yet powerful deity of Kish.

Enki could not believe it. Everything, in an instant, was taken from him. The crowds had abandoned him. His best friend was taken by death. And Aya... He slowly drifted backward and then out of sight of the crowd as Lugulbanda continued his comforting appeal to the people of Uruk and beyond. He felt as though he were now in another world. And then Lugulbanda pulled Haran and Aya together to join their hands to one another. Enki's heart broke. He turned and quietly slipped out of the room.

***

Malki and Shulpae followed him as he began to wander aimlessly through the palace grounds. They said nothing but simply kept their sights on the Prince afraid of what he might do. Enki eventually wandered into the streets by a lesser used exit from the palace. The streets were empty – all were on the other side of the castle in the palace courtyard listening to Lugulbanda continue to dismantle his reason for living. He had nothing. His destiny was destroyed. His name was in ruins. His family and his sweet Aya had simply let him go without a word. He knew deep inside that he deserved it with the way he had treated both, but still the feeling of rejection was toxic and quickly produced in him an aching despair. She had said she would always love him no matter what happened. Now those words came back and haunted him. She had known all along and had told him nothing. But what could she say? What could she do? When the mighty King Lugulbanda decreed something it was done. She was trapped and he knew it.

He walked on in silence. He suddenly was unable to feel anything. His emotions were suddenly just gone. He felt nothing. He cared for nothing. He would just walk out into the desert and die. There was nothing left to do.

He passed out of the city and proceeded to the banks of the Euphrates. As he began to cross the bridge Malki and

Shulpae felt they had to intervene at last.

"Enki, where are you going?" Malki began.

"My lad, this is not the end for you. Pain and tragedy can yet give birth to hope," Shulpae said.

"Ha!" said Enki. "Speak not of hope."

Enki continued to walk on.

Malki repeated his inquiry. He asked, "Where are you going, Enki?"

Enki suddenly stopped and turned. "Malki, the gods have destroyed me. I must face them. I go now to find them. I will walk into the desert till death takes me and if there is a world beyond this one, then I will know and I will demand justice of them."

"Enki," Shulpae said. He spoke now with a deep look of empathy in his eyes. "I… know a bit of how you feel. I once lost something dear to me as well." An anguished look of pain suddenly swept Shulpae's expression. He paused for several seconds and seemed as though he would not be able to go on. He regained his composure though and continued. He said, "It made me lose all will to live. It's what prompted my search for life's meaning as I sought for Utnapishtim. Enki, don't give in to despair. Use the despair to drive you to seek for the answers. I never found it. You can succeed where I failed."

Enki turned and was about to lash out in mockery of the old man, but the memory of the Voice suddenly enveloped him. *Come away with me.* He almost felt as though he had heard it again. He desperately wanted to believe in something and at this moment the Voice he'd heard was all he had to go on. Everything else had abandoned him. But hadn't the Voice abandoned him as well? He proceeded with the mockery.

"You're a fool, old man! Why did you waste all those years searching for some mythical survivor of the Cleansing? Were you afraid to face the despair of death? You succeeded in avoiding it for many a year, but you'll face it all the same. It will come upon you in the end. I choose to face it head on. There is no such person as Utnapishtim, certainly not now living. You wasted your life looking for him. But I am just as much a fool. I thought I had a destiny to fulfill. And I have wasted my life seeking it. But alas, death comes to us all, sooner or later. I choose sooner, for at least then I can choose."

Enki turned away from them both and walked on into the darkness of the desert. Shulpae continued to call out to him to return, but his voice grew more and more faint as he proceeded further on into the desert wastes. Malki did not call out and he was tempted to turn around to see if he was even still standing there watching him. Then Enki smirked as he thought, *even my loyal slave has turned on me and given me up as lost.* He walked on.

***

He walked on for what remained of the night and then well into the next day. Dawn had been clear but as the morning proceeded, dust storms began to form in the distance and soon the wind picked up. He was not sure how long he could continue walking like this. The heat of the day began to slow him down. He had ceased to think at some point. At first he replayed certain events of his life. Waves of rejection came and went. Now he was just numb again. He had ceased to care about anything. He had ceased to even question why. He sat down for a while under the shade of a large stone. After an hour or so he arose again, emotionless and empty. He now proceeded to walk, then to run. He ran with all his might. All the pent up energy and repressed emotion of the last few hours came welling out in a burst of speed. He ran on and on for hours. Further and further into the desert he went. Night came. He continued on. The moon was bright and lighted his way. *Nanna is luring me to my death*, Enki considered. *It is her final revenge for all my blasphemies.*

About the third watch of the night, he began to finally collapse. Food, of course, he could do without for many days, but not water. His body was almost spent. But the exhaustion and dehydration numbed his emotions and came almost as a relief. He lay down to die.

He stared up at the night sky looking at all the stars. He started to count them like he used to do when he was a child. It suddenly made him think again of the Voice. *To where would you have me go?* It was a sudden reply he finally gave to the Voice. *Come away with me* it had said. Funny that he had never thought of replying to the Voice until now. *Where would you have me go? I've nowhere else to go. If you speak to me again, I'll go where you tell me.*

The reply was only silence. A gentle night breeze blew sand across his face. His eyes began to water. He rubbed his eyes and wiped them clean of the sand. But his eyes watered again and then he realized he was weeping. He was weeping like he had not cried since he was a little boy. He cried out in anguish. He called out to the Voice. He cursed the day he was born. He implored Gil to forgive him. He told Aya he loved her. He wept through it all until his consciousness finally gave way and sleep took him. His last thought was that he had lost count of the stars.

***

Enki woke in a tent of some kind. He was lying on a thatched mat couched in between cushions of ornate design. The tent opened to his right and the flap of the tent flittered back and forth in the warm desert wind. Outside through the tent's opening he could see the night sky. *How long have I been here*, he wondered. Then he realized a better question was, "Where am I and how did I get here?" and he spoke it out loud.

"You owe your life to your slave," he heard a strangely familiar voice say. He turned in the direction of the voice and saw its source. *Zoreth!*

"How? Where!?" Enki began several times to query the desert warrior but each time was left speechless.

"How did I find you and where did we come from and where are we now?" Zoreth said in an attempt to aid his speech.

Enki just nodded dumbly in reply.

"Your slave Malki found us and told us the general

direction you had been heading when you went walking off to fight your gods. Foolish and desperate prince. Why cast your life away in such a manner? There are better and more noble ways to die."

Enki did not respond. His pride could no longer be wounded any more than it already had been. He simply lay back down and stared at the canvas ceiling. He felt again that detached numbness inside that had come and gone in the last day and a half. Then he thought of Malki. At least he knew now that Malki had not really abandoned him. It brought some comfort, or at least he felt it should. But then he became dismayed that his only possible cause for encouragement had come from the thought of a faithful slave. His family and his love Aya had rejected him. His slave he owned. What else could he do? But he knew that was not fair. Malki had done an act of great selflessness. And what act of selflessness had he ever done? The thought condemned him. Even his slave Malki was more noble than he.

"Where is Malki?" he asked at last.

"Resting. He nearly killed himself in finding us. And when he found us we nearly killed him for approaching our encampment. He's safe now though and he has proven his worth in the eyes of the clan. He will be well cared for."

Enki considered this as he lay there. Then he asked, "And why care for either one of us? Especially me? I am of no more use to you. You must know now that I have lost all favor in the eyes of my people, my family and my king. I can offer you no leverage and can win you no favor with the High

King or even with my father Terah the ensi of Ur."

"Bah! I care not for any of it. Do you think I made peace with you Prince Enkidu because I wanted to win the favor of New Sumer? No, I made peace with you because you are one of our own kind."

"And because we both would have killed each other had you not succumbed to my bargain."

"Well, yes that may have been a factor," Zoreth said with a smile. And now a second wave of warmth washed over Enki. What was this he was feeling? Was it hope? But at what cost? To rely on a slave and on an uncivilized desert chieftain for a feeling of acceptance – was not this the greatest rejection?

He decided to return the smile, but only mildly.

Enki said, "I was ready to die, Zoreth. I suppose I still am. And yet… for the first time since leaving Uruk yesterday I feel I could go on living at least one more day."

"It's been longer than that Enki of Ur. You've been feverish and unconscious three days now in this tent. And it had been a whole other day between the time we found you and brought you back to our camp. It's nearly been a week since you left Uruk I'd wager."

"Oh," Enki said profoundly.

"Rest now, plainsman. We shall talk of better and more noble ways for you to end your life later."

And with that Zoreth strode out of the tent.

Enki slept for a while.

When he awoke again, light was streaming into the tent. The night had passed and day had come. He sat up and drank some of the water that had been left next to him. Just then a woman entered. She was robbed in traditional desert garb. She looked curiously at him. He must have been quite the spectacle for this desert tribe. She spoke something in a language he did not understand. Enki indicated that he did not understand her tongue. She spoke then in a broken form of the common speech.

"You are well now, plainsman? You food eat?"

Enki didn't realize how famished he was till she mentioned food. Enki nodded.

"I bring." And with that she left the tent. Very shortly she returned with a bowl of broth and a piece of roasted mutton. He ate gratefully.

When finished, he stood up and found he was able to manage the feat reasonably well. The rest and water and food had restored him. He almost felt as though he were not in complete turmoil. But then he thought of Aya and a wave of pain again enveloped him. He closed his eyes as he lay back down. He tried to think of anything but Aya, but all he could picture was his sweet Aya holding his much older brother Haran's hand. He knew she did not love him and probably never would. His brother was respectable but not very lovable. And he was twice her age with two children about as old as she. Milcah was his oldest daughter and the second was Iscah. Poor Haran. He had never had a son. His wife had died giving birth to Iscah. Milcah was the only one to carry on his name, if she could be married off to one of the noble houses. But now Haran may have a chance for a son after all and for a direct heir. He tried not to think about

Haran and Aya together. It was absurd.

Life was absurd. Where was the meaning in any of this? Were there truly gods and were they just punishing him? Perhaps. But then he thought of Sadiq and the two times he saved him. And he thought again of the Voice. And then he thought of the chamber of the Annunaki and the strange letter from this Orion figure from before the Great Cleansing. And then he thought of the mystical Utnapishtim who Shulpae believed was still alive and secluded somewhere. Well, if he was still alive he might have some answers and perhaps he would know of this Orion, this Nephilim who forged the Axe. And then he thought of Kreon and the Great Cedar. And he thought of Kreon's final fateful words of lamentation. *Dellan, Dellan*, he had cried out. What was the sin of Kreon against his brother Dellan?

Suddenly, the thought became more real for him – the thought that there was a vast world and history beyond his own petty life. Of course he had always known that, but it hit him now in a fresh new way. The extraordinary things that had happened to him stood before him now as a rebuke that he would seek so carelessly to end his life. No, he really didn't have anything worth living for now, but life was life. Perhaps, he could seek out answers. He doubted he would find any real answers, but he could die trying and it would be a better way to die. It would make Zoreth happy. He smiled at that thought. Why had this desert chieftain saved him?

And then he thought again of Shulpae and his quest for Utnapishtim. Did he really have the answers to life's meaning? And did he have access to the fountain of everlasting life as the legends said? And would he know who Orion was and why there was this letter that had apparently been meant for him. That thought again suddenly raised his thoughts beyond his own personal despair and tragedy and made him think suddenly of something greater and beyond himself. He was already dead. His life was over. Nothing really mattered for him personally anymore. But perhaps he yet did have some role to play? Certainly the extraordinary events could not be without meaning. He had been blinded to this plain truth during the early hours of his great grief, but now he could see it.

And yet, how foolish. How possibly could he find this Utnapishtim if he even still lived or ever really had? Shulpae had spent years looking for him and had never found him, never even come close. Reality crept back in to his thinking. No, he was not now sure he could end his life so carelessly as he had been about to do, but he could think of no really good reason to go on living either. But he was fairly certain now that he could find some other mode of existence devoid of ambition or pain or disappointment. Perhaps, he could become a trader. Perhaps he could join Zoreth's clan and raid Uruk's countryside just to create havoc for Lugulbanda. He was jesting though, of course. He was still a man of New Sumer at heart. He would not betray his people like that. But he was determined now to fade from the scene. He would not return. He may live a while longer yet. But his days as a prince of Ur were over. And the dream of being a conquering general was finished.

He got up and exited the tent for the first time and

stretched his arms upward in the bright sunlight of late afternoon. As dusk settled he could see the fires being lit and the evening meal being readied. He strode over and sat around the emerging campfire. He did not notice at first, but Malki was sitting outside a tent nearby. Their eyes met and Enki allowed a look of gratefulness to pass between them. Malki rose and came to sit with the prince. A look of understanding passed between them as Enki allowed Malki to see in his eyes both a look of thankfulness that he saved him along with the tortured look that betrayed the deep ongoing anguish of his heart. Malki nodded in sympathy. Then they both turned their gaze toward the fire and sat in silence.

Soon others came and sat around the fire. There were many such gathering fires, but with Enki the strange plainsman present, many now gathered about *their* fire. Zoreth also came and sat down and motioned that the meal be brought to them. As they ate and drank and as darkness began to settle on the surrounding terrain, a festive mood emerged. Dancing girls began their joyful dance about the fire. Their clothes were a colorful flowing tapestry of reds and blues and gold. Musicians played skillfully on their lyres and flutes. But the music and the food and dancing did not move Enki. He saw it all through detached eyes. His heart had been broken. But the despair that had led him to end his life had subsided to a point of simply an ongoing throbbing painful angst. He could live with that in time he supposed.

As the night wore on and the dancing girls migrated to the center of the camp, the musicians migrated with them and audible conversation became an option.

"Well, my prince, have you considered more your fate?"

Zoreth's speech woke Enki from his private thoughts. He looked up at Zoreth emotionless but with less of the crazed look of one seeking to end his life. He had come to some kind of truce with the gods… for now.

"I don't know Zoreth, I really don't. I feel lost. So sure have I been all my life. Now all is foggy. I don't mind telling you, I am ruined. But you need not be concerned." He gave Malki a quick glance. "I'll not quite so carelessly end my life now."

There was silence for a while as they watched the dancing girls now on the far side of the encampment.

Enki smiled and began to speak, then stopped. Zoreth waited for him to speak. Enki chuckled then as he considered what to say next. He finally spoke, "It's a silly thought, but old Shulpae, a dear old teacher in Uruk, and something of a scholar, or so he likes us to think of him, thinks I should go off in search of the meaning of life." Enki smiled at the thought and Zoreth laughed out loud.

"Ha, the answer to that question is clearly known to us in the deep desert. *Sing great songs, dance wild dances and love your woman with passion and delight – all else is vain*, or so our poets have said."

Enki forced a smile and a response. He said, "Wise are your poets." He maintained the smile but inwardly he groaned as he thought of Aya and knew his life would now forever be in vain without her.

Zoreth realized the angst he had just caused the prince and quickly spoke again before Enki could fade back into his morbid thoughts. "And what else does this Shulpae say? Where does he suggest you search for this meaning of life? Does he propose you ask the sea nymphs or approach the rock giants of our children's tales?" Zoreth spoke this with a light hearted laugh and the rest of those gathered about the fire joined him in the jest.

Enki smiled and then laughed along with them as he considered how foolish it was that Shulpae had taken so seriously this search for Utnapistim, this supposed sole survivor of the Great Cleansing.

"Yes, it is something like that," Enki laughed. His laughter faded to a sly smile as he decided to tell them of Shulpae's ridiculous quest that he almost had hoped was truly viable. "He spent a good portion of his younger years searching for some mythical survivor of the Great Cleansing – Utnapishtim we call him. We have tales of such an individual surviving the Cleansing in a great sea craft and now living out his days at some secret lifespring."

The laughter around him immediately stopped. Enki was still smiling as was Malki. But soon both ceased their grins as they saw the dead seriousness on every face around the fire. Each looked to each other with surprised, but curious looks. Then all eyes fell upon Zoreth.

"Your *Utnapishtim* lives," Zoreth said at last. "*Manu* we call him."

Zoreth appeared as though he were about to say more but then fell silent.

Several seconds passed as Enki absorbed and processed these words. Finally he asked, "You have stories of

Utnapishtim too?"

Zoreth looked thoughtful before responding. Then he said, "We have more than stories."

Enki felt an odd sensation of hope well up inside him.

After another several seconds of astonished silence Enki asked, "What else do you know of him?"

Zoreth looked around the circle and received several nods from some of the elders in the group.

"We know where he is."

THE END

THE ABRAM TRILOGY

Book One – The Breaking
Book Two – The Seeking (forthcoming)
Book Three – The Believer (forthcoming)

DID YOU ENJOY THE BOOK? WOULD YOU LIKE TO HELP SEE THE REST OF THE STORY UNFOLD? YOU CAN HELP!

The Abram trilogy of books depends upon you, and others like you, to see it through to completion! Here's what you can do to help:

- Post about the book, and link to it on Facebook, Twitter, LinkedIN and other social networking sites.
- Review it on Amazon, GoodReads and anywhere else people talk about books.
- Tell your friends and family about it. Blog about it.
- Sign up to get email updates when new books are released: http://www.therebelplanet.com/getnews
- Follow Peter Churness on Facebook and Twitter (@peterchurness).
- Also "like" the Rebel Planet Creations Facebook page and follow @therebelplanet on Twitter to help promote future products (video games and books) relating to our epic pre-flood fantasy world! For more information see www.therebelplanet.com.

ACKNOWLEDGMENTS

First I want to thank my wife Sandy. We're going on 20 years now and each year you bring more and more joy to my life. In my dedication I noted that you live in the present. You neither dwell on the past nor worry about the future – which is very fortunate for me on both counts. I love you more each day. Thank you for sharing with me this adventure of life together and of mutual devotion to the God of Abraham.

Special thanks to Tyrean Martinson for proofing the book and making great editing suggestions. Each suggested tweak was spot on. Any remaining errors or poor wording is certainly because I did not take her advice on something. Tyrean is a seasoned and truly gifted writer. Check out her blog at http://tyreanswritingspot.blogspot.com/ and buy all her books!

A word of acknowledgement is also in order for my good friend Tom Hilpert. Parts of this story dip into the elaborate backstory of the pre-flood fantasy world he and I fashioned together during our seminary days when we should have been studying our Greek. Tom is also a much better writer than I and a masterful storyteller. Check out his excellent Lake Superior mystery novels at www.tomhilpert.com.

I should note as well that Tom and I "stole" some of our pre-flood ideas (touched on more so in forthcoming book two) from a very creative Old Testament professor named Harold Hosch. Harold, I don't know if you are still on this planet or are now in the Blessed Realm beyond, but thank you.

Made in the USA
Middletown, DE
26 November 2015

ABOUT THE AUTHOR

Peter Churness lives in Gig Harbor, Washington where h
the pastor of One Hope Church (www.ohcgh.com).
been married to Sandy for nearly 20 years (all of t
blissful) and has three fantastic kids, Hannah, Megan
Caleb. In addition to doing church stuff and writing he
has been involved in making spiritually themed video g
(see www.TheRebelPlanet.com). He also sings and
guitar and has composed and recorded an acoustic
version of Handel's Messiah (you know, because Ha
version wasn't good enough). Check that o
www.MyMessiah.org.